CARSON'S LEASE

DENNIS L. BOYKIN

GREAT PLAINS PUBLISHING

Carson's Lease

Dennis L. Boykin

First edition published 2005 by Morrison Publishing.
Second edition published 2017 by Great Plains Publishing.

First edition edited by Adelaide Myers and Debbie Riley
This second edition edited by Kellie Quinn and Kellie Boykin

Cover design by Debbie Riley • aesopF@msn.com

ISBN: 978-0-69288-316-7

Printed in the U.S.A.

Another book published by Dennis L. Boykin:
The Boykin Boy ©2003, 2017 • ISBN: 978-0-69284-178-5

This book is dedicated to a man who inspired me to write it.
The man who doesn't need to read it—my son, Doug Boykin.

ACKNOWLEDGMENTS

No one writes a book alone. So, once again it is time to say a thousand thanks to everyone who has been a part of the fun of writing this novel:

My gratitude is endless to Adelaide Myers, my principal editor, who guided me throughout the first edition of this book with humor, guarded words of praise, and constructive criticism. It has been a joy to work with her.

A special thanks to my friend, Debbie Riley, for guiding me through the first edition of this book, her many hours on the cover design, and her constant expressions of approval and support.

A big note of praise and gratitude to my daughter, Kellie Jo Quinn, and my granddaughter, Kellie Anne Boykin, for taking time out from other important projects to provide a final edit to this second manuscript.

FOREWORD

Sooner or later we all have to struggle with our demons, and often as not, those demons will lead us to a fork in the road. Do we follow blindly in the footsteps of our parents, trusting that what they have promised us will indeed come to fruition? Or do we, instead, strike out on our own, forsaking all that we have been given in the gamble that we may create our own, larger destiny?

For Reed Carson, the only truth he knows is the rugged, unforgiving landscape of rural Wyoming. Like a true Wyomingite, he clings to the reality that he understands, right or wrong, and the rancher's way of life that has defined him and his kin for a century, even as it gives way bit by bit to subdivisions and corporations.

Carson's Lease follows this conflicted young man through a series of events that will test his will to carry on and hold fast to his birthright—a concept that evokes a visceral reaction in anyone who was raised to believe they would inherit the land they were raised on. But he will come to find out that he *is* his birthright, and he can assume control of his own destiny. He can get out from under the thumb of a domineering mother and a shameful past, but he has to look within himself first.

His lease on a small piece of pasture is more than the piece of paper allowing him to bunk and graze his cattle there safely; it is his ticket to freedom, and the beginning of his relationship with the community as an independent man, not merely the foreman of his mother's ranches.

But that's just my take on this story. It is, dramatics aside, a play that takes shape all too often in families whose wealth is measured in acres. When land is at stake, rationality seems always to be the first thing to go—and its vacancy is quickly occupied by feudalism and infighting, often acted out old west style. A reader unfamiliar with this part of the world might find it a stretch that these things still happen, but stepping into rural Wyoming is somewhat like stepping into the past.

About halfway through the book, Reed thinks to himself, "In this world, kindly people like them don't exist, except in fairy tale books." But Boykin knows, as I do, that people like Claude and Mabel Cadwaller, the subjects of this musing, *do* exist in rural Wyoming. I know that the "fairy tale books" that someone like Reed Carson would read (ahem, westerns) are populated with such characters, and so is the un-named town that *Carson's Lease* is based on.

It was Boykin's grasp on the real town that I lived in that made this book compelling to me. I was working as a reporter in a town of about 1,200 surrounded by nothing but prairie when I read Dennis' first book, *The Boykin Boy*, a novelized memoir of a child rejected by one society and embraced by that same society of which we now speak. I was struck by the way the community that he described, though taking place almost a half-century before, hadn't changed all that much when I came to live there.

I was struggling to capture that reality in newspaper articles when my editor characteristically hurled *The Boykin Boy* onto my desk and demanded a review the following week. I read the book in two days and looked up the author to interview him for my article. He was cordial and answered all of my questions as diplomatically as possible, and he asked for a copy of my review after it was published. What has developed over the next year and a half has been a surprise to me, as his second work, and his first attempt at true fiction has followed me across the country to Louisiana, and I have sent it back again and again with my comments and criticism. I wouldn't call myself an editor, per se, as much as a test reader.

Dennis has been extremely patient with the time that it has taken me to read and re-read *Carson's Lease*, although if he was fussing at me, I wouldn't know it because we are separated by thousands of miles and brought together only through email, *sans* cuss words. It has been a rewarding experience, though, and we have both learned a lot about the writing process—and each other.

Writing from experience and writing in the vacuum of true fiction are two different worlds, and authors don't often make the leap without falling through the cracks. But the strength of *Carson's Lease* lies in the fact that it *is* based on at least one experience that is universal, and one that we all must face even if our parents *don't* own thousands of acres of ranch land. But if you want to know what *that* feels like, here's your book, it is the next best thing to actually visiting that rugged, unforgiving landscape that people either love or hate. Enjoy,

Adelaide Myers
M.L.I.S. candidate
School of Library and Information Science
Louisiana State University, Baton Rouge

ONE

Reed Carson stopped in the middle of the living room to take one last look at the surroundings where he had spent the last nine years of his life. His trophies hung on the walls—heads of elk, deer, moose, bighorn sheep, and coyote—relics that he couldn't take and didn't know if he would ever see again. Each stuffed animal told of a different adventure—of swapping stories with hunting buddies, of campfires, and of dragging carcasses down steep, snowy mountainsides.

With his sleeping bag, rifle, and flashlight in hand, he paused another moment, then whispered, "Let's go Mister," to his Border collie mixed-breed companion. He ducked his head through the doorway and merged into the blackness of a moonless night.

A horse nickered. Hooves shuffled on the floor of a livestock trailer; his diesel pickup hooked on the front, idling. Reed placed his rifle on the seat of the truck and threw the sleeping bag in the back of the pickup, already loaded with saddles, tack, and most of his remaining personal affects.

He fumbled through the bed of the truck until his hand touched a roll of canvas tarp, covered his belongings, and began wrapping everything with a lariat rope. He was taking the last lap of the rope around the load when he heard Mister's low growl, then saw a flash of car lights in the distance.

The vehicle was fast approaching, and less than a half-mile away. *Who could it be?* He had so few visitors, except his mother, and she was probably at the Fort Collins livestock sale with his replacement, Justin Bullock, the new foreman of all three of the Teardrop Ranches.

'Reed was as cool a hand as there was in the country,' his grandfather had often bragged—'as calm as a horse trough.' At the moment, he didn't feel calm at all, watching the strange headlights bounce in and out of chuckholes on the road. Two weeks, or even a week ago, he would have given little mind to the strange vehicle. Tonight, he had a hunch that the unsteady headlights weren't guiding the way for any good news.

He struck a match on his pant leg, lit a cigarette, and leaned his tired body against the pickup to wait for the fast approaching vehicle. The car pulled within fifty feet of Reed's horse trailer and stopped.

He recognized the marked car even before Sheriff Jim Logan swung the driver's side door open and pried his jumbo body out from under the steering wheel. Sheriff Logan wasn't a tall man, maybe five-eight or nine, and, as anyone could see, he wouldn't be the first one to push away from the dinner table.

Logan gathered his balance, hitched at his pants with one hand, and wobbled a few steps toward Reed, in front of the headlights. The dog stood rigid, hair bristling across his back, baring his teeth and growling low in its throat. The sheriff stopped and danced back two steps, lost his balance and nearly fell. Reed raised his hand toward the truck cab and the dog leaped onto the seat, sat on his haunches behind the steering wheel and continued growling.

The passenger side door of the sheriff's car swung open. "Stay where you are Billy. I'll handle this," Logan called out over his shoulder. Reed heard a car door slam.

Reed laughed. "That your backup, sheriff?"

"Carson, you know I don't need a backup. You don't know him. That's Billy Schultz. I borrowed him from the Laramie police department to fill in while Duane is on vacation … nice kid, and pretty cop-savvy, too."

Reed focused squarely on Logan's round face, pulled on his cigarette, and pushed out a cloud of blue smoke, frowning. "Okay, Logan, I know you didn't drive sixty miles for a social call, and I don't need scolding. This is my last load. There's still some personal affects in the house that I can't take. I'll let you know if I decide to come back for them."

Logan pushed a thumb into his pants pocket, and took a step back to balance his weight. "No, Reed, this is more serious than that. As bad as I hate to say it, I got a warrant for your arrest."

Reed fought back his rising anger. He'd known Sheriff Logan ever since he could remember and didn't have any strong feelings for him one way or another until five days ago, when the sheriff served him an eviction notice. A single sheet of paper that turned his world upside down—the little white sheet of paper that made his stomach knot and his throat thicken painfully.

"What in the world are you talking about, Logan?" Reed said, straining to keep his composure. "Has she totally lost it this time?"

I don't know anything about your mama's health, Logan replied. All I know is, she filed charges against you this morning for stealing her cattle. Her ranch foreman, Justin Bullock, and your brother, Kirk, were with her. Seems they think you've been trucking cattle out of here with her brand on them."

Reed lit another cigarette, drew deeply and pushed a cloud of blue smoke toward his boots. He shifted his legs into a square stance. "You know anything I hauled off this ranch belongs to me."

"Well—Reed, it ain't for me to say. All I know is, I'm just doing my job; and you're going back to town with me in cuffs."

"Well—Logan, maybe it's not for you to say, but you aren't cuffing me and you better know you're not taking me back to town—with or without the cuffs."

"Carson, don't make it any harder than it is. All we wanna do is book you, then you can go about your business. Judge probably won't even ask for a bond."

"I trucked a hundred head of Hereford cows with calves and two bulls out of here yesterday. Every one of those cattle wore my brand. Shadow Truck Line can verify that."

"Reed, listen, I ain't personally doubting your word, but…."

"Forget about your doubts and just listen to me before things go any further," Reed said. "I got a little place leased up on Dry Creek …. you know the area. That's where my cattle are and

7

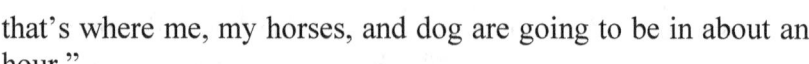

that's where me, my horses, and dog are going to be in about an hour."

Logan stepped back and palmed the top of his revolver. "Okay, Carson, put your hands behind you. I'm gonna cuff you or I'm calling for backup."

Reed took the cigarette from his mouth, dropped it between his feet, and ground it out with his boot. "Sheriff, you can call for backup, or you can shoot me, but I'm not going anywhere with you. My horses need feed and water and my cattle are probably scattered and gone because I haven't had time to repair the fences. I'll go see the judge tomorrow ... and you know I'll keep my word."

Reed swung his long legs under the steering wheel, put the truck in gear, and slowly drove off. Sheriff Logan took a few steps toward the disappearing taillights, like a bloated cow chasing her calf, shouting words Reed couldn't understand.

———

Logan slowly struggled back to his patrol car, opened the door, and allowed his large bulk to slump into the well-worn seat. Sitting quite still, gripping the steering wheel with one hand, he tipped his Stetson back and let go a deep sigh.

"He's big for an Indian," Billy Schultz said. "I wish you would've let me take him."

"He ain't a full-blood Indian," Logan said, catching his breath. "His dad's a full-blood. Now, *there's* a big Indian, but he ain't around here no more. Anyway, Billy, you're new here and you can thank me for not letting you get rough with him."

He inhaled another long breath. "I could've arrested Carson. He'd a let me cuff him, before I shot him, or he decided to take my pistol away from me. But neither one of us was gonna let any of that happen. You see, I've known Reed all his life—since he was a baby. I've always considered him to be a good kid. He's only had two scrapes with the law, one minor, and one serious. But, he doesn't go asking for trouble. Maybe he's getting a raw deal, I don't know. It's happened before. Anyway, you were in the car and had nothing to do with any of this tonight ... and you didn't hear anything .... you got that?"

"Yeah, I got that, Sheriff," Schultz said, with deep sarcasm. "What was this serious thing Carson got busted with?"

Logan looked away from Schultz, shook his head and turned the key on the police car. "It's a long story, and I don't feel like getting into it right now. Tell you later .... maybe." Slowly idling the patrol car in a wide three-sixty, he turned again to face Schultz. "Maybe I let him go too easy tonight, but I know the boy is good for his word."

———

Reed's pickup was pointed toward the back entrance to the Homestead Ranch headquarters, which caused him to travel another five miles out of his way to reach the county road. Better to travel a few miles out of his way, he reasoned, than try to turn around and get past Logan's war party.

Sheriff Logan had entered the ranch by way of the main gate, through the huge rock and stucco archway—the giant ranch marker that was jokingly referred to by some of the neighbors as 'The Grave testimonial.'

Reed reached the county road and turned east. State Highway 167 would be eight miles, then another sixteen miles before he could feel comfortable again on dirt roads. Dirt roads that would take him to his small cabin—the place he now, strangely enough, called home—only the second place he'd called home in his young twenty-seven years.

During the past six days of moving his cattle and personal effects, Reed had dreaded and anguished over his life being uprooted, losing his home. Now—at this moment—he was almost looking forward to it. It would be a place to clear his mind, to think, and, deep down, he even welcomed the chance to be totally on his own for a while.

The cattle stealing charges would go away and maybe he would conquer his need to be shielded by the security of the home ranch before his mother's mood changed and she realized the damage she'd caused. But whatever came of the cattle stealing charges, or her change of attitude, he had an unsettled feeling that his life would never be the same again.

Turning off Highway 167, Reed stopped, inspected his load, and allowed Mister to check the tires. Fighting sleep, he stood behind his trailer, moved his head in circles, stretched his arms, and walked a few high steps in place.

His thoughts returned to the present and he felt an urgent need to know how this mess had come about. *What was going on?* First his own mother evicted him and now he was accused of *rustling?* What had he done wrong?

How long had it been since he'd felt so isolated from his mother ... from the world, for that matter? Not even thinking about it very hard, he silently answered his last question to himself.

It had been eleven years ago. He could still picture in his mind that beautiful girl being dragged from a muddy creek bank and placed on a gurney, not twenty feet from where he imagined himself to be watching in a haze of disbelief. The isolation, shame, and despair stayed with him, and from time to time throughout the years, he thought he could see it in his mother's hollow-eyed stare when she was most upset with him.

Still searching his tired mind, he wondered if he had gone wrong somewhere else. He'd tried to do everything right, by her standards anyway—forfeiting his own plans for college to help her run the three ranches while his brother, Kirk, was in law school—managing the ranch to her last details, staying out of her way during her spells of depression, comforting her when he could, and sitting patiently while listening to nonsense chatter for hours on end.

Kirk never listened to her, not even for a minute. Kirk would roll his eyes and get the hell out when he saw an episode coming. But how many times had he dropped his own plans to run his mother to the hospital when she became a danger to herself and anyone near her. How many times had he battled her attempts at self-destruction in the confines of a truck cab?

She'd been in and out of a mental ward more times than he wanted to remember. But she always seemed normal (normal for her, at least) when she was on her medication. Maybe she was a little nervous and uncertain about who was doing what; nothing to cause him to think she could do something like this. True, communicating with her had become increasingly difficult in the past two years, but he attributed that to his brother, Kirk, and Justin Bullock's increasing influence.

Reed thought about his older brother, Kirk. His stomach twisted. Even with the bad blood between them, he couldn't help but feel sympathetic and sick at heart, considering Kirk's lonely, tortured, self-hating life. Reed could easily understand part of Kirk's problems. But knowing how Kirk felt didn't bring him any closer to his brother. Reed couldn't remember if he'd ever had anything with him, even before his own problems started. Kirk never allowed anyone near him (not even his mother), and Reed never pushed the issue.

And what about Justin Bullock? What part was her lovesick foreman playing in all of this? It was useless. His thoughts were jumbled and going nowhere. He needed sleep. He called the dog and swung back into the pickup, trying to convince himself that tomorrow he would wake up and all this would just be another nightmare to forget.

Five miles off the highway, he stopped and opened a wire gate. A few yards left of the gate, in a large opening cleared for the purpose, stood a cattle loading chute. Surrounding the opening and as far as the eye could see were stands of scrub oak brush and scattered pine trees. The road got rough and steep from here on to the cabin—too rough for cattle trucks. This was the spot where Shadow Truck Line unloaded his alleged 'stolen' cattle yesterday. Reed smelled cedar, pine, and sage, mixed with the pungent scent of fresh manure of over a hundred head of cattle.

Reed pushed his shoulder against the stubborn wire post holding the gate together, drove his load through, and closed the gate behind him.

Two more miles, through a small creek bottom—with the banks starting to freeze from the night's frost—then up a steep hill, before Reed's new home was illuminated in a widening tunnel of headlights.

The little one-room log cabin, a small outhouse, horse barn, surrounded by a small pole corral and feed rack, were the only visible buildings on the rolling landscape. The corral came off of a rickety barn, and even in the limited light, looked like fair game for the next windstorm. To the left of the corral stood a large stack of baled hay, hauled in the same day he signed the lease with old man Cadwaller.

"Okay, Mister, we're home," Reid said to the dog and ran the palm of his hand over his faithful companion's alert head. He squinted at the clock on the dashboard and saw that it was midnight. "Home early tonight," he said aloud. Leaving the motor running and the lights on, he slowly opened the pickup door. Mister jumped out behind him and disappeared into the darkness.

Reed untied the halter ropes on the horses, unlatched the trailer gates, and watched while they slowly backed out of the trailer. Leaving them in the pole corral, he checked the water trough and threw a bale of hay over the fence. Returning to the truck, he grabbed his flashlight and turned off the headlights.

With flashlight in hand, he found his sleeping bag under the tarp. Too exhausted to unload anything else, he carefully replaced the canvas over his tack and strode toward the cabin.

Two split logs served as steps into the cabin and the door swung open on two large steel hinges. There was a metal latch where a lock could be placed, but it didn't cross his mind to buy a padlock for the purpose. Once inside, he struck a match and lit a gas propane lantern.

Some of the chinking between the logs was cracked and had fallen out in places, allowing for a slight breeze through the cabin. There was a small cook stove in one corner and a tiny wooden table near the wall by a small window. In the other half of the cabin stood another wooden table, two straight back chairs, and a wire frame cot. The floor was made of wooden planks with lots of creak to them.

He rolled his sleeping bag out on the bare bedsprings, yanked off his boots and stretched his long frame, heard his backbone snap several times, and fell asleep.

TWO

Reed sat at the little table and stared into his coffee cup. He watched his cigarette burn out on a jar lid, fought back glimpses of the confrontation with Sheriff Logan, and stole glances at Mister begging for his breakfast. He kept pushing the thoughts from his mind. There'd be plenty of time to think on his way to town to see old Judge Ledbetter.

Feeding his horses hay, he glanced at the sky, watched low submarine-shaped clouds racing eastward, felt a shiver from the cold breeze, and sensed there was something very different in the air. He hurried over to his truck and turned on the radio, where he got his answer soon enough. The first words he heard were a cattleman's warning. Two feet of snow had already fallen in Salt Lake City with more expected. Snow already moving east into Wyoming and ….

Reed flipped the radio off and looked toward his barn where the wind was making a rat-tat-tat sound on the loose tin on top of the barn. He glanced at the sky again and his thoughts turned to his cattle.

It was the last week in March, and it had been so mild. He thought about the big snowstorm about this time last year and cursed himself for not keeping up with the weather forecasts the past few days. Would they have enough protection in the bottoms to survive a blizzard? There was plenty of old grass, but could the cows get to it? If a front was coming in, would he have time to haul hay into the treed bottoms? Garfield was a two-hour trip—one way. If he left now it would still be four o'clock before he returned to the cabin. But he had given his word to the sheriff. He had to make the trip and get back in time to haul hay to the bottoms.

It was ten o'clock. Reed parked his pickup and jogged half a city block to the courthouse steps. Taking the steps two at a time, he breezed into the clerk's office. Sheriff Logan looked up from his newspaper, inspected his watch, and managed a weak smile.

Reed paused to catch his breath. "What's the schedule, Sheriff? Can I see the judge, now? There's a storm coming and I got to get back and throw some hay to my cattle before all hell breaks loose."

"Judge's still in court. Margaret says it shouldn't be too much longer."

"How much longer?" Reed asked, a little too loud.

Logan lifted his felt with the tip of his thumb, showing his red, irritated forehead. "Carson ...." Logan started very slowly, "you blow in here like a dust devil expecting everyone to be at your beck and call, and it just don't happen that way. The judge don't plan his schedule around your cattle feeding problems. So, you just settle down and he'll see you in his own good time. Any more questions?"

"No, Sheriff. Guess I owe you an apology, though. None of this is your fault."

Ten minutes passed. Margaret pushed a button on her desk. "The judge will see you in his chambers, now," she said.

Reed had met the judge only once in his life. The one time he wished he could forget. He was only sixteen then, and he was praying the judge wouldn't recognize his face or his name.

Reed trailed the sheriff down a short hallway before the portly man stopped at a closed door, cracked it a few inches, and stole a quick peek. He opened the door wider and nodded for Reed to enter.

Reed took in the large, theatre-like room at a glance. It was easy to see nothing much had changed in eleven years. There were metal folding chairs lined on each side of a long passageway that led to a small platform, and nothing else to attract much notice. Judge Eliot Ledbetter was sitting in a large, worn, over-stuffed chair behind a shiny desk as if he hadn't moved in eleven years.

Reed fixed his eyes on the man in the old chair and remembered a much younger man. The judge was holding his reading glasses on his nose with one hand and studying a single sheet of paper in front of his face with the other. Reed and the sheriff moved to a small desk directly under the podium, and stood, staring at the judge. To Reed, it seemed like forever before the man looked up and said, "You can be seated."

"Are you Reed Carson?" the judge asked, with only a glance toward him.

Reed cleared his throat. "Yes, sir" and felt a slight nudge from Logan's elbow.

"You will respond to me as Your Honor, Mr. Carson."

Reed cleared his throat again. "Yes, sir, Your Honor."

"Are you represented by counsel, Mr. Carson?"

"No, sir, Your Honor."

The judge penciled something on a notebook, "Well, I'd advise you to get one. However, you can represent yourself at this hearing, if you so desire. I'm not going to require a bond. But, when I see you again I pray you will have confident counsel."

"Yes, sir, Your Honor."

"Mr. Carson, since we're not holding formal court, I'm going to make things very simple. Lucy Carson, your mother, has charged you with removing two hundred head of cows and calves from her Teardrop Ranch without her permission. By law, that is stealing, and that is what she is charging you with."

Judge Ledbetter read off some legal terminology, mentioned some dates, numbers, and asked Reed if he understood. Near the end of the second sentence, Reed's mind was lost to thoughts of the fast approaching storm, buying needed groceries and supplies before the trip home, and getting hay to his, soon-to-be, helpless cattle.

"Do you understand the charges against you, Mr. Carson?"

"Yes, sir, Your Honor, I understand," Reed was finally allowed to muster. But all he really savvied was that he had already been tried and convicted of stealing his mother's cows, and he needed to get the hell out of there.

"Mr. Carson, do you have anything to say about these charges?"

By now Reed Carson was visibly shaken, not only by the seemingly cold treatment from Judge Ledbetter, but by his need to get back to his cow herd. "Your Honor, all the cattle I removed from Mom's ranch belonged to me. As Sheriff Logan can testify, two days ago I hauled off a hundred head of Hereford cows and calves and two bulls from the Teardrop Ranch. Every one of those cattle bore my brand, bar-teardrop-quarter-circle. I don't have a bill of sale from my mother, Lucy Carson, but I can prove those cattle were given to me in lieu of wages over the years I worked for her."

"Okay, okay, Carson. Tell all that on your day of court. I'm putting you down as pleading not guilty. Sheriff Logan has assured me that he knows where you are keeping the allegedly stolen cattle, and I'm allowing you to keep them in your possession until after your trial. Your counsel will advise you of your court date. Good day, gentlemen."

Reed glanced at his watch, then up at the dark, roiling storm clouds as he waited for traffic before pulling out of the parking lot. It was eleven-forty. He was thankful for the early hour, and that snow hadn't started to fall, yet. There was still plenty of time to stop for groceries and pick up a few bags of cow cake at the Co-Op and get back to the cabin before four o'clock. With any luck he could get a two-day supply of hay hauled to the bottoms and spread some cow cubes on top of the hay. The extra feed would keep the cows from scattering to look for grass.

A small grocery store was on his way out of town; the Co-Op was a little further down the street. Reed grabbed a cart with both hands, wheeled down the aisles as if being chased by a sheriff's posse and was out of the store in less than ten minutes. His stop at the Co-Op was nearly as fast: fifteen bags of cow cake— weight for added traction in case he got behind the storm, and enough supplemental feed for several days for his cows.

An hour out of Garfield, snow started spitting on his windshield. An hour later, Reed turned off Highway 167 on top of three inches of fresh snow and near zero visibility. His heart sank. If he couldn't get hay and grain to the sheltered area in the bottoms, the cattle would wander with the blizzard until they crowded into a drift fence, where most of them would smother or freeze to death.

Inside the cabin, Reed dressed in coveralls, discarded his Stetson for a winter cap, grabbed warm mittens, and with Mister at his heels, rushed toward his still idling pickup.

Blinded by snow, he could only guess his way to the haystack where he loaded thirty bales of hay. Following the cross-fence to the creek bottom, he found his cattle bunched near the fence with their tails pointed toward the storm. The hunched, snow-covered animals paid little or no attention to him as he scattered hay amongst them and covered the hay with three sacks of cow cake.

The cows were fed and protected by a deep gulley where a small stream flowed that supported some scattered willows and a few cottonwood trees.

Back at the cabin, Reed built a fire and removed his wet coat and coveralls, soaked from the driving snow. Mister shook his body violently to remove crusted, frozen snow from his long hair, then jumped on Reed's sleeping bag and lay still, his eyes following Reed's every movement.

A small blizzard raged through the slits in the logs where the chinking had weathered and fallen out. He scraped two inches of snow off his eating table and hurriedly stuffed the cracks with underwear, socks, and old newspapers he'd been using to start fires. Soon the fire was crackling and steam was rising from the snow melting on top of the stove. His stomach rumbled. Mister raised his wet head into the air and perked his ears. He'd fed the dog his breakfast before they'd left the cabin that morning. Reed couldn't remember when he'd eaten his last prepared food.

Reed's first complete meal in his new home felt like paradise. He couldn't recall when he'd been so hungry. He peeled and sliced potatoes, placed them in an iron skillet, and covered them with pieces of bacon and onion. He slapped two sirloin steaks in another iron skillet and watched them sizzle while pulling on a cigarette to put down that hard, empty feeling in his stomach.

"Yeah, you little mutt," Reed said, "I cooked enough for both of us." A slit of a smile creased his lips, and he dished out some dog chow cubes for Mister to tide him along until the steaks were cooked.

Reed tackled his meal like a man three-quarters starved, consuming enormous amounts of steak and fried potatoes. Mister ate half a pan of fried potatoes, two slices of wheat bread, and a complete sirloin steak, medium rare. After his meal, the dog grasped the bone between his teeth and jumped on the bed, making grinding sounds that reminded Reed of a rat gnawing through the pantry floor.

After supper, Reed touched a match on top of the hot stove, lit a Marlboro, then walked to the door and peered into the swirling snow.

The storm waged with increasing force. His little camp was supplied with plenty of food, water, and wood. He wished he could just hunker down in his warm hutch, relax, and wait it out. But his mind was too busy. His cattle were in danger of freezing, he was accused of being a cattle thief, his mother had deep-seated mental problems, and for the first time in his life, he was truly alone in body, heart, and spirit.

THREE

Reed's latest trouble with Sheriff Logan had started early the morning of his last trip with material possessions to his new home—less than ten hours before Sheriff Logan would try to arrest him for cattle theft.

While Reed was pulling on his second Marlboro over his third cup of coffee and wondering if one more truckload would see him off the Homestead Ranch, the second largest ranch of the Teardrop spread, Lucy Carson was glancing at the clock on her nightstand at the North River Ranch, telling herself she would have to hurry.

Lucy wasn't looking forward to her business with the district attorney this early in the morning. The Fort Collins cattle sale, later that day, would be stressful, too. All of her cattlemen friends from several counties and some from out-of-state would be at the sale as usual, but it wouldn't be the same. Today, she would be thinking about her latest legal actions against Reed, and she would be scrutinized by her son, Kirk, and her new ranch foreman, Justin Bullock.

Justin would be coming from the bunkhouse at any minute. Kirk had already arrived from the South River Ranch. She pulled her ladies Levi's over her smooth hips, sucked in her stomach, zipped the front and turned to look in the full-length mirror. She stared at her tall, slim figure for a full half minute, turning one way then another. "Not bad for a fifty-two-year-old mother of two," she mused. From her jewelry box she selected her favorite earrings: dangling turquoise Indian jewels she'd bought on her last trip to Santa Fe. She bent to pull on her red, hand-made, Lucchese boots. Then she stood to brush impatiently at her long, dyed-red hair. She finished her wardrobe off with a pure white, cotton, button-down western shirt, and checked herself in the mirror again. There was a knock at her bedroom door. "Justin, is that you?"

"No, Mom, it's me, and we're late. Justin is here, pacing the road and kicking rocks, as usual."

"Do you have the papers with you?" Lucy asked.

"Yes, Mother … without the papers we wouldn't be making this trip."

Lucy seized her leather purse from the counter, shoved a jar of bottled water inside, and trailed Kirk's footsteps down the hallway. She locked the house door, then with long strides, overtook him at the yard gate. Taking his arm, she asked in nearly a whisper, "You okay with this, Kirk?"

Kirk didn't break his stride. "You know how I feel, Mom. Do we need to keep going through this?"

Justin Bullock was strutting around the car, smoking a cigarette, looking for a stray rock to send on its way. She glanced his way and met his glaring, impatient gaze. He flipped his cigarette butt into the wind and opened the rear car door, all in one motion. His actions struck her as an ill omen. Not a good way to start the day, for any of us, she thought—especially herself. The next two hours would be stressful, then the day—the world—would get better for her, she tried to assure herself.

Tim Barkley, assistant district attorney for Mineral County, was sitting at his desk with wet palms, shuffling papers. He was expecting Lucy Carson—actually looking forward to seeing her again. Barkley had been widowed for four years now and had tried for three of the four years to interest Lucy in a romantic way. He knew she was a stern, disciplined woman and would probably prove too much for him to handle; and he knew the history of her mental problems. But none of this dampened his enthusiasm for the chase, or stopped him from admiring her flowing, confident beauty. They'd had several ˙luncheon dates,˙ as he enjoyed thinking of them, but he had so far been unsuccessful in talking her into anything further.

Justin Bullock held the door open for Lucy to enter the district attorney's waiting room. Lucy strode past the matronly woman sitting behind a clean desk without a word or glance in her direction. She stopped at the doorway to Barkley's office, brushed a lock of stray hair from her face and waited for Bullock to open the door.

Lucy never just walked into a room—she made an entrance, piercing and dominating the space with striding confidence, head held high, knowing that all eyes were probing her direction. Such was the way she entered Tim Barkley's office that Monday morning to sign papers.

Barkley rose abruptly and extended his hand. "It's really nice to see you again, Lucy," he said, beaming with a smile as wide as a dinner plate. Lucy dropped her head to avoid his admiring gaze. She cared not a whit about Tim Barkley, and it always irritated her to see his naked, fawning affection. "I'm so sorry the situation between you and Reed has come to this," Barkley said. "But, Lucy, you can be sure …."

"Look, Tim…let's just get on with this. I need to be in Fort Collins for the livestock sale in less than two hours." She was in no mood for his admiring prattle.

"Oh sure," Barkley replied, nervously removing a handkerchief from his pocket to wipe his reading glasses and the sweat from his overheated, bald forehead.

Flanked by Justin Bullock and Kirk, Lucy leafed through the several papers required for her review and signature   papers that could put her younger son behind bars for a crime she was certain he didn't commit. Kirk, the habitual nervous twitch at the corner of his mouth working overtime, practiced his lawyerly smirk. Justin Bullock sat straight up with a boot slung over his knee, wearing a thin smile.

Kirk and Justin exchanged glances just as Lucy was signing the last papers and excused themselves to look for a bathroom.

"Okay, Tim, now it's in your ballpark," Lucy said, looking straight at Barkley, but not really meeting his eyes. She swiveled around in the chair and rose to her feet. Barkley pushed his chair back, hurried around the desk, and followed her to hold the door open.

Lucy made a half-turn toward Barkley and said, "Thank you."

Barkley replied, "Hey, it's all part of the service...and, Lucy...can we have lunch again some time?"

Their eyes met for a split second. Her lips parted as if to say something. Then, without a word, she turned, tilted her head back and strode toward the door with long, purposeful steps.

Lucy's Cadillac El Dorado was parked less than a block from the district attorney's office. Kirk slid behind the wheel and turned the key. Justin opened the door on the passenger side of the car and cast a smile in Lucy's direction. "Want to sit in the front, sweetheart?"

"No, Justin, you and Kirk can talk cattle, tell jokes, or whatever. I'm going to get a couple of hours of shuteye."

Lucy sat upright in the soft, luxurious seat, opened her brown leather purse, and removed a bottle of water and four small pill containers. She quietly dropped two capsules from each container into the palm of her hand, threw them into her mouth, and drank from the bottle. Then she stretched her long legs across the comfortable seat, eased her aching head down on a pillow and closed her eyes.

Sleep was the last thing on Lucy's mind, though—not the least was Reed's eviction notice she'd signed just five days ago, then the cattle theft charges filed today.

So much had happened the past two years, and now Lucy could feel it all coming down on her. Kirk had settled in his little law office in Riverdale, and she had installed both boys as ranch foremen on two of her ranches: Kirk on the smaller South River Ranch and Reed on the Homestead Ranch, where she had lived all her life—until her mother died.

Now everything was going haywire again. Reed was putting more pressure on her to sell him the Homestead Ranch, her new backhoe tractor suddenly disappears and Kirk comes to her accusing Reed of stealing cattle—all of this when she thought her life was finally under control.

The North River Ranch was the biggest of the three ranches with nearly twenty-thousand acres of rich grassland-sagebrush range, with a forest permit for five hundred pairs of cows and calves, and two thousand acres of high producing hay land. For Lucy, it was the new home ranch and headquarters of the Teardrop Ranches Empire.

She didn't want to move to the North River Ranch after her mother died. It was her father who thought the change would help him cope with the constant reminder of his loss.

Even after all these years, she still missed the old Homestead Ranch, but she couldn't think about moving back. Her house on the North River Ranch was a showplace. The house was built by a Texas oilman a few years before he died, and the ranch became the property of her dad, Sheldon Graves. It wasn't long after her own father died that she realized the spaciousness, elegance, and charm of the six-bedroom, Colonial style home was perfect for her new social status in the community.

Not long after Reed was out of high school, Lucy settled him as foreman on the old home ranch, located not five miles from the North River spread. He was dependable and steady and she had promised to sell it to him in the near future if he would take the job.

Lucy thought it would be nice to have him close enough to manage the old ranch and help her make some difficult management decisions on all three ranches. But it wasn't long after he was firmly established in his new job that she realized it was all a big mistake. He became obsessed with the notion of buying the old Homestead Ranch which prompted her to regret her decision as it would reduce the size of her ranch empire substantially.

From age fourteen, the year of her mother's sudden death from a car accident, Lucy had worked and planned with her father, Sheldon Graves, to become the heiress of the Graves' ranches. An only child, her father doted upon her and spoiled her to a point she could barely stand herself at times. Daddy Graves' primary concern was keeping the ranches together and training his only child to take over in his absence. When her father died, the Graves' ranches became the Carson ranches, and she made them her life.

People didn't look at her any more as the spoiled brat daughter of Sheldon Graves. She'd proved her worth as a manager of a large ranching empire. She relished the attention and recognition by the community and certain state senators. And she relished the power it gave her over local politicians. All this she wasn't ready to surrender for the sake of satisfying Reed's ranching ambitions.

Justin Bullock was another concern, but nothing she couldn't handle, she thought. Still, she felt like she should have been more discrete. In the two years that Bullock had worked for her, she had never divulged her plans to get all three ranches back under her sole control. But he must never know that he had been a player in her ambition to get Reed completely off the Homestead Ranch. Yet to do so she had had to secretly compromise her true feelings towards this bully of a man, who could make her life unbearable if he even suspected the truth.

The sedative Lucy had taken upon leaving the district attorney's office was starting to work. She was in a softer mood now. Her eyes burned, but she was no longer seeking the peacefulness sleep would bring to her troubled mind. Her headache was gone. She sat upright in the car seat, feeling more alert, stared at the brim of Bullock's Stetson for a moment, and drank from her water bottle.

Kirk was speaking, his voice barely audible, telling a joke—something about three preachers in an airplane. Bullock laughed heartily. Lucy closed her eyes again, tilted her head back on the soft leather seat and allowed her thoughts to drift—back to the night when she allowed Justin Bullock to become more than just a hired man in her life.

The housekeeper had served dinner to just the two of them, then excused herself, saying she would return later to clean the kitchen. Throughout the meal, the conversation between Lucy and Justin had been light, mostly about ranch activities. When dinner was finished, Justin rose from the table and moved to the living room, where he made himself comfortable at one end of the soft leather couch—the most presumptuous thing he had done in the short time he had worked for the ranch. But she said nothing, followed him into the living room, and asked him if he would care for a drink before returning to the bunkhouse. Lucy reached for a new bottle of Black Label Scotch as she was speaking. She poured Justin Scotch on the rocks, and she had a rum and Coke.

By the time she had refilled their glasses for the fourth time, Justin had spilled, what she guessed to be, a carefully crafted version of his life history, of lost love, and of life's disappointments.

By his body language and his soft tone of voice, she knew he was hitting on her, making his move. She didn't counter his confessions with any of her own. Her mind was busy with other thoughts. Thoughts about how she could use this, seemingly simple, hired man to further her own personal goals. Despite an induced haze, she came to realize that Justin Bullock would prove to be more valuable than just an ordinary ranch hand.

That was two years ago. With Justin Bullock's unwitting help, her plan had worked. Reed was off the Homestead Ranch and the Carson Ranches were intact, again. No more harassment from her younger son about taking away part of her empire.

"Time to wake up sleeping beauty and spend some money," Lucy heard Justin whisper.

The sale barn was packed for the monthly breeding cow sale. Except for a few out-of-state buyers, Lucy and Kirk knew every single rancher, their wives and their kids. Among them, Lucy was treated as an equal—a savvy cattle buyer and a successful rancher.

But today wasn't a good day for keeping up relations. She kept her head close to her clipboard and avoided long conversations. Reed was known by every ranchman in that part of the state, and she was sensitive and defensive when every casual conversation ended with, "Hey, how's that big, tall drink of water son of yours?" or "Some gal got Reed off on a picnic today?"

They found three empty seats in the bleachers. Kirk and Justin Bullock flanked her on either side. Justin turned in his seat toward Lucy. "Sorry about you having to answer all those questions about Reed," he whispered.

Lucy placed a hand on Bullock's knee. "It's okay, Justin, I've handled worse. It'll all be over tonight. Then there's the trial, and who knows what then…."

Bullock put his arm around her shoulders, leaned closer, and whispered in her ear. "I'll be right there beside you."

"What do you think, guys?" Lucy said in a subdued voice, changing the subject, staring at her clipboard. "Are the figures we discussed about right to replace our missing cattle? I mean, the mother cows Reed has somehow found necessary to haul off the ranch—to hell knows where."

Her chest tightened with a jolt of guilt. She settled back in the hard, wooden chair with a deep breath, hoping to release the pressure in her chest. She'd allowed herself go along with the façade thus far, and everything had gone as planned. She had to remind herself to be careful, to say just the right things at just the right time. There was no turning back now, she thought. Later, much later, after the Homestead Ranch was securely under her control again—and after Justin was on his way—she would smooth Reed's ruffled feathers.

"I walked through the lots while you and Kirk were getting reacquainted with the locals," Bullock said. "I don't think there's enough good cattle here to buy two hundred head. We could maybe buy a hundred or a hundred and fifty."

"I'll be happy with a hundred head," Lucy said, now staring straight ahead at the cattle being herded into the sell ring. "It's early. The grass hasn't started to come real good yet, and there'll be another sale in May."

By six o'clock, she had bought eighty-seven head of different age breeding cows. "I feel really good about what we were able to buy," Lucy said, as they made their way out of the sale barn. "We were lucky to get the last of the Peter Redfield herd. Poor Peter, lost his ranch, then his wife leaves him, and his only son comes out of the closet and volunteers for the Army. I'm glad I didn't run into him today. I'm not *that* good at consoling people. Let's stop by the desk and make some trucking arrangements, then get something to eat at the Rancher's Restaurant before we go home."

The restaurant was crowded. Some of the ranchers had seen Bullock with Lucy at social events and were starting to give him the once-over. This all added to her general discomfort. She cut her steak in deliberate motions and ate quietly. Sensing her mood, Justin and Kirk became silent, too.

Kirk unlocked the doors to the El Dorado with one click to the remote. Bullock moved to the rear door, held his hand on the handle until Lucy tilted her chin, her sleepy green eyes meeting his inquiring grin. She lowered her head, and settled her tired body into the cushiony seat. He closed her door, winked at Kirk's questioning gaze and strutted around the car. He removed his hat and slid across the smooth leather seat until their legs touched. Lucy moved away from an arm that encircled her shoulders.

It was going to be an uneasy ride home—for both of them, Lucy imagined. Her stomach was churning, to the point of being sick, still feeling the resentment and humiliation from seeing her cattlemen friends giving Justin the once-over, picturing them as a couple. The thought of any man sharing the glory of the Carson Ranches nauseated her—a state senator, a wealthy cattleman, or even a doctor—maybe. She knew what Justin wanted. She didn't want to do this, especially after today. She hated it already. But most of all she hated Justin's assuming attitude, the excitement in his eyes—and she was blaming herself for all of it. There had been times these past two years, after consuming too many rum and Cokes, when she'd let her guard down just enough to give him some hope. She agonized with the thought.

Under different circumstances, and at another time in her life, she could even imagine herself feeling differently toward his advances. Justin was an attractive man, with his six-foot-three height, broad shoulders, and wiry, ropey muscles. But she wasn't a reckless teenager any more, she reminded herself. She was Lucy Carson, heir to a large cattle empire, a respected member of the community. It turned her stomach to think she would have to continue playing the game with a common hired man to keep things going her way.

But she had to get through today—and the long ride back to the ranch—then she would have a talk with him, let him know where he stood. Lucy waited with fear and disgust as the big Cadillac backed away from the restaurant: fear that Justin's temper would erupt and cause a scene in front of Kirk if she refused his advances, and disgust, with a nausea coming from deep within, if she allowed it to happen.

Lucy reached for Justin's hand, held it lightly, wanting to make conversation, anything to distract him from what she knew was foremost on his mind. Now she was holding both of his hands and staring straight into his intense blue eyes. "Justin, do you think we did right by filing those charges against Reed today?" she whispered.

"Sweetheart, we should've had him arrested six months ago. He's been nothing but trouble for us. And I'm still convinced he stole that backhoe tractor and sold it out-of-state somewhere."

"Really? Sheriff Logan said he made a thorough investigation. I asked him outright if Reed could have been involved and he didn't waste any time assuring me of Reed's innocence. But, you've always been so right about everything, Justin. I'll take your word over that sloppy sheriff's any day."

It was working. She almost smiled at her own deviousness. Bullock was agitated, yet feeling safe. Time was her enemy, but if she could just keep the conversation going her way….

Bullock turned in his seat, his face flushed, daring Lucy to disagree with him. "Lucy, you know the proof I've given you, and Kirk has told you himself that Reed has been stealing our cattle. What's to say he has any conscience about stealing a backhoe from his mother?"

Bullock's remark cut deep. She'd only resented him before. Now she was sure she hated him. Lucy wanted to end this conversation—now. It wasn't going the way she'd hoped. Better to be sick at her stomach than risk a shouting match in front of Kirk.

"Justin, let's stop this and enjoy our ride home together. Okay…?" Her voice was smooth, while making quiet, cooing sounds with her lips and running her long fingers through his thick blonde hair.

Lucy tilted her head toward Bullock and closed her eyes. He kissed her fully on the mouth, positioned his left hand on her leg, far above the knee, and applied a light pressure. She resisted the urge to make a fist and slam it into his face.

She grimaced, gently pushed his hand away and reached for her purse, retrieving a container of pills and a bottle of water. "I'm so sorry, Justin, but I have the worst headache in the world. You understand, don't you? We'll be home in no time."

FOUR

Reed fell asleep on top of his bedroll, as he had done the past five nights. Sometime during the night he awoke, chilled to the bone. The cabin door was ajar, flapping with the wind, allowing part of the storm to be deposited throughout the cabin. With stilted movements, he pulled himself out of bed and bolted the door. After stoking the fire, he removed his boots, shirt and pants, and crawled between the folds of the warm sleeping bag.

He came wide awake in an instant, from the first pull of the cabin door. Mister's growl broke the stillness before the door latch groaned the second time. Reed didn't know what time it was, but he knew he hadn't slept long after securing the door. He hunched his shoulders up on one elbow, stared into the darkness, and listened to the wind scream for release from the structure. Maybe a minute passed before he was brought wide awake by two solid bangs, like a rifle butt or the end of a shovel handle hitting the door.

Reed sat straight up in bed. The dog was growling, barking, jumping at the door, backing up and jumping again. "What the hell!" Reed said in a voice loud enough to be heard above the noise of the howling storm. He sprang out of bed and reached for his pants and shirt, folded on a wooden chair near his bed.

He dressed quickly, found his flashlight and hunting rifle and went to stand by the door. Mister was barking and foaming at the mouth like a rabid dog. Reed did nothing to stop him. A minute or two passed, while he stood, waited, and cleared his head. Three more bangs at the door, this time with more intensity. "Who are you?" Reed shouted.

"It's Butch Morgan."

Reed didn't know anyone by that name but he knew that whoever it was had to be hurting if he'd been out in that weather very long. "Okay, Morgan, stand back a pace or two and I'll unlock the door." He glanced down at the dog, now settled down to a deep, guttural growl, "Sit, Mister—stay."

Cradling his rifle, Reed pulled the latch on the door, and pushed it hard with his foot. He moved backward two quick steps and shined the flashlight directly through the opening.

In the snow-tinged light of the flashlight beam, Reed thought he was looking at something out of a horror movie—a huge caricature formed in ice and snow. He froze. The eerie creature had spoken, but it couldn't be real. He was dreaming or his mind was playing tricks on him. They stood, staring at each other, until the creature raised his hand slightly and said, "Can I come in?"

Reed didn't trust his own voice. He backed up a step or two more, leaned his rifle against the wall, and motioned it inside.

The caricature wavered, like a gut-shot grizzly, stumbled forward two steps, and Reed helped him squeeze his huge bulk through a normal-sized door. Mister was having no part of it. The dog jumped on Reed's bed and sat on his haunches, teeth bared.

Once through the door, the caricature laid his rifle on the floor, yanked off his mittens, and headed straight for the stove. Reed backed off a step or two and stood motionless, staring at the stranger trying to warm his hands over a lukewarm stove.

After closing and latching the door against the howling wind, Reed shook the grate on the little stove and grabbed a piece of firewood in each hand. The stranger moved to the side to allow him to open the top and chunk the wood onto the warm coals.

In a few minutes, the air inside the cabin turned warm and the ice and snow covered hulk started to melt.

A puddle of water formed at his feet. The seemingly frozen body, that Reed now recognized to be a man, moved to remove an ankle-length beaver garment. Reed made a movement as if to help him.

With his lips barely moving, the creature-like figure managed to say, "Thanks, friend, but I can take it from here. I just need to thaw out a bit more."

Reed stood back and looked at the man more closely, now dead certain he'd never seen him before. The stranger brushed back his beaver cap to reveal a thick head of shoulder-length, dark brown hair. "Sure glad you let me in ... don't believe I caught your name."

"You didn't ask. I'm Reed Carson."

"Hmm...," Morgan uttered, quietly, while stroking his tobacco-stained beard.

Reed was surprised to see the man looking at him with a curious expression now, sizing him up. "Don't guess we've ever met, but that ain't surprising, since I spend most of my time roaming the hills. You any relation to Jesse Carson?"

"How do you know my dad?" Reed asked, trying to hide his surprise, while looking directly into the stranger's deep-set, brown eyes.

"We've spent some time together."

"Where is Jesse these days?" Reed asked, still trying to keep his voice calm.

"I don't know, haven't seen him for awhile."

Morgan reached deep into a shirt pocket, came out with a new pad of Days Work chewing tobacco, numbly removed the wrapping and bit off a large chunk. Positioning the chew in his mouth as he talked, Morgan said, "Since I'm imposing in your diggings, you can call me Butch, and, if it's okay, I'll call you Reed."

"Fair enough," Reed said. There was a long silence. "So, Butch," Reed finally said, "Now that we're on a first name basis, what are you doing out on foot in *this* weather?"

Morgan had placed his ankle-length beaver coat on a wall peg above the stove, and was warming his hands, watching the steam rise from the wet fur. "It may surprise you, but I don't have wheels or a mount. Years ago got used to getting around on my own power."

Reed thought he could see a crack of a smile through the tobacco-stained hair surrounding his lips. "But to answer your question, son, I got lost. You see, I got a little lean-to not far from here, and a diggings the other direction. Your cabin here lies smack-dab in the center of both. I'd left my hut in early afternoon. I could see a storm coming, but figured I could make shelter before the storm broke loose. I've known about your cabin here forever...used it some in the past. So when the storm got really bad, I just naturally felt my way here. Surprised me when the door was locked, then your dog barking kind of gave me a spook."

"You're welcome to bunk it out with me as long as you need to," Reed said. "I've got plenty of grub and firewood."

"Appreciate the gesture, son. I won't take up more room than need be. Expect this storm will be blown out of here by morning and I'll be moving on."

Reed stifled a laugh. There was hardly enough room for him and his dog and this guy would make nearly two of both of them. But he was glad for the company, and there were a thousand questions he wanted to ask this strange hulk. He didn't want to pry, though, not just yet, anyway. He took Morgan to be a man not easily pushed into volunteering any more than he cared to.

Reed pegged the man to be about forty-five or fifty. He could be six-feet-six, or even a little taller, massive shoulders and a chest as dense as a black bear. He tried to remember the last time he'd seen anyone this big, with so much bearing. His own father maybe, but he didn't have a clear picture in his mind what he looked like, just that he was big.

Reed stoked the fire, walked to the door and tossed coffee grounds and stale coffee into the swirling snow. He refilled the pot and placed it back on the stove. Soon the fresh brewed coffee aroma filled the room. Reed filled two tin cups and the two big men sat across the table from each other, like heavyweights preparing for an arm wrestling contest. They cradled their coffee mugs, stared at the table in front of them, drinking in silence.

Morgan's words, 'We've spent some time together,' played over and over in Reed's mind as he sipped the hot coffee. *How much did this stranger really know about Jesse Carson?* He was determined to find the answers before the grizzled hulk trekked back to his mountain domain, maybe never to be seen again. He was hungry for any news about his dad, even if it came from a stranger who looked and acted like Paul Bunyan.

Reed almost couldn't remember when he'd seen his dad last. It was probably fifteen years ago, when he was twelve-years-old, he thought, but when he put his mind to it, he remembered it clearly. He and Kirk had been tossing a ball about in the yard when an old pickup drove into the ranch driveway. A large, dark-skinned man sat at the wheel, wearing a black, flat-brimmed hat. He didn't get out of the truck, just sat there, his eyes glued on the two of them. Reed opened the yard gate and started toward the truck, when his mother appeared at the door. "Reed, Kirk! Come to the house, right now!"

The man in the truck didn't move.

Inside the house, their mother dialed a number on the telephone. Kirk disappeared into another part of the house and Reed hovered at the living room window, keeping a sharp eye out for his mother, while watching the man in the old truck.

The pickup sat there for a good half-hour, until a sheriff's car appeared, and two uniformed men got out and approached the driver's side of the vehicle. The dark-skinned man with the big black hat drove off, without looking back.

It wasn't until several days later that his mother told the two boys about the dark-skinned man in the old pickup: 'If you must know, it was your good-for-nothing father. And if he shows himself around here again he'll be doing some time behind bars.'

At the time, Reed didn't care all that much. There weren't many days she didn't remind him that his father was a drunken, lazy Indian, who cared nothing for his kids, and had no self-respect. It didn't occur to him until he was a grown man that maybe his mother had been deliberately poisoning his mind against his father.

It was another hour before they finished their third cup of coffee. Neither man had spoken a word since sitting down at the table. Reed glanced at his watch and scraped his chair back. "There's some blankets behind the seat of my pickup that you can make do with—if I can find the truck." Reed stretched his long arms, wrestled his body into a pair of insulated coveralls, and plunged into the blizzard. Within five minutes, he returned to the cabin, stomped the snow from his boots and handed an armload of blankets to his unlikely guest.

Morgan reached for the blankets. "Much obliged, son, I'll be out of your hair tomorrow, and you and old dog there will have your space back."

Reed helped him move the table, chairs, food cooler, and assorted tack to make enough room to stretch his large frame out on the floor. Morgan's deep snoring disturbed the silence before Reed finished stoking the fire and preparing the coffee pot for morning.

It was late, but Reed didn't know if he could sleep. Something about the man and the name, Butch Morgan, disturbed him. For sure he would remember the man if he'd seen him before, but the name rang a bell somewhere in his mind. There weren't any Morgans in Riverdale, or nearby towns for that matter, that he knew about. Then it hit him and he 'almost fell off the milk stool,' as his grandfather would say. There was a skinny little Morgan girl, maybe in the seventh or eighth grade, the year he graduated high school. She didn't come from a ranch family, and he didn't know her parents, or if she had sisters or brothers. Could she be kin to his bunk partner? He mulled on this until he fell asleep, still trying to answer his own question.

———

Reed heard the stove lid clang on metal, and the familiar sound of wood chunked into an empty grate. He sat up straight, struggled to pull himself awake, turned his head and squinted at Morgan's mass moving in the near total darkness. He sensed it was late morning; it was impossible to tell. The window above his bunk was packed with snow, and the wind squalling so loud it drowned out Mister's steady growl. Morgan struck a match to the Coleman lantern wick, adjusted the hissing flame, and glanced at Reed. "Coffee'l be ready 'fore long, son, but you may want something stronger."

Reed grunted, pulled on his pants, and walked to the door. The wind caught the door and it was all he could do to keep it from slamming against the outside wall. "Shoot! It's worse than last night!" He braced himself, closed and bolted the door, walked to the stove and stood there, staring at the coffee pot. Without a word, he donned his heavy clothes, and forced his body against the wind to the horse barn, where he found most of the tin roof gone and the horses bracing themselves against the clapboard walls of the shed. He twisted the wires off a bale of hay and threw it into the middle of the two hunched-over horses.

Morgan divided a pan full of fried eggs between two plates. He reached in the wooden cabinet for a jar of jelly and a loaf of bread, and pulled up a chair. "Hope you like your eggs over hard, cause that's what you got."

Reed pulled off his coveralls, and dropped them on the floor, then slid onto the bench facing Morgan. He glanced at his plate, and frowned, before digging into a heap of charred eggs.

For the moment, Reed didn't permit himself to think about the welfare of his cows. He couldn't. Those one-hundred cows and calves and two bulls were all he had left of his self-esteem, and everything tangible that he had in the world. Sure, he had fifty thousand dollars in his bank account, money he'd saved from six years of salary and sale of cattle. But that was just paper—paper that he was counting on to buy supplemental hay and grain for his horses and cattle until he could find a permanent home for them. Without his cattle, the money meant nothing. He couldn't possibly replace his herd, buy feed, and pay expenses for another year with that amount of money. And what would he do if he couldn't continue ranching?

———

The day he received his eviction notice, he had no idea where he would go, or where he could pasture his small herd of livestock. Then he remembered the Cadwaller place, up on Dry Creek—six sections of native pasture and good water. Thirty-eight hundred and forty acres—enough grass to see his cows through most normal years.

He had heard old man Cadwaller mentioned in the household as long as he could remember, for up until two years ago, the Carsons had leased his land for summer pasture. But that was before his mother and Cadwaller had had a falling out. Cadwaller wouldn't spend any money to fix the fences, saying he couldn't afford to keep the fences up on the kind of lease money she was paying him. His mother refused to renew the lease. But since the Cadwaller place was surrounded by Carson property, she continued to use the pastures, and didn't reimburse old Cadwaller a dime.

Reed didn't have a hard time finding Claude Cadwaller. The Cadwallers had always lived in Riverdale, where Claude worked for the county maintenance department. He'd bought the rangeland with the idea of helping his only son, Roy, get started in the cattle business. But after high school, Roy went off to college, married, and moved back east with his new bride.

Reed explained his situation to Cadwaller in as few words as possible. Mabel, Claude's plump little wife, listened without saying a word.

"Never trusted, or liked your mother much," Claude said, in an apologetic tone of voice. "Now, your dad, he was a nice guy, plum decent and a hard worker, too. Sure should've used a bullwhip on that mother of yours."

Reed winced, but let the remark stand and changed the subject, with an offer to pay the Carson Ranches' back debt for the privilege of obtaining a new lease. Cadwaller would have none of that after hearing about Reed's falling out with Lucy Carson. Reed signed a new three-year lease with the old man, and for far less money than the previous Carson leases.

Reed crushed his cigarette into a jar lid already full of cigarette butts, lifted his chair back and stood up. "What do you think my chances are of reaching those cows in this storm?" he asked Morgan.

Morgan studied the tin coffee mug between his hands for a while, leaned to the side and shot a wad of Days Work into a can, before meeting Reed's steady gaze. "I can guess what those cattle mean to you, son, but I think you would be crazy to wander a hundred feet out in this storm. And even if you could find them, there ain't a thing you can do for them. Loco or not, though, I'll go with you if that's what you decide to do. But consider this before you get us both froze to death—those cows of yours are in the best shelter this country can provide. There's trees, rock outcroppings rising fifteen or twenty feet above the creek, and you said they have plenty of hay. This storm ain't gonna last forever. As soon as we can get out of this cabin, I'll help you in whatever way I can to find and care for them cattle."

Reed threw a leg over the straight-back chair and sat down hard. With his elbows on the table, he rolled his powerful shoulders forward and eyed the older man. "You've been in this part of the country a lot longer than I have. What do you think this storm's gonna do? I mean, how long do you think it'll last?"

Morgan sipped once on his coffee, taking his time to answer. "I don't know. This is a different kind of storm. But my guess is, it'll blow itself out some time today or tonight. But you gotta remember, son, this kinda weather comes around every March and April in this country, and I'm just guessing those old cows of yours have been through worse. And I'd bet a whole bunch they ain't half as worried as you are."

Reed crossed his arms on the table, and lowered his eyes to the smoke curling off the cigarette in a jar lid. "I hope you're right, about all of it. And I'll take you up on that offer to help dig those cows out when the storm breaks."

Reed walked to the door and chanced another look at the angry, swirling storm, then moved to his bunk and sat down. A dreary cloud settled over his mind.

Mister took a position on his haunches, staring up at Reed, who was leaning forward, running a hand through the dog's hair. Reed grinned and cupped both hands behind the ears of his curious-faced companion. "Dog," he said, locking eyes with the animal, "this is one day you can be thankful you ain't no ordinary ranch mutt, or you'd be freezing your ass off in the snow with the other critters on this outfit."

Reed smiled down at the dog, as he remembered the day the black dog with a white patch of hair above each eye had become an important part of his life. Reed had gone to the Fort Collins livestock sale with his mother. He was in the parking lot retrieving a pack of cigarettes, when an old pickup pulling a battered one-horse trailer stopped beside his car.

Reed turned his head toward the truck and smiled. "Skinner Moralez, long time no see. Are you buying or selling today?" Reed never knew if Skinner was his real name, but that's what everyone called him, and it seemed to fit. Skinner was a small man, maybe five-six or five-seven, and narrow at the shoulders and hips. A broad pair of suspenders held his soiled Levis in place below a potbelly.

"Reed, have I got deal for you today," the peddler said, smiling, exposing one yellow upper tooth and three lower.

"No time for a deal today, Skinner. Just came back to get my cigarettes. Sale is about to start."

Reed started to move away, when he heard a whining sound coming from somewhere behind the truck. Reed guessed the fretful disturbance was coming from the bed of the horse trailer and walked back to have a look. He unlatched the trailer door and bent to his knees for a better view. Five little black and white puppies scampered out of a pile of straw and waddled toward him. One lone puppy stayed behind, huddled in the corner, standing stiff-legged and straight, his watery black eyes staring right at Reed.

"Their mama and daddy are the best damn cow dogs in the country, Reed."

"Skinner...I don't have time to haggle with you over the price of a cross-bred pup. Mom's waiting in the sale barn, and I gotta hustle back there and buy some cows."

"Reed, I ain't trying to *sell* you nothing. I was aiming to *give* you one, just to show you my heart's in the right place."

Reed laughed heartily. "You mean you're feeling guilty about that little scam job you pulled on Mom a few months ago, selling her a 'broke-to-death' cow pony that's bucked off every cowboy on the ranch?"

"Honest, Reed, I didn't know that 'ol horse was an outlaw. Scared the bejeezus out of me when word got back I'd bushwhacked Lucy Carson. You and your mama have bought a lot of stuff from me, and I just want to do something nice back for you."

Reed turned to the little pitchman and smiled. "Okay, Skinner, I'm going to make you good for your word this time. Hand me that scared little critter huddled in the corner there. He acts like a loner, just like me. We'll hit it off just right."

Skinner stepped over the noisy litter of squirming whelps, scooped up the lone pup with a white patch over both eyes and handed him to Reed. "He don't look like much now," Skinner said, "just a little ol' runt, but just you wait…. And you're right about him being a loner. He won't hardly associate with his own brothers and sisters."

———

Morgan dressed in his winter garments and went outside. Reed was still stroking Mister about the head when it hit him: *Butch Morgan's the guy who shot the game warden, burned his own cabin and hasn't been seen for six years.* Reed recalled that law enforcement officers gathered from all over the state, joined by game wardens from Colorado and Montana to hunt for the killer. Most thought he'd burned himself up in his cabin fire. Nothing was found in the ashes to prove one way or the other. The cops were hell bent on frying this guy proper. Search details dominated all the local papers for almost two years.

Reed felt that cold prickly feeling up between his shoulder blades to his neck until he remembered the other part of the story: another man, not Butch Morgan, had been charged with the crime—voluntary manslaughter. Reed was out of high school and working long hours on the ranch at the time and didn't read any newspaper accounts, just word of mouth stuff.

So, he had hid out in the hills, Reed thought. If the killer had been convicted, and Morgan was no longer a suspect, what was he doing still tramping around the mountains? Reed was still pondering all of this when the door blew open and Morgan squeezed his snow-covered body through the small entrance. Morgan removed his beavers, hung them on a peg above the fire and poured himself a tin of black coffee. Reed's eyes steadied on the man standing over the stove rubbing his hands together—a seemingly kind giant. Could there have been two killers of the game warden? *Why not?* Morgan had been there—burned his own cabin and was never seen again....

Reed got up slowly, walked to the stove and stood near Morgan. Without looking at the other man, he poured himself a cup of coffee, walked to the door, fingering his tin of muddy brew.

"Something on your mind, Reed?" Morgan asked, in a quiet voice.

"Maybe," Reed said, without looking at him.

"Let me guess," Morgan said, still warming his hands over the stove. "Your memory has been working overtime, and you've put my name together with the dead game warden?"

"Yeah, guess that's about it," Reed allowed. "But I don't have a problem connecting you with the murder," he quickly added. "And maybe it's none of my damn business, but I was just pondering why you've lived like a hermit four years after the law got their man and quit looking for you. Word around the valley is, nobody's seen you since the murder, and it might be for a good reason."

"Not surprised about your curiosity, son. I wouldn't even be shocked if you hadn't heard I'm not still on the most wanted list. I was front page on every paper in the country for two years. Then when the hunting buddy of that loud-mouthed Chicago dentist ratted him out for the killing, most papers listed the incident on the third page, in print too small for most folks to read. You see, I know all of this because I have a good friend, lives on the other side of Saw Mill Road, who's supplied my camp, and kept me informed. Other than you, he's the only one I've talked to for all that while."

Reed gave out a short breath and eyed Morgan more closely, trying to form a mental picture of everything Morgan was telling him.

The grizzled man fingered his cup and moved to a chair at the table. Reed followed suit. "I'm gonna tell you the rest of it, Reed—not because I'm desperate to get it off my chest, but because I've taken a likin' to you. Not to mention you may have saved my life, taking me in out of the blizzard and all."

Morgan sipped on his coffee again, leaned back in his chair, and studied the younger man's face. "We have a lot in common, you an' me. You're near as big as I am, and that ain't all. I've watched you some. You're strong as an ox, but there's something inside that's pulling you down. I thought at first it was your stranded cattle, but that's just part of it—something else's got you by the short hairs. It wouldn't surprise me if you're running from something, maybe even hiding—not the law, though, something worse."

Reed stared at Morgan in a stunned moment of silence. "I'm not running, Butch—maybe harassed a little by my conniving brother and my poor sick mother, and her good-for-nothing boyfriend. But that's all going to change soon as I get my feet on the ground." He didn't think Morgan was buying it, but that was all he was going to say.

There was a long silence, with Reed saying all he was going to say and Morgan not wanting, or needing, to press for more.

Reed was relieved when Morgan broke the silence. "I want to finish telling you how I got here, and ask you for a favor—if you will—something that I can't bring myself to do." Reed was puzzled. *What could he possibly do for such a man that he couldn't do for himself?*

"Go ahead, Butch, let me have it with both barrels, and if I can help—so be it."

Morgan cut off a huge chunk of Days Work, slowly placed it in his mouth, and settled back in his chair. "I was raised on a farm, in a little town not far from Joplin, Missouri, with my four sisters, and my dad and Mom. My dad skidded logs all his life and we were poor as dirt. But that's what I wanted to be, a skidder. Doesn't sound very ambitious, but I didn't know any different then. When I was sixteen, and a sophomore in high school, the logs were playing out in the woods and my folks were barely making it. I left home and headed west. I got as far as Laramie and found a job driving a log truck. That's where I met my wife, Julie. Then six years later, along came our daughter, Anne."

That's the name, Anne Morgan, Reed almost said aloud. Morgan had an easy, unhurried way of talking, like a man who never raised his voice or got excited. And now Reed was more curious than before and wanted him to hurry along with it.

"Well, sir," Morgan said slowly, "Anne finished the seventh-grade the same year the logging business petered out in Woods Landing. That would be about in '88 or '89. We packed our gear and headed toward Riverdale. I got a job working at the sawmill and Julie waited tables at the Antlers Café. Anne started to school in the eighth grade in Riverdale that fall."

Morgan paused long enough to refill their coffee cups. "We had a little money saved, but not enough to buy a good house in Riverdale. Julie and I both loved the mountains. So, we decided to buy a little cabin near the headwaters of Bitter Brush Creek.... that's when all the trouble started.

I spent most of my spare time trapping and prospecting near our cabin, and Julie idled away her free time visiting Howard Dibbs, the local game warden. I found out about the two of them, pounded old Dibbs' head into the ground real good, and the word got around.

They didn't see each other for a while, and I thought it was all over between them. Then things got a little better for Julie and me, or so I imagined." Morgan took a deep breath and another sip of coffee.

"Elk season had been opened for about three days, and there'd been a big snow. I couldn't work, so I headed for our

cabin. I got up early and hunted all day. It was getting dark, and I'd heard several shots earlier that sounded nearby. By now, I'm tired as hell and headed back. I was unlocking my cabin door when I heard two quick shots, not a hundred yards away. I'm thinking someone got something down and I wanted to see it.

There was something down, okay, a bloody game warden— lying on his back, blood all over him, just starin' at the sky and seein' nothing. Even with all the blood, I could see it was Howard Dibbs, shot through the chest. About that same time I hear a motor running, and the sound was going away."

"I'd never been scared of much of anything in my whole life, but I was scared! I held my hand over his jugular, felt his wrist— just to be sure he was really dead—got blood all over my hands, and part of my sleeves. I stumbled back to my cabin, trembling like an aspen leaf in October, cleaned myself up, sat down on my bunk and cried. That poor man was shot in the back, clear through with a high-powered rifle, something like the 30-06 I was carrying."

"So you just started running, and never looked back?"

"I did, but not until I thought on it some. I was sure they would string me up if I hauled him into town. I could just picture the reception I'd receive with a dead cop, stiff as a fence post, in the back of my pickup. Everyone knew Dibbs was having his way with Julie, and that I had threatened to kill him. Now here he is—deader'n a can of corned beef, within spitting distance of my cabin. There wouldn't be any question in anyone's mind who put the bullet in him. So…I wanted them to think I was dead.

I gathered everything I needed—ammunition, bedroll, change of clothes, poured a two-gallon can of gas on my little cabin and lit a match. I walked away without looking back. That was six years ago."

"I'm not proud of what I did," Morgan continued, "but at the time I wanted to live more than I wanted to hang."

"Today—who knows what I would do," Morgan said. "But that was then and today's today."

"Butch, that was six years ago. You've known for four years, so you say, that the law wasn't after you. What about Julie, and your daughter, Anne? Didn't you want to see them again, or, at least, let them know that you were alive?"

Morgan frowned, and turned away from Reed's steady gaze while he cut off a fresh chunk of chew and pushed it between his teeth and gums. "That's just it," Morgan said. "I had two years to think about my wife with that game warden, and after awhile I even got to smiling to myself when I thought of him laying there in the snow with a bullet hole through his back. I gotta tell you, I had a pretty sour attitude. I imagined that Julie didn't care if my ashes were in the cabin or if I'd froze to death in some dark cave. And I didn't want to face any of those people that pegged me as a murderer and chased me for two straight years."

Morgan moved to the stove and refilled their cups with coffee, before he dropped back on the bench facing Reed. "I missed Anne like fire. But after I found out the cops had turned their attention to someone else, she'd had two years to adjust her life around the belief that her daddy was a cop killer. How she managed, I don't know. Anyway, I couldn't come slinking back into town and admit that I'd left her and ran like a scared rabbit—which is exactly what I did."

There was a long silence. Reed waited, wanting Morgan to finish his story. Finally, he cleared his throat. "And that favor you mentioned earlier…?"

"Don't know if I can go through with it, Reed. Maybe it's too late." Morgan's voice trailed off. "I've thought about it a lot, and I was about ready to give up the notion until a few hours ago. If there was some way I could let Anne know that I'm still alive, short of facing the whole town myself, I'd do it. If you could find her and just give her a message…."

Reed didn't know what to say or quite how to act. He'd never had anyone confide anything personal to him before. And he sure hadn't seen a man near tears—crack right in front of him.

"I don't know if I can do this, Butch. I wouldn't know where to start looking. There's no Morgans in Riverdale, or in any other nearby town that I know about. Julie could've remarried and gave Anne her new married name. How old is Anne—twenty-one or twenty-two? She's old enough to be married herself with a new name." When Reed glanced up from studying the smoke curling off his cigarette, he knew he had made a mistake. It was all over Morgan's face.

Butch had spilled his guts, and he'd let him down. "Tell you what, big guy," Reed said, in as cheerful a tone as he could muster. "When this storm is over, you help me dig my cows out of the snow and I'll high-tail it into town and do some detective work."

FIVE

The cattleman's warning was all over radio and TV, and Kirk had prepared for the worst. With his cattle fed and sheltered in the dense trees of the river bottom, Kirk Carson and Justin Bullock were sitting out the bad weather at the Pronghorn Bar, drinking beer, and shooting pool with Kirk's hired hands, Cole Rusling, Blackie Dubois, and John Pratt. The hired men were in a good mood, laughing, joking and telling each other how they were going to spend all the money promised to them by Kirk Carson—money enough to supply themselves with marijuana, crank, and loose women for at least six months. Not in this place, though, they all agreed. Pretending to be cowboys, riding horses, bucking bales, feeding cattle, and irrigating wasn't the life for them. They were going to Florida, sun themselves on the beaches, eat and drink from pushcart vendors during the day— make the beach bars at night.

Kirk Carson and Justin Bullock were planning bigger things. Kirk despised all four of the ex-cons. He hated Justin Bullock the most. Bullock, the slimy ex-convict, insisted upon one-third of everything gleaned after they grabbed control of the Carson Ranches. Kirk had no intentions of divvying up several million dollars. Bullock was on probation and knew better than anyone that he was walking a fine line—and Kirk wasn't stupid enough to believe that Bullock would go down alone. He would find ways to deal with Bullock, though, and they wouldn't include giving away a fortune.

Bullock's cellmates were easier to deal with—hired men's wages, and a few hundred dollars after each load of stolen cattle was hauled to a Montana cattle sale, plus all the marijuana and crank to satisfy their addiction.

The men were all in their early or late thirties. Kirk didn't credit the lot of them for having enough brains to fill a thimble, but he knew each had particular skills perfect for what he hired them for. Cole Rusling was maybe five-eight or five-nine, ill-tempered and wiry. He could hotwire a tractor blindfolded and operate any piece of equipment rolling out of Detroit. Blackie Dubois was a prison bodybuilder, barrel-chested, arms as big as stovepipes, and nearly as tall as Bullock. He was the biggest doper of the three, and when he wasn't tripping out, could fight his way through a mill saw. John Pratt, the quiet one, had cold blue eyes and a long, blonde ponytail. He was of medium build, sinister, and cowardly. He'd committed first degree murder, but he got off with second degree on a plea bargain. Between numerous prison terms, Pratt had spent some time on a ranch in Montana and could at least handle himself around cattle.

They'd all met in the Wyoming State Penitentiary. Rusling—car theft, Dubois—grand larceny, Pratt—second degree murder, Bullock—forgery, assault with a deadly weapon, and resisting arrest. What kept them together in prison, and after their release, was a plan they'd hatched during their four years together behind the walls. It was a plan that didn't even include Kirk Carson. But here he was, offering them more money than their scheme to rob the Pine Tree Savings and Loan in Riverdale—with a lot less risk.

Bullock was released first. He had no priors and walked free in four years, two months, and six days. Bullock wasted no time in returning to his old haunt, Medicine Park, Wyoming. Kirk would be waiting in the Pronghorn Bar, which he jokingly referred to as 'my office.'

Bullock had worked for some rancher in the area six years ago, he couldn't remember who, the summer he'd busted a cop's head open with a tire iron who came to the bunkhouse to arrest him for passing bad checks. He'd met Kirk Carson at the bar that same summer, and they had become more than just drinking buddies; they shared a common interest—money. Now, Kirk Carson, the lawyer, had helped him with an early out, arranging a work release for him. That was two years ago, and it was starting to pay off for both of them.

At first, stealing cows and an eighty-thousand-dollar backhoe tractor was enough for Kirk. And it was easy, especially with the help of his four new hands. Stealing and selling his mother's cows was especially easy, since his name was listed as co-owner of the Teardrop-Quarter-Circle brand. It was a little slight-of-the-hand job he pulled when his mother was strung out on rum and Coke and a strong dose of antidepressants.

His dealings to-date were chump change. Kirk dreamed of having it all in his name—the North and South River Ranches and the old Homestead Ranch. All he had to show for his law degree, and two years as manager of the South River Ranch, was what little money he'd stashed beneath a loose board under the kitchen floor. He garnered it from his small meth lab, from sales of his mom's backhoe, and a few stolen cattle.

Early on, Kirk knew if he was to get control of the ranches he had to have an inside partner. He needed a man about his mother's age, ranch savvy, mannerly, and smooth-tongued. He also had to be greedy, conniving, someone totally loyal to their objectives, and someone without a conscience who could play his mother's mental illness like a fine fiddle. Justin Bullock was perfect.

In Kirk's mind, his mother was already a certified fruitcake, spending half of her time in the nut house. What if she was bonkers enough to sign the Teardrop Ranches over to Reed? It could happen, Kirk reasoned, and he was going to see that it didn't.

Getting Justin Bullock in position to implement their plan was the easiest part. He knew his mother desperately needed a good ranch hand. Kirk had the perfect man for the job. It had been two years since Kirk cooked the scheme to get Bullock hired on the North River Ranch, but he still found humor and a sense of self-satisfaction with his cleverness.

Lucy Carson had never heard of Justin Bullock until the day she picked up the phone and heard a smooth, masculine voice on the other end asking for a job. He could do anything on a ranch—maintain ranch machinery, handle cows, irrigate. It sounded all too good to be true, especially since good hands were hard to come by. He had a reference, too. But Lucy couldn't know it was pecked out by Kirk on her own father's old Underwood typewriter—then signed by Justin Bullock himself.

Kirk looked at Justin Bullock who sat on the stool next to him. His elbows were resting on the bar with both feet planted on the brass foot railing. Bullock glanced across the room at his three cellmates shooting pool. Justin then tipped a glass of bar whiskey to his lips and squarely returned Kirk's gaze. "When are we going to look for that high and mighty brother of yours and get our cattle back?"

Kirk stared at the liquor bottles lined up in front of the ancient bar-length mirror and lightly wetted a fresh cigar between his nervous lips. He was in no hurry to oblige an answer to Bullock's dumb question. He bit the end off his cigar, spat it across the bar, and showed an irritated frown. "Starting to miss your old prison chow, Bullock? Or maybe you're just plain stupid. We can't just go rustling cattle under his nose—cattle with his brand on them. Besides, old Judge Ledbetter said he could keep the cattle until the trial."

Bullock glowered, tipped his glass, and did a slow burn. "Okay, so we can't get the cattle for awhile. Guess I'm just anxious to get a piece of that brother of yours. He's made my life miserable the past two years and almost threw a monkey wrench in our plans."

Kirk grinned. "You'll get your chance, Bullock, a lot sooner than you think. You see, I know where he is. Old Cadwaller called Mom, gloating that he had leased his place to Reed. Mom called me before the ink was dry on the papers, not the least bit upset, probably tripped out on Zoloft. Anyway, I played along. The less she knows the better."

"So, when can we get him?" Bullock shot back.

"Get him?" Kirk repeated, with a curious smirk. "Whattaya wanta' do, *kill him*?"

"Oh buddy, nothing like that. I just want to harass him a little. Make him squirm like he did me for two straight years. Maybe beat him for an encore."

Choking with laughter, Kirk coughed out a lung full of cigar smoke. This he would enjoy seeing. He hated Bullock, and he always wanted to see him kicked good and proper.

"Storm's breaking," Kirk said. "How would tomorrow suit you, partner? He'll be digging out what's left of his cow herd, and we'll be coming in from the other side. Maybe a little harassment is just what he needs. Keep him from getting too cozy in his new digs."

SIX

The morning broke clear and bitter cold. Morgan was up first, kindled the fire, and had coffee boiling before Reed stirred from his bedroll. Reed pulled his clothes on, centered his hat, and stumbled to the door. Mister dashed out between his legs. He stood in the doorway and stared into a perfectly still, bright, snow-covered landscape.

Reed was struggling with his coveralls when Morgan glanced his way. "Whoa there, big man," Morgan growled, "it's gonna be a hard day. Better stow away some grub. Supper is a fer stretch."

Reed nodded and continued what he was doing. Butch handed him a plate with burnt eggs and three slices of wheat bread. He stood on his feet, gulped down the offering, and was out the door before Morgan had his huge body covered with beaver skins.

The sun was just an orange blur on the eastern horizon when Reed stood surveying the blinding white landscape. The snow covered Sierra Madre mountain range stood out like a store-bought picture post card. He cautiously looked toward the west, trying to see into the valley, not a half-mile away, where he had left his cows to weather the storm. Only the tops of the leafless cottonwood trees were visible. He shuddered and turned toward the barn, or what was left of it.

Anxious to check on the condition of his horses, he made his way toward the barn, not a hundred yards away. Here, most of the snow had blown off—deposited in huge drifts behind the haystack and what was left of the corral and other structures. The horses were crouched between the fence and a snowdrift higher than the remaining wall of the barn. Reed threw a bale of hay between them and walked to his pickup. The Dodge diesel fired after the second preheat. He breathed a sigh of relief, pushed his way out the door, and walked to the cabin.

Morgan wrestled his way out the cabin door and met Reed halfway to the idling pickup. He blotched a patch of snow with a mouthful of Days Work and looked seriously at Reed. "It's your show now, partner. What's the plan?"

Reed flipped a cigarette butt into a far snow bank and paused a moment, staring at Morgan. A picture of a fair-sized grizzly flashed through his mind. He wanted to laugh, and would have, except for the seriousness of the moment. "I got chains for all four wheels, and I got a feeling we're going to need them. Let's chain up and grab some snow shovels, ropes, and tow chains. We'll take a load of hay for traction and feed those we can get to."

Morgan looked toward the corrals and pulled twice on his tobacco-stained beard. "Reckon it would hurt to take a saddle horse? We might be able to pull something out stuck in the deep snow that we can't get to with the truck."

"I must be losing it," Reed said. "Yes, we'll take saddle horses! You can ride Lurch, that tall gray gelding, and lead Brownie, the big bay. I'll break trail with the truck."

The sun was riding high in the sky before snow was shoveled away from the corral gate, horses saddled, hay loaded, and chains and ropes readied. Mister jumped on the topmost hay bale, pointed his nose toward the west and barked once. Morgan left first, riding Lurch and leading the bay horse, Brownie.

From the cabin, the land sloped toward Dry Creek. Reed pondered the fate of his livestock as the Dodge effortlessly plowed down hill through the four or five inches of snow left between sagebrush clumps. They were nearly halfway to the creek bottom before the brush got thicker and taller, and where the truck bottomed out in four feet of snow.

Reed was struggling with snow against the pickup door when he heard Mister bark and Butch calling to him. Reed's breath quickened with the sight. A line of cows and calves were breaking trail out of the creek bottom and heading straight for the pickup. "Let's get this hay spread!" he called back.

Morgan dismounted, dropped the reins, and jumped on back of the truck, tossing hay bales toward the horizon. Before long, the truck was surrounded by forty or fifty cows and calves munching on fresh feed. Reed let out a big sigh. "That's a start, Morgan, but it's horseback from here on. That pile of junk is buried."

They put their horses at a slow walk, eyes straining to catch sight of anything alive or moving in the stillness of the pristine landscape. Mister easily ran ahead of the horses, burying his nose into the snow and occasionally following a fresh rabbit track to the right or the left. This went on until Reed stopped his horse, whistled, and motioned the dog to jump on behind his saddle. Morgan glanced at the animal comfortably balanced on the gelding's rear end and shook his head.

As they worked their way through the tall oak brush, the snow deepened. The horses were busting through snowdrifts chest high—still no sign of cattle or tracks. Then, suddenly, Reed let go a loud call, "Yaaah cattle!" In less than a minute came the mooing answer. He glanced at Morgan and smiled. "Let's go get 'em. They're under the outcropping."

The huge shale overhang wasn't far from their position—across the creek and up a steep bank to a level area that extended under shale carved out by a thousand years of rushing water. The cattle were trapped where they had been protected from the blizzard, but they were now without feed or water. They sat on their horses, feet in the stirrups, their legs buried to the knees in snow, listening to the hungry cows lowing for help, or so it seemed. Reed looked at Morgan. "Our horses can't break any further, we'll be lucky just to get them backed out of here. There's some shovels in the pickup."

The two geldings were turned loose to nip on hay with the cattle around the snowbound pickup. Morgan buried the business end of his scoop shovel deep into the snow and was leaning on the handle with one hand, waiting for Reed to dig his shovel from the pickup bed. "Some of that snow is six and eight feet deep, but we should have a path shoveled by sundown," Morgan said, "then we can start on the truck."

Reed found his shovel, struck a match with his thumbnail, lit a cigarette, and lifted the shovel to his shoulder. "Digging this old Dodge out is going to be a bigger job than the cows, and I've been thinking on it. There's no need for all that shoveling. If you just lift one side at a time while I shove a bale of hay under the tires..." Morgan laughed.

They had walked about ten feet toward Dry Creek when Mister barked twice, and Reed turned in his tracks. "What the...?" The sound was unmistakable. A vehicle of some sort was approaching from the east fork of Dry Creek, the only road into the property. "What do you make of it, Morgan?"

Morgan turned his face to the side and discharged a brown stream of juice onto the fresh snow. "Sounds like your neighbors are coming to help you out. And it ain't no small rig—a big tractor or motor grader most likely."

"Clyde Cadwaller is the only one who knows I'm up here, and he sure doesn't own a snow plow," Reed said while straining his eyes in the direction of the sound.

"Our mystery is solved. This is our lucky day," Morgan brightened, gesturing toward the east with a beaver-skin-clad mitten, just as a huge, blue tractor popped the hill, pushing an eight-foot blade of snow. A red Dodge pickup, chains on all four wheels, followed behind the tractor.

Reed felt his chest tighten and the hair stand on the back of his neck. "I don't need this—not today," he said to the wind. "Butch, there's going to be trouble. That's my brother, Kirk, and there'll likely be three or four of his hired men with him. It's not your fight. Just hang back. I can handle it. There's no need of you getting into trouble."

Morgan grinned, removed his mittens and tossed them in the snow, near the pickup.

They stood, unmoving, and watched the big snowplow push a mountain of snow against the tailgate of Reed's truck. At

Reed's side, Mister went rigid, emitting a low, throaty growl. The smiling driver reversed the tractor and backed off about ten feet. Reed recognized the operator as Cole Rusling. He knew Kirk, Dubois, Pratt, and Bullock would be in the pickup. Rusling waited for backup before climbing down from the tractor cab.

He didn't have to wait long. Kirk opened his door, turned, and motioned Rusling to join them.

"Who's the little fella with the black ponytail?" Morgan asked.

"That'll be Kirk," Reed said. "I had to look twice myself. I was looking for his freshly pressed shirt and a red necktie." Kirk was wearing brown coveralls, snow boots, a rabbit fur cap with upturned earflaps, and lined mittens.

Kirk and his hired men were nearly upon them when Morgan said, almost to himself, "He ain't no more'n half your size."

The five intruders stopped about six feet from Reed and Morgan. Kirk wore a smirky grin and carried an unlit cigar between his thumb and forefinger. Reed and Morgan stood motionless, Reed staring directly into Kirk's watery, black eyes. The hired men stood, with mouths slightly open, dividing their attention between Morgan and the snarling dog.

Reed spoke first. "After you push that hill of snow away from my truck, you can turn around and get out of here, and take your thugs with you. This is my property now, and you can consider yourself trespassing."

Kirk calmly dug into his coveralls, found a silver-colored lighter and touched the flame to his fresh stogie. "You're the one trespassing, Reed. You know this place has been leased to the Carson Ranches for longer than either of us can remember. And I know you've moved a hundred or more head of Mom's cattle up here. If you leave now, without the cows, I won't report you to the sheriff again, and maybe you can stay out of jail for a little longer."

Reed started to smile—he couldn't help it—even with Kirk's sour face staring at him. Kirk was using his deep-chest voice, again. The voice he used when he wanted to impress someone.

Reed stopped smiling. "Kirk, you should get your own comedy act, charge admission, but around here we don't pay for slapstick humor. "Kirk, you know I wouldn't be here if Mom had any right to it."

Kirk's face turned a different shade of red. "You son of a—," he muttered, checking himself in mid-sentence.

Reed stared down at his brother for a minute before responding. "Now that we both know that you're trying to pull a big bluff—for whatever reason I can't guess—you can stop grandstanding and get out of here. I don't have time for any more of your humor. I got starving cows buried in eight feet of snow, and...."

"You mean Mom's cows, don't you, Reed?"

"Kirk, you're an idiot, among other things, and if Mom knew what you were doing she'd kick you off the ranch."

Kirk bristled, touched the cigar to his trembling lips, and took a short pull at the stogie. "Reed," Kirk started, nervously out of breath, "You...."

"Forget it, Kirk. I've heard enough," Bullock said, stepping forward in a crouch, fists raised. His eyes were full of rage. He lunged the short distance separating him from Reed, still talking. "It's payback time, half-breed. Remember all the sh....?"

Kirk winced and dropped his cigar at the sickening explosion of knuckles bursting against flesh and bone that silenced Bullock's outburst. Bullock hit hard on his back in the soft snow, arms outspread, a startled look across his splayed face.

Reed was standing over Bullock, watching him slowly pull himself to a sitting position, when he felt a force slam him to the ground. Flat on his back, gasping for breath, Reed vaguely remembered seeing a man's boot just before it landed against his forehead. Dazed, blood trickling over his ears, he rolled to avoid a second deadly blow aimed again at his head and caught the boot heel from his attacker. Yanking upward with all the strength left in him, he recognized the upended face and body of Blackie Dubois.

Reed was up and standing on rubbery knees when Dubois made his second charge. Reed stepped aside, swinging a right that grazed Dubois's cheek and sent him sprawling to the ground. Dubois was back on his feet quick as a dropped cat. Blinded with fury, he rushed Reed with fists raging like a windmill in a gale. Reed came from all the way under to catch Dubois with an uppercut to the chin that sent him down hard— and he stayed there.

It had been less than a minute since Reed's first punch landed in Bullock's face. No time for him to think about what Morgan was doing. Reed was checking for life from Dubois when he turned toward the direction of a startled cry. Cole Rusling was flying through the air. A dull thud sounded from the pickup tailgate. Reed glanced to his right. Morgan's arms were still in the air, as if following through with the winning hoop at a state basketball championship.

To Morgan's left, John Pratt was struggling with the deep snow, trying desperately to reach Kirk's pickup, while dragging a snarling dog attached to his rear end. Morgan turned a half-circle to his right and saw Reed slowly making his way to his pickup, then, he turned back toward Pratt and planted a size thirteen boot into Pratt's ribs, turning him over, face first into the snow—with the dog still attached, tearing at tender flesh.

The two big men leaned on Reed's truck bed, slightly out of breath. Reed was torching a cigarette and Morgan was reaching for his chew when they suddenly became aware that Mister was sitting very erect, cocking his head from side to side, not five feet in front of them, staring at one, then the other. Morgan bit off a hunk of Days Work, stuffed his cheek, then looked squarely at Reed. "Is that mutt bragging—or asking if he can chew on that feller's ass some more?"

Reed laughed. "Pratt had better hope he's bragging."

With searching eyes, Reed turned his head one way then the other. "Where's Kirk?" he said to Morgan. Morgan glanced toward the red truck and lifted his chin. Blue smoke was

chugging from the exhaust, the windshield fogged completely—
except for a small round area cleared from the inside.

"The little coward," Reed said under his breath. To Morgan,
he said, "Let's have a word with him."

They were less than a dozen yards from the red Dodge when
the driver's side door swung open. Kirk stepped out, rifle in
hand, and jacked a shell into the chamber. He raised the rifle and
sighted down the barrel in the direction of the two men, and said,
"You better just back off, now, or I'll blow both of you away."

Reed started forward. Morgan held a tree-stump arm straight
out to block his advance. "You stay put, Reed...you hear? I've
dealt with the like's of him. He ain't shooting nobody."

"Butch, let me handle him. I don't think he'll shoot his own
brother, but he's scared. He might shoot you out of fright."

Morgan kept his arm in front of Reed, never removing his
eyes from Kirk. "No...and that's final." Reed dropped his arms
in desperation. The argument was lost. There was no point in
trying to reason with someone with a skull as thick as a wild
bison.

"Okay, Butch, but don't rush him."

Morgan dropped his arm and slowly walked toward the red
truck. "Put the rifle away, Kirk. I'm not going to hurt you,"
Morgan said, as he slowly approached the truck with measured
steps.

"What do you want from me," Kirk said, through a nervous
chatter. "Just let my men go, and we'll get out of here.
But...if...if...you keep coming I'm going to shoot you."

Morgan stopped a short distance from Kirk, hands at his side,
staring into Kirk's panic-stricken face. "You're not gonna shoot
anyone. Lower that rifle or I'm going to break every bone in
your cowardly little body, and you can spend the rest of your life
in a wheelchair."

Kirk slowly lowered the rifle and tossed it to the side.

Morgan retrieved the rifle from a snow bank, walked to the
pickup, and shattered it against the metal bed.

Reed's heart quickened. Unknown to Morgan, Reed, with the dog by his side, had followed Morgan step-by-step—standing not ten feet behind him when Kirk tossed the rifle.

Reed opened the door to Kirk's truck, grabbed the keys and shoved them into his coverall vest pocket. "You asked the man what we wanted. I'll answer that question. Since you screwed up our whole day, you're going to help put it back in order. Gather up what's left of your sorry crew and keep them out of our way while I use that tractor and plow to rescue my cattle and pull my pickup out of that mountain of snow."

Kirk nodded, started to say something, but the words didn't come until he turned and started calling to his men, three of them standing perfectly still, like lost calves in a blizzard. Pratt was still lying face-down on the snow, unmoving.

Reed turned toward Morgan, both men smiling honestly. "Keep your eyes on them, Butch. I won't be long. Mister will stay with you. If he gets bored, give him something to chew on."

A half-hour later, Reed was widening the snow path back toward the pickup, trailed by the rest of his cows and calves, or most of them, he guessed. Surrounded by a herd of lowing cattle, Reed pulled his pickup to high ground and tossed the pickup keys in Kirk's direction.

Reed walked over to Butch, who was leaning against Reed's pickup and watching Kirk's lame crew load up for the trip back to town.

"I've never seen the likes of those tinhorns," Butch allowed. "I figure that cowardly brother of yours just ain't bolted together right. He's got more problems than a whole corral full of shrinks could solve. The rest of that sorry bunch are just a bunch of lily-livered drunks off the street. You'll need to watch your back from now on."

Reed glanced at Morgan's serious face, their eyes holding for a moment, without speaking, then he turned his attention toward Kirk's efforts to gather his faltering crew. Without moving, a wave of sadness flooded his mind. It wasn't right, brother fighting brother. Blood was supposed to be thicker than water.

Why did Kirk hate him so much? It wasn't his fault that Kirk had quit growing and talked with an asthmatic voice. He'd done it to himself. Reed shook his head, already seeing himself and Kirk in future scrapes.

Kirk was stumbling and out of breath while pushing and pulling Bullock and Dubois to the pickup. With some effort, Rusling climbed and lifted his limp body into the tractor cab, slumped over the steering wheel, started the machine, and turned eastward. Pratt hadn't moved from his face-down position in the snow— both hands clasped to his midsection. The back of his pants were shredded and covered with blood—ugly torn flesh exposed to the elements.

Kirk rolled Pratt over on his back, amid the sound of loud moans. Kirk bent over with his back to the pickup, grasped both hands of the limp body, dug his heels in and pulled. Inch-by-inch and foot-by-foot, he narrowed the distance to the truck—less than one-hundred feet. He was groaning and out of breath when he finally dropped Pratt's head and shoulders in the snow near the front bumper. He looked toward the truck, his eyes begging for help. Dubois, blood still dripping from his nose onto the front of his coveralls, pushed himself out the door, and the two of them rolled the limp form into the crowded front seat.

Butch Morgan spewed a stream of ugly tobacco juice into the snow and trained his eyes on the departing red Dodge. "We haven't seen the last of that bunch."

"You're right, but you can bet we won't see them coming next time."

SEVEN

Reed checked himself in the tiny mirror. He was wearing a clean, gray and maroon striped western shirt, Levi's, and his newest gray Stetson. Satisfied there were no coffee stains on the front of the shirt or barnyard spots on his pants, he turned to Morgan, who was sitting at the table, blowing on a cup of coffee. "Thanks again for your help. Maybe I can even the score a little today."

"Reed, it ain't like we're keeping score. Anyway, slapping those skunks around a little was more fun than work. You don't owe me a thing. Anne may not want to see me, but at least she'll know I'm alive, and I'll have the satisfaction of knowing how she's doing."

The two big men headed out of the cabin together—Reed to his truck, Morgan toward the horse corral, bridle in hand. Reed fired the diesel engine, rolled down his window and called to Butch. "Those two loads of hay we fed this morning will tide the cows over until tomorrow. If I'm not back by then, throw hay out of the stack. They'll either find it or you can catch up Lurch and push them over this way. Mister can help you."

___

Butch Morgan looked back over his shoulder and watched as the Dodge disappeared over the hill. He waved, but he didn't know if Reed saw him. Morgan urged the gray gelding toward the crest of the hill where he could see Bridger peak and over toward his claim. He couldn't see his mine, but he knew exactly what little hill it lay under, and he knew every inch of the area between here and there.

Morgan hadn't slept well, wondering if he had done right by telling Reed about Jesse and Anne, and the rest of it. Then he got to thinking the same thoughts now that he'd thought every day since he walked away from his burning cabin. At first he was just scared of being hanged for something he didn't do, then after a while, he got to thinking about being locked up, waiting for the trial, and what all this would do to Anne—herself not knowing if he was guilty. He guessed that Anne didn't know about Julie and Harold Dibbs. But it would all come out—her dad in prison, and her mother around town with another man. If he just left things the way they were, the way he had thought all along, Anne wouldn't think of him as a coward. She'd get used to the notion that her dad was dead and go on to make a life for herself. And Julie…she'd go off and marry someone else. But, no matter, he never gave up the notion that some day he would go back and try to work things out with Anne, and explain, in his own way, why he had to do what he'd done.

Finding Reed the way he did—that was something he was still trying to work out in his mind. Reed Carson, Jesse's son, of all people in the world…a big strong man, with more troubles than ten men could handle. Maybe it was just destiny, or maybe it was just luck, or maybe it was the Lord taking a hand, as he remembered the preacher saying so many times as he sat between his dad and Mom in church—a long time ago.

It didn't matter, he finally decided, now smiling to himself. Even if Reed couldn't find Anne, he knew now that he would come out of the hills and scour the whole damn country if he had to until he found her. He couldn't let Anne live out her life thinking all along that her dad was a pile of ashes.

"And that ain't all I'm gonna do," Morgan said to himself, unloading a stream of brown juice off the gray's left shoulder. As soon as he could leave here, he would go back to the mine and see Jesse, and let him know that one of his sons was a right decent young man.

Where to start looking? Reed pondered, while dodging exposed rocks on the muddy road between his cabin and the highway. Riverdale would be the logical place, but he was fairly certain it would be a dead end. He needed a phone, a regular phone, to get numbers from information. He'd heard of getting phone numbers and addresses from the internet; he could manage that. Then he pictured a computer taking up part of his cabin space and almost smiled.

Reed had friends in Riverdale who would gladly let him use their phone or computer for that matter, but he didn't want anyone knowing his business. *Claude Cadwaller*, he mouthed the words. The old guy wouldn't ask any questions, and he couldn't hear very well, anyway.

Claude and Mabel Cadwaller were regulars at the Riverdale Senior Center for potluck dinners and an occasional card game, but they seldom ventured anywhere else. Visitors to their home were a rarity because Claude considered sitting around jawing with a bunch of old codgers 'a damn waste of good time.' But Reed knew he would be welcomed into their home. On his last visit, to sign his lease, they treated him as if he were another son.

As Reed expected, they greeted him with warm smiles and offered coffee and freshly baked cinnamon rolls. With very little explanation, Mabel positioned a portable phone on a nightstand in a small bedroom, searched the house for the least out-of-date phone books, handed him paper and pencil, and quietly left the room.

Alone in the tiny bedroom, he finished his roll and coffee, while trying to organize his approach. Mabel had carefully laid out six phone books on the bed, organized in alphabetical order: Baggs, Middlecamp, Laramie, Garfield, Riverdale, and Cottonwood. All the books were current except Laramie, which was two years old.

No Morgans were listed in Baggs, Middlecamp, Riverdale, or Cottonwood phone books. Reed expected this. In Laramie, he found Robert, John, Donald, and J. Morgan. No Anne Morgan or Morgan with initial "A." In Garfield there was one Morgan with initial "C." He called numbers and information operators in Laramie and Garfield, without success. He didn't want to divulge to anyone the purpose of his search, but would the Cadwallers know something—anything—to give him a lead? They would be more than willing to help, and he was sure they wouldn't spread it around the community.

Claude and Mabel were sipping coffee and munching on fresh rolls when Reed ducked his head to enter the doorway into the cozy little kitchen. Claude was reading the *Riverdale Weekly*. He removed his "store bought" magnifying reading glasses and turned toward Reed.

"Any luck, son?"

"Not an ounce."

"Is there some way we can help?" Mabel asked, in a sweet old lady's voice.

"Maybe," Reed replied, massaging his stubby chin with a forefinger. He had to tell someone, sometime.

The old man scraped his chair around to face Reed and fixed his eyes on the young man's worried expression. "Who you're looking for ain't none of our business, son, but we'd like to help. And what you tell us ain't going anywhere."

Reed took another bite of roll and raised his coffee cup to wash it down, thinking about it. "What I'm about to tell you is not my business to share. Butch Morgan can tell his own story when and if he comes out of the hills," Reed said. Mabel smiled, and Claude nodded. Reed could feel his face getting warm. He inhaled deeply, then in as few words as possible, Reed explained about Butch Morgan and his daughter, Anne. Claude never changed his expression. Mabel didn't try to hide her feelings, while she soaked up tears and honked on a dishtowel.

When Reed finished, Mabel pushed her chair back and reached for a dry towel. After wiping her face again, she poured three cups of fresh coffee and fixed a teary gaze on Reed. "Son, that is the saddest story I've ever heard. Those poor people!"

Claude responded in a raspy voice. "I felt so sorry for that girl after her pa disappeared. Never liked her mother much, she was a looker, though. Always figured she was the cause of everything. Everybody knew she was messing around with that no-account game warden. Like everybody else, I pegged old Butch to be guilty, but I never blamed him much."

There was a long pause. Reed looked at Claude and noticed his eyes searching Mabel's quizzical face. The old man turned in his chair, facing Reed. "I didn't know any of those folks very well. Only what I heard about town, and at the senior center, and most of it I didn't believe. Not too long after old Butch disappeared, they moved out of town. Some of the old geezers at the club seemed to think the mother married some feller from Garfield."

Reed's expression brightened. "There's a Morgan in the Garfield phone book with initial 'C.' Could that be one of them?"

Mabel had composed herself by now. Reed studied her worried face and guessed she was desperately trying to recall something to be of help.

"Reed, honey," Mabel said, "I think it would be worth your time to just get in your truck and drive to Garfield—talk to some store owners and the like up there. If they're around, someone will know. I remember the names of a few old hens in Garfield from when they visited our senior center. They know everybody's business. Shoot, honey, if I wasn't so old and stoved up I'd go with you myself."

Reed stood and pushed his chair under the table with a smile playing across his lips. "Appreciate your help, and thanks for the coffee and rolls. I'll let you know how my trip to Garfield turns out."

———

Reed ducked through the doorway and pushed a pair of already soggy boots through the six or eight inches of soft snow still lying unshoveled on Cadwaller's sidewalk—his mind deep in thought. He swung his body into the truck seat, grasped the steering wheel with both hands, and sat for a moment, thinking. Mabel was right. Garfield would be the place to start looking. Maybe he'd start at the county court house, or the sheriff's office, then talk to some of the locals.

This was a new game for him. Most anyone would know better how to find a missing person, he agonized. But he owed

Morgan, and he was determined to turn the country up-side-down, if necessary, to find his daughter. He didn't want to think about how differently things could be today if Morgan hadn't been there. He pictured Cole Rusling shooting through space like a circus clown shot out of a cannon.

The main highway was slushy with melting snow and iced-over spots. The trip would take longer than he expected—time to pull himself together, plan, worry. Foremost on his mind was the twenty calves and fourteen cows he'd lost in the blizzard. After the count, they had searched until dark, probing into drifts more than six-feet deep. Maybe the cows had wandered with the blizzard and found shelter upstream? The calves wouldn't have cow milk, but they were old enough to scratch for forage through areas where the snow had blown off.

A shade of guilt came upon him. He questioned his motives about running off on a wild goose chase when he could be looking for his lost cattle. No, he satisfied his conscience, he was lucky to have such a small loss, and the missing cows and calves couldn't be found until some of the snow melted.

Garfield had received its share of the spring storm. Streets were unplowed. He guessed the city was saving money by waiting for the sun to turn the snow to slush and dirty water.

It was ten o'clock. The Clerk and Recorders office was empty save for an older, stocky woman at the counter and a slim, college-age girl sitting at a computer near the back of the small room. Both women turned their heads and looked when Reed entered. "May I help you?" the older woman asked in a pleasant tone of voice.

"I hope so," Reed answered, returning her friendly smile. "Fact is, though, I'm not even sure this is the right place to ask. I'm searching for a young lady by the name of Anne Morgan." The woman put on a baffled expression.

"Do I know you?" She asked, holding to her puzzled face.

"I'm Reed Carson, son of Lucy Carson."

The woman's face lit up with a smile. She extended her hand. "Reed Carson! I've known you since you were a baby. I'm Sara Westerfield." She pointed toward a nameplate displayed on the counter. "Lucy and I used to belong to the same bridge club— until your grandpa passed on, and I guess she got too busy with the ranches and all."

"Nice to meet you, Ma'am…Mrs. Westerfield. Sorry I didn't recognize you."

"That's okay, son. Now, back to your missing person. You say her name is Anne Morgan? And you've checked the phone book, of course?"

"Yes ma'am, first thing this morning. There's one Morgan, with initial 'C', and I wondered if that might be her."

"Well, I don't think we've got any official records that can help you, but I know a Morgan girl here in town—not Anne, though. The Morgan I know works at the high school—a secretary, I believe. She would be the one in the phone book. Cindy is her name. Maybe Anne is her middle name, or visa versa."

That lunkhead Morgan never mentioned a middle name, Reed muttered under his breath. He lowered his head, staring at the blank wooden counter, then looked up and exchanged a smile with the woman. "Thanks, Mrs. Westerfield," Reed said. "I'll check it out."

Reed had one hand on the long brass doorknob when the woman's voice stopped him. "Oh, Reed, um, …why do you need to find this Anne Morgan?"

Reed turned and smiled. "An old schoolmate—thought I'd look her up if she's still in town. Thanks again, Mrs. Westerfield."

"Thankfully it's Friday, the school will be open," Reed mused, doing a little skip in his half-run, half-walk trip to his truck. Could it really be Butch's Anne, now going by her middle or first name? Reed pondered the chances while gripping the steering wheel with both hands and staring at the empty snow covered street ahead of him. He'd go to the school and ask for Anne Morgan at the desk—maybe get lucky.

Reed found the school principal's office and stood outside the glass-paneled door a few seconds, catching his breath—rehearsing his approach. He'd never considered himself shy around the opposite sex—awkward, yes—not shy. But this was different.

"Can I help you?" A man's voice asked, as he reached his arm past Reed and pushed the door open. Reed gathered himself and looked down at a short, stocky, man, about fifty, dressed in a dark blue suit and a yellow tie. Before he could answer the man, someone caught his eye at a long counter on his left. The stranger opened the door wider, and they both moved one step inside the front office. The door closed.

"Thanks, but I have business with the girl at the counter, Reed said. The stranger shot a scowl in Reed's direction and moved off.

A tall, thin girl with long, brown hair and wearing an ankle-length, red, ruffled skirt with a blue, long-sleeved blouse stopped scribbling something on a notepad and turned her attention to Reed. He covered the girl's face and tall, slim features in one glance. She looked up at him and smiled.

In a flash, Reed knew he had blundered. This tall, pretty woman with the beautiful smile standing before him bore absolutely no resemblance to Butch Morgan—not the least. But then again, he reasoned, suppressing a grin as an image of the grizzled giant flashed before his eyes, what woman outside a carnival freak could match any of Morgan's appearances? He was trapped, though. He had to say *something* to explain his presence.

"Sorry to bother you ma'am. I'm looking for a person by the name of Anne Morgan, and I can see I've come to the wrong place," Reed murmured, while fumbling with his Stetson between his sweaty palms.

The tall girl ushered out a short chuckle. "Is Cindy Anne Morgan the girl you're looking for?" she asked, with a curious little smile.

Reed inhaled a short, quick breath to relieve his tight chest. He was suddenly feeling the pressure from his clumsiness and searching for the right words to respond. Standing away from the counter, still nervously handling his hat, Reed finally found his voice.

"Are you telling me your name is Cindy Anne Morgan?"

"That's right. Now, what can Cindy Anne Morgan do for you?"

This time Reed collected his bearings before speaking. "Did you go to school in Riverdale, and is your father Butch Morgan?"

"Yes, I went to school in Riverdale through the eighth-grade. And my dad's name was Butch. Did you know him?"

"No, I didn't know your dad then, but I knew you." Reed smiled. He was feeling more comfortable talking to her. "You don't recognize me. I'm not surprised, though. You aren't the same skinny little girl I remember, either."

Cindy cracked a smile and her face changed to a shade of red. "When did you last see me?"

"You were in the seventh or eighth grade, and I can see that you still haven't placed me. I'm sorry I should have introduced myself right off. I'm Reed Carson."

"Oh yeah, I've heard of you," she said smiling. Then she quickly added, "I don't remember you from school, but if Lucy Carson is your mother, I *should* know who you are. I can't believe you remember me."

"Well, I couldn't put you two together today, but you kind of stood out as the shy, skinny little junior high girl the year I graduated from high school."

"And you were probably the big football hero. Too bad I wasn't a cheerleader; I could have watched you play." There was an awkward silence. Then she said, "Did you come just to say hello?"

She had stopped smiling, when Reed lifted his eyes from the counter top and asked, "Cindy, do you have a few minutes we can talk, maybe during lunch or after you're off work?"

"Sure, I guess so, but you sound awfully sinister. Am I allowed to know what our topic of conversation will be?

Reed cleared his throat. "Uhhh….it's about your dad."

"My dad?"

Reed gripped the brim of his hat, and twisted it hard. "Well…yeah, sort of…. You see, Carson ranches own property near the site of your dad's old cabin. One day, while chasing stray cattle, I found some things that look like personal items that may belong to him. If they're his, maybe you would like to have them."

Cindy's face took on a strained look. "Well—sure, Reed. Of *course* I would like to see anything that belonged to my father. But, I'm really surprised. It's been such a long time. What did you find? Do you want to bring them in?"

"There's only a few things. I left them in my truck, parked down the street. I would rather not bring them in here. Could we meet for coffee, or something after you're off work today?"

"I have playground duty at noon with no one to replace me. But I can get off work early—say three o'clock. I'll pick up my daughter at the babysitter and meet you at my apartment about that time. Will that work for you?"

"That would be just right," Reed said. "That gives me time to buy supplies for the ranch."

She scribbled something on a small piece of paper, folded it twice and gently placed it in the palm of his hand. "My address and phone number," she said.

———

Before turning the ignition key, Reed lit a cigarette. He inhaled deeply, pushed out a lung-full of acrid smoke, and felt a weight lifted from his body. He had a small sense of uneasiness about lying to her. But what else could he do? He couldn't just belt out that her dad was alive right there in her work place.

Cindy's appearance had unnerved him more than the little lie that he was forced to tell. Everything about her—her turned up nose, her perfect white teeth, and a face he wanted to keep staring at. That wasn't the picture he had of her in his mind at all. She would be tall and wide, with long, hairy arms, and hands as big as frying pans. *But what did it matter, anyway?* He thought. He could return to camp with good news for Butch, and get on with his own plans.

But his mind wouldn't let it go at that. Cindy had a daughter—Butch's granddaughter. What about her husband, and her last name, Morgan? Why did he feel a slight pang of disappointment when she mentioned her daughter, which instantly created an image of a husband in her life? Of course she had a husband, how else could she have a kid? That's what people did—get married and have babies! Reed pulled harder on his cigarette, and gripped the wheel tighter. He hadn't thought about having to explain about Butch Morgan to a husband and wife. Maybe it will be easier this way, he thought—a husband's shoulder to lean on, or cry on, if she's the emotional type.

By two-thirty, he had finished his shopping at Safeway, loaded ten bags of Co-Op cow cake in the back of the pickup, and read the *Garfield Daily News* three times. At exactly three o'clock, he was holding his Stetson in one hand, and pushing the small doorbell ringer at Cindy Morgan's apartment with the other. The door handle wiggled several times before it slowly opened. The small hand holding onto the knob was attached to a tiny little blonde-haired girl, he judged to be about four years old. "Are you Mr. Carson?" the serious child said, straining to look Reed in the face.

Reed smiled down at the small child. "Yes, I am. I'm here to see your mother."

"I know, Mama told me. You can come in if you want to. She's in the bathroom. I'll go tell her."

"Thank you," Reed said, and stepped past the little girl into a sparse, tastefully decorated living room, with a full-size TV, a couch and love seat—that appeared to be new—and an antique wooden rocker. The wall with a door to the side, leading to the kitchen, was adorned with family pictures—dated photos of Cindy and a little girl, and several baby pictures. A middle-aged, attractive blonde, standing beside a husky, dark-haired man about her same age caught his eye—pictures of her mother, and probably her new husband, he ventured. To the far left of the display was an eight-by-ten color photo of a burly man he recognized instantly, even without his beard. He could have been thirty or thirty-five at the time. Reed smiled. A picture he judged to be very recent caught his eye at the center and near the top of the photos, a small girl, flanked by Cindy and a tall, craggy, blonde man, about Cindy's age. Cindy and the man were smiling, each with an arm about the tiny girl.

The man looked familiar and he was having a closer look at the picture when Cindy stepped through a door from the other side of the room. "You and Kimberly have met," she said, smiling. She brushed away a stray lock of hair out of the little girl's eyes, then offered an outstretched hand toward Reed. "Thanks for coming."

Cindy bent to her knees, held Kimberly's hands in hers, and spoke softly. "Honey, Gary is coming over. He wants to take you to the Dairy Queen for ice cream. Then when you come back, you and Gary and I are going out for dinner. Does that sound like fun?"

Kimberly screwed her face into a scowl. "I want to stay here with you and Mr. Carson."

"I know, honey, but Mr. Carson and I have some business to talk about that you wouldn't be interested in."

The doorbell chimed. Reed recognized the craggy, smiling face who stepped forward to embrace Cindy as the man on the wall, and again as the son of the president of Tri-State Bank in Garfield. Kimberly didn't move to greet the man, or change her expression. Reed accepted a weak handshake from Gary Stockton. "It's been a long time, Gary. How've you been?"

"Great, since my shoulder healed from that hit you gave me in our last football game. What was that—about ten years ago?" They both laughed.

"Are you ready, darling?" Cindy asked Kimberly. Stockton grasped the little girl's hand, managed a weak smile, and led her out the door without looking back.

Cindy had followed them to the door and watched as Gary Stockton fastened Kimberly's seat belt. She waved, and closed the door. "Gary is wonderful with Kimberly." Cindy said, turning to face Reed. "I just wish she could look at him in the same light." She paused, inhaled a deep breath, and gestured toward a long couch.

"Let's sit down, Reed. I'm so nervous...and excited, too. Did you bring the things...the personal items?"

Reed breathed deeply and let it all out before answering. "Cindy, there are no personal items. I had to—"

"What...? Is this your idea of a *joke?*"

"No. No...it's not a joke. I have some news about your father, but I couldn't just blurt it out at your office. I had to tell you *something.*"

"News? What news?"

"Cindy, your dad is alive. And he wants to see you. He's on my ranch at this very moment, wondering if I've found you and delivered his message."

Cindy's lips moved, as if to speak, but no words came. Reed froze, not knowing what else to say, or what to expect. Cindy searched his serious face for a long moment, before she turned away and stared out the window. Reed thought she must be crying, but he didn't know for sure.

When she turned again to face him, her cheeks were dry, not a tear. Her face was red and drawn, and her eyes were tightly shut. She took a deep breath, and bit her lower lip before she started to speak.

"I'm okay, really," she said. "I just don't know what to say. It's too overwhelming." She excused herself, slowly rose from the couch, and walked into another room. Reed heard a door close—water running.

She could control her voice, but not the mind-racing shock on her face. Had she gone to the bathroom to cry, to let it all out? He felt tightness in his chest and he had a bellyache. He wanted to run, hide, disappear, smoke a cigarette, anything but just sit here and stare at a blank TV screen and listen to water running in the bathroom. He'd played it out in his head a thousand times after he had left her office, but it didn't happen that way. Now he was berating himself for how she was feeling. Butch should have been the one to break the news, not him. He had to be nuts to think he could pull something like this off. He was trying to put together some words to excuse off Butch's absence without actually blaming him when he heard a door close.

Cindy returned with a towel in her hand and eased her hips down on the couch opposite Reed. "Six years, Reed. Six long years of hoping and praying, and now, to learn that he is alive is almost too much to accept all at once. And all those ugly rumors, cop killer, coward, burned himself up in his own cabin...why did he wait until *now*? It just doesn't make sense!"

"I can't answer for your father, Cindy. But I can tell you that he wants to see you. No, he doesn't just *want* to see you—I think he would give his right arm to see you again. I know you have a thousand questions you'd like to ask, but all I can tell you is how Butch Morgan came into my life, and what little I know about him. Fair enough?"

"Fair enough," she said, through a weak smile.

Reed turned his body slightly more toward Cindy, to allow direct eye contact. He needed to gauge her emotional reactions to help him to pace his comments, if that were possible. It wasn't something he felt qualified to do, but he could see that she was doing her best to make it easy for him.

He began with the minute Butch Morgan entered his world, telling her what he thought was important for her to know about the man—leaving out the fight scene with Kirk and his goons.

When he stopped talking, he averted his eyes to the blank TV screen, and waited for Cindy to collect her emotions.

They sat for a while, without speaking. Reed continued to stare at the dark TV screen. Finally, Cindy got to her feet and started pacing the floor, talking, making gestures with her hands.

"I don't know what's wrong with me, Reed. You've just given me the best news of my life. I should be yelling, shouting with joy, and crying like a baby. Maybe all of that will come later, but right now I'm just feeling really hurt and relieved at the same time. Sure, I'm so happy that I can hardly stand it to know that Dad is alive, and I can hardly wait to see him. But how could he let me go on thinking that he was dead? And why did he have to *send* someone to tell me? Is he sick, or crippled?"

"There's nothing at all wrong with your dad, Cindy. But I'm afraid he'll have to answer for himself." What else could he say? This was the part he dreaded the most, and was the least prepared for.

"Reed, please don't think I'm being ungrateful. You're wonderful and kind, and all this can't be easy for you. If Dad had to send someone, I'm glad it was you. I'm just so...so *shocked!* It really doesn't matter *how* I got the news. He was such a terrific Dad, and you can't know how it makes me feel to know that he's alive. I never once thought that Dad had killed that game warden, then when the news came that he was innocent; I just knew he would be coming back into my life—sooner or later."

"Did you ever think that he was still alive, but wouldn't come back to Riverdale for reasons of his own?"

"I never allowed myself to believe he was dead, but I wasn't totally convinced that I would ever see him again. I just held on to my memories of him and prayed. It's so wonderful, Reed!" Through a nervous laugh, she continued. "You're a brave man. I couldn't have done the same for you." She grasped his hand with both of hers and squeezed. "When...when can I see him, Reed?"

"What's your schedule for tomorrow?"

"I'm free."

"How about eleven o'clock. And lunch is on us, if you can eat deli food."

Cindy smiled. "We can do that!"

They continued talking until Reed glanced at his watch. It was four-thirty. They had talked for over an hour, with Cindy asking more questions about her dad than he could possibly answer. Reed looked at his watch again and stood. Together, they slowly walked toward the door without speaking. Reed had one hand on the doorknob, the other holding his hat, when he said, "Have you thought about how your mother is going to take the news about your dad?"

She shrugged her shoulders. "It doesn't matter. A long time before that thing happened with Dad, I knew they didn't have any kind of a marriage. I never saw her cry after he left, and when she caught me crying she would leave the room. Mom has to know how much I miss him."

_____

Cindy had never felt such mixed emotions. After Reed left, she went back to the couch and sat very still, hands clasped between her knees. The only sounds came from an occasional car door being slammed in the apartment parking lot or cars passing on the street. Reed Carson, a total stranger until a few hours ago, had given her the best news of her short twenty-two years of life—news that would change her life and her daughter's life forever. She should feel like the luckiest person in the world. She should be shedding tears of joy.

Instead, she sat silently, staring at the blank wall, brooding, her mind torn between resentment and delight. The dad whom she never allowed herself to believe was a murderer, refused to accept that he was dead and out of her life forever, had chosen to send a perfect stranger to tell her that he was healthy and well. How dare him! She felt like shaking her head violently, as if that would bring everything into focus.

After a while, she decided she was responding too much like the girl who first learned that she was unwed and pregnant. She would have given anything to bring her father back to her, even if the good news came from a stranger. There had to be a reason—some mysterious reason that she could not possibly know about. Anyway, she reasoned, what difference did it make *how* it happened. She had just been handed a chance for a new life with the father she remembered loving and adoring. She could feel sorry for herself later, after he explained why he kept his presence hidden for six years, while his only child lived with an insufferable heartache.

EIGHT

Lucy Carson advanced from malaise to flat-out depression on her third day of being housebound by the vicious spring snowstorm. She had never been one to minimize her troubles—Daddy Graves had not felt it necessary to instill that quality in her—and she saw her troubles multiply ten times over in three short days. With Reed permanently off the ranch and Justin Bullock firmly installed as ranch foreman for her entire spread, she should have felt an upswing in her mood, but the opposite was the case. She had not resolved in her mind exactly when and how she would dispense with Justin Bullock, nor had she totally justified her recent legal actions against her younger son, Reed.

She had been unable to contact either Justin or Kirk at any time during the past three days and nights of the blizzard, and did not know if the cattle were being cared for on either of the other two ranches. What if they were trapped in their vehicle, unable to find shelter? Over-and-over, as she lay in her bed, or walked the floor rubbing her arms, she pictured them sitting side-by-side, in their truck, shivering, waiting for help that wouldn't, or couldn't come.

After three long days and nights of isolation and worry, she could stand it no longer. She doubled her dosage of antidepressants and added a sleeping pill. Sleep is what she needed. Real sleep, not the fitful sleep she was experiencing, accompanied by ghoulish nightmares about Kirk and Justin freezing to death in a snow bank, and her helpless starving cattle lying dead.

She had not bathed or combed her hair for two days, and her only nourishment came from refrigerator snacks. Her arms were red and raw from rubbing them. She was moving slower than usual that morning, but managed to function enough to remember her resolve to double the prescribed number of pills.

She picked at the poached eggs and toast prepared by her housekeeper, Mrs. Stinson, then returned to her room, laid down on the bed, and curled her tired body into a fetal position.

At twelve-thirty that afternoon, Mrs. Stinson lightly knocked on the door of Lucy's bedroom. There was no answer. She knocked again and again, harder each time. Finally, she pushed the door open, walked to Lucy's bedside, all the while quietly calling her name. After five minutes of shaking and shrieking, "Wake up, please wake up," she called Kirk Carson, left a message on his phone then called Dr. Wisner's office.

An hour later, two ambulance attendants entered the Lucy Carson residence without knocking, followed some indistinct whimpering sounds to Lucy's bedroom and found her on the bed, curled into a fetal position. Shirley Stinson was bent over her bedside, wiping mucous from Lucy's mouth with a wet towel.

Several hours later, Lucy Carson rode a stretcher into the emergency room of Cheyenne Mercy Hospital. A staff doctor checked her vital signs, ordered detox treatment be started immediately, and called Dr. Harold Whiting.

Dr. Whiting arrived at the hospital two hours later, briefly examined the patient and prescribed a private room and a twenty-four-hour watch.

———

It was a silent ride home after Kirk and his hired mens' encounter with Reed and Butch Morgan. Bullock left straightaway for the Teardrop Ranch. Pratt, Rusling, and Dubois scrambled for the bunkhouse to finish off a liter of sour mash, smoke pot, and nurse their wounds.

Kirk abandoned the crowded pickup without a word to the others and crept to the main house, where he touched the button on his answering machine for the first time in two days. He listened to a message from Cheyenne Mercy Hospital, and another, frantic, recording from Shirley Stinson. "Crazy old bag, she never does make any sense. Why didn't she just say, 'your mom's in the nuthouse again,' without all the dramatics?" Kirk grumbled to himself.

Later that evening, he returned the housekeeper's call to hear the same story, worn thin ten years ago. He sighed and decided to give Dr. Whiting a call, then drive to Cheyenne, spend the night in a motel, and visit his mother early the next day.

"Dr. Whiting will see you now," said a pleasant receptionist with a clinical smile. Kirk followed her down a hallway and into an office decorated with large, ocean-view murals. A plump, balding man in a white coat and a matching white beard greeted him with a firm handshake and a serious face.

Kirk felt his lips twitching as he eased into a comfortable leather chair, facing the doctor's desk. "Would you like a cup of coffee, Mr. Carson?"

"I'm good, sir, thank you."

"Very well then, I'll get right to it. As you know, Mr. Carson, your mother was brought to the hospital by a private ambulance about eight o'clock yesterday evening. The information given to me is sketchy, but as I understand it, her housekeeper was unable to awaken her from what she perceived to be a deep coma. She failed in her efforts to contact either you or your brother. In desperation, she called Dr. Wisner in Riverdale, and he sent an ambulance to the Carson residence."

"How is my mother?"

"Resting. She was irrational and hallucinating when she arrived at the hospital. A staff doctor immediately ordered detoxification, and by the time I arrived her condition was stable."

"Mr. Carson, I've treated your mother for depression for the past fifteen years. Prior to yesterday, she has always admitted and dismissed herself at will. Her longest stay was five days— unfortunately, not long enough for me to do a proper diagnosis of her illness."

The corners of Kirk's lips danced. "Mother has been under tremendous pressure the past few weeks. You will need to know what's happened between her and my brother, Reed, to understand why her condition has worsened."

"Perhaps Mr. Carson, but everything about her life should be considered. However, my hands are tied. The minute her condition improves, she will check herself out and we will expect her back again in a very short while."

"I'll do anything in my power to help Mother get well. Just say the word, doctor."

"That's why I called you here, Mr. Carson. I only wish your brother could be with you. I've reviewed Mrs. Carson's complete medical history with several of our staff psychiatrists. To be candid, our consensus is that she exhibits some classic symptoms of paranoia. Understand, this doesn't constitute a diagnosis by any means. And that's where you and your brother must enter the picture."

"Paranoia?"

"Yes, Mr. Carson. Paranoia is a symptom of schizophrenia, a serious mental illness, characterized by a slowly progressive deterioration of the personality, involving delusions and often hallucinations, in which the person feels persecuted, and believes the actions of close friends and relatives are threatening. Your mother exhibits some form of all of these symptoms. Again, let me emphasize, I am not giving you a diagnosis. I'm saying she needs a psychiatric evaluation, and probably, long term treatment."

"How can I help, doctor?"

"You're a lawyer, Mr. Carson. You know better than I that we can't keep your mother confined unless she's declared mentally incompetent. I can certify to her mental condition, but I can't keep her here unless you and your brother take the necessary legal steps to commit her to an indefinite stay in the hospital. I know Lucy Carson well, and I'll have a fight on my hands when her condition improves. But your mother is also a sensible woman, and in time, I think she will come around to my point of view, especially if you and your brother are behind it."

"Can I see her today?"

"You can, but I advise against it. As I've said, she's resting, and I should also add, she's under a twenty-four hour suicide watch."

"I'll take your advice. I will do anything to help my mother get well—to be herself again. I know Reed feels the same way. I'll prepare the necessary papers in my office tomorrow, see the judge early Monday morning, and have them back to you by the afternoon. Thank you so much for your time and concern, Dr. Whiting."

Kirk removed a fresh stogie from his vest pocket, rolled it between his skittish lips, and danced a little jig in the hallway. In the hospital parking lot, he eased himself into his mother's luxurious Cadillac leather seats and touched a flame to the cigar. He took a short pull, pushed the smoke out an open window, and smiled before turning the key. *What a break!* Could he ask for more? Maybe he didn't need that bunch of jailbirds after all.

———

Kirk didn't tell Bullock about Lucy's episode before he left to pick up her Cadillac at the North River Ranch for his trip to Cheyenne. He'd learn soon enough. Now, on his way home, relaxed to the smooth purr of the big engine, he enjoyed the aroma of a fresh cigar and occupied his mind with his new plans.

He was in no hurry to get back to the ranch. He would stop by his office and prepare the papers for Reed's and his signatures. He laughed to himself as he thought of Reed's signature. How many documents had he forged in Reed's name? While he was at it he would set himself up with Power of Attorney, with complete control over his mother's entire estate, which would also require Reed's signature. His last act, before closing the door and locking his office, would be to write Justin Bullock's last paycheck.

———

Kirk pulled into the driveway of the North River Ranch, expecting to see a green, 1990 Ford pickup parked in front. Lucy had helped Bullock buy the old clunker after his first week of work for her. His mother was too generous. Or maybe she thought a bit of kindness on her part would give him incentive to pull his lazy ass out of bed at six in the morning, like the rest of the hired help, and set an example. Now, Bullock had the title to the pickup, and he still owed his mother for more than half of the cost. Kirk had forgotten to deduct the remaining twelve-hundred dollars from Bullock's final check. A small price to pay in exchange for the fortune Bullock was expecting, he thought.

Kirk checked the garage and the machine shed, where the hired men often parked their vehicles, then used his key to enter the bunkhouse. Dirty dishes were scattered about the table and sink. Several full ashtrays littered the coffee table. "What a pig," Kirk murmured.

"Hey, Justin, you about?"

No answer. Kirk scowled, mumbling to himself, "Justin is probably at the Pronghorn Bar getting oiled. I'll sack his stuff and take it to him. Fire him right in the bar. "Serves the worthless puke right," he said out loud to the empty bunkhouse.

He didn't find Bullock at the Pronghorn Bar, but he *did* leave his bag of personal affects with the bartender to give to him on his next visit.

Bullock and Kirk's three hired hands, Pratt, Rusling and Dubois, were standing in the driveway of the South River Ranch, leaning against the green Ford, drinking beer, and passing a joint when Kirk returned.

He ignored them, parked the Cadillac, and walked straight toward the house. Bullock turned and kicked a rock across the road, scowling at being dismissed. "Hey Bossman, what's your hurry?"

Kirk felt his face burn, but didn't turn around. Bullock followed on his heels. Kirk wasn't accustomed to being addressed in such a manner. It occurred to him again that letting Bullock in on his plan to take the ranch was a big mistake from the beginning—all the more reason to fire him today.

Bullock had no solid evidence on him …yet, but it was just a matter of time before he would have enough to take both of them down—hard. Despite this worry, Kirk was feeling a wave of

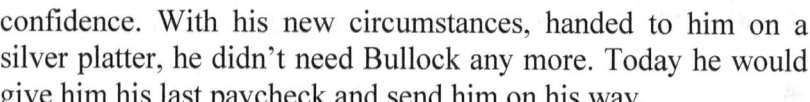
confidence. With his new circumstances, handed to him on a silver platter, he didn't need Bullock any more. Today he would give him his last paycheck and send him on his way.

Kirk entered the porch and let the door slam. Bullock burst in behind him. "What the hell is it with you, big shot?" Bullock said. "You're too good to speak to your new ranch foreman?"

Kirk reached into his shirt pocket and pulled out a neatly folded envelope. He pushed it toward Bullock and said, "As of now, you're not the foreman of anything around here. You're fired."

Bullock didn't say a word until he'd torn the envelope open and stared at the check as if he couldn't read. "So that's it? You talked your mama into firing me?"

"Let's just say that Mom and I are in accord, not that you would know what that means. Anyway, considering the amount of work you've done lately and your performance yesterday, I can't think of any reason you're needed around here."

Bullock leaned forward, his beery, marijuana-laced voice threatening. "If what you say is true, about Lucy agreeing to fire me, I'll see that you're put away so far they'll be piping daylight to your piss-ant little eyes. You think you can let me go, just like that? With everything I know? You're forgetting about the stolen backhoe, and all those cattle Pratt and Rusling hauled to Montana…and I'll bet the sheriff would love to taste some of that rotten stuff you cook in the old barn."

"And you forget that I'm a lawyer, and you're an ex-con. Who would believe *you?* If anyone finds my stuff in the barn, who's to say it isn't you that's been cooking it? I want you to take your paycheck and get out of here—now. If you put one foot on any of the ranches again, I'll see you in court. Judge just might decide to throw you back in prison for breaking parole. As for anything you might say about me…it's your word against mine, and your word means nothing. And by the way, you'll find your other change of clothes at the Pronghorn Bar."

A vicious scowl darkened Bullock's scarred face. He whirled and stamped toward the door. Midway, he stopped, and without

looking back, hurled one last menacing threat: "You'll pay." He strode past the three curious hired hands, fired the green truck, and peeled gravel.

Five minutes later a patrol car pulled into Kirk's driveway. A uniformed cop eased out and gave the three nervous hired men a once-over, hitched at his gun belt, and strode toward the house. Kirk met him at the door. "I'm Deputy Sheriff Billy Schultz. Sheriff Logan dispatched me. Is everything alright?"

"Yes, the crisis is over. I fired a man when I found out he was an ex-convict. I've known him to have a violent temper, and I wasn't sure how he'd react to the news. You may have heard of him, Justin Bullock, resisted arrest and beat up a policeman several years ago."

"Umm…the name rings a bell. I passed a scruffy looking guy driving too fast in an old green Ford. Could that be him?"

"That's him."

"Where do you think he's going?"

"You can probably find him at the Pronghorn Bar. He didn't commit any crimes here—that I know of—but he did make some threats. One can't be too careful with a character like him."

Schultz tightened his lips and stared at Kirk. "The fool was driving too fast. Shoulda' gave chase. But I was on this call and the sheriff said it was urgent."

Schultz turned to leave. "I'll be getting along now. If I don't get another call on my way, maybe I'll pay that fellow a visit at the bar. Call me if he causes you any more trouble."

"Thanks sheriff," Kirk called out, as Schultz sank into the seat of the patrol car.

NINE

The shadows were long and the air was starting to chill when Reed arrived back at his cabin. Butch Morgan was nowhere to be seen. Lurch was missing from the corral, and the dog wasn't there to greet him. He unloaded the supplies and packages, and found room for them inside.

Coffee was boiling, and he was preparing supper for two when he heard a horse whinny. Mister burst through the opened door. Reed playfully scuffed his ears. "Hey guy, I thought you'd left me." The dog smelled Reed's pants leg and licked his hand before moving to the door and barking twice toward the horizon.

Several minutes passed until Morgan darkened the doorway with half of a deer carcass strung across his shoulder. Reed stepped back and eyed the hairy carcass. "Looks like we've got camp meat for awhile," Reed said.

Morgan cut a stream of brown juice to the side. "Thought a little change of diet wouldn't hurt either of us."

Reed sat two cups on the table and filled them with steaming coffee. "You look ruffled. Did our company return today?"

"Naw, nothing like that. Old dog and I been trailing crazed cows all over the mountain, packing back motherless calves and breaking snow up to our belt lines."

"So you found some missing cattle?"

"Yup, guess we earned our pay today. Those fourteen mother cows wanted to do a search on their own, so we cut the fence and let them have at it. They were bent on looking for their calves, and we just followed along—brought you back six calves and four cows. There's more tracks leading on up the creek, and where there's tracks there's gotta be cows, but we wuz just too tired to go any more."

"Butch, that calls for a celebration. But first, you've got to get rid of those smelly beavers and put on some decent clothes."

"You think I've been out shopping all day for a fancy suit? Or maybe you'd prefer a tux?" Morgan grinned suspiciously.

Reed moved to his bed and grasped a large plastic bag he'd carried in with other supplies and emptied out the contents onto the bed. He turned to Morgan and said, " I bought you some new duds today, but they're not for the party tonight. Come on over here and try them on."

Morgan hesitated, then he slowly moved to the bed. With thumb and forefinger, he picked up a black and white plaid shirt and gingerly held it toward the light from the window. "What is this? I thought we were friends, and here you are trying to freeze me to death—giving me a shirt thin enough to watch a girlie show through. And, those pants…."

"Hey, if you want to wear those stinking beavers when you meet your daughter tomorrow, it's okay with me."

Morgan's weathered face took on a look of serious disbelief. "You did it, didn't you?" Morgan shouted, grabbing Reed and lifting him in a bear hug. "How'd you do it?"

"Never mind the details. She'll fill you in on everything. And before you put those clothes on, dunk yourself in the horse tank. My horses won't thank me for it, but Cindy will. Yes, her name is Cindy, Butch—did you know that? Why didn't you tell me she had a first name?"

Morgan ran a hand through his long hair. "I don't rightly know. Guess I plum forgot. We never called her anything but Anne."

Reed slowly shook his head, looked away, and said, "Oh yeah, before I forget, be prepared to say hello to your granddaughter."

"Granddaughter!"

"Reed, I cursed you all day, every time I dug out of a snow bank. Now I gotta take that all back. Tell me how we're gonna do this, man. Is she coming here?"

Reed leaned back in his chair with a satisfied grin and set a match flame to another Marlboro. "At eleven o'clock we're gonna meet Cindy and your granddaughter, Kimberly, where our road joins the highway. We need to be there a little early so she won't miss the turnoff. I gave her some written directions to the cabin, just in case."

"Are you sure she can find her way?" Morgan asked anxiously.

Reed grinned at him. "Don't worry, she didn't inherit your sense of direction—*or* your looks."

"Reed, tell me some things about her. Was she happy to know about me, I mean that I'm alive? Is she pretty, like her mom? Did you meet her hus…?"

"Now hold on there, big guy. I'm not telling you anything else, except to say that she isn't just pretty, she's a real knockout, and so is your granddaughter. And I guess it's safe for me to say that she was glad to learn that you're not a bucket of ashes. Oh yeah, before I forget, I invited them for dinner. I bought a couple of roast chickens and some other fixings. We'll serve them in our spacious dining room."

———

It was a clear cool, Saturday morning. A gentle pine-scented breeze moved a loose tin on the barn roof just loud enough to be heard inside the cabin. After a hurried breakfast, with Morgan silent as a scared dove, Reed threw four six-gallon plastic Wal-Mart jugs in the back of his pickup, filled them at the creek, and unloaded the lot beside the cabin door.

There wasn't a chance he was going to allow Morgan to meet his daughter without bathing. "It's your turn first," Reed said. "There's a tub in the barn. Heat some water on the stove, and if there's any left, I'll douse myself after I feed the cows."

"Let me help feed. It won't take me long to scrub…maybe five minutes."

Reed turned toward the door. "No way, man! We both smell as bad as a sheepherder's socks. Maybe you haven't noticed the cows staying upwind when we're scattering hay. You couldn't scrub the dirt out of your toenails in five minutes." Morgan slowly shook his head as he fumbled in a pocket for tobacco.

An hour later, Reed slowly cracked open the cabin door, afraid of what he might see. They'd talked very little that night. Morgan chewing, spitting, smoothing his tobacco-stained beard, and doing his best to get Reed to tell him more about his daughter. Reed was chain smoking, reading a James Michener novel by lamplight, and ignoring Morgan's endless questions. Morgan was standing with his back to the stove, stroking his beard, when Reed stepped inside. "Whadda'ya think, little buddy? Tell me before I freeze to death in these city duds."

Reed turned away, not wanting Morgan to see how he really felt. Then he couldn't hold it any longer, and burst out laughing. "You look as silly as an Eskimo in Phoenix on the Fourth of July."

Morgan took on a silly smirk, shoved both hands out, exposing three or four inches of hairy arms not covered by shirtsleeves, and performed a showy turn.

Reed wiped tears from his eyes and tried to get control of himself. "Where did you buy clothes before half the beaver in the county outfitted you? Garfield doesn't have *Tall and Big Men* shops like they do in Denver, you know. I bought the tallest pants and the biggest shirt they had on the shelves at Wal-Mart. The chubby little clerk couldn't stop smirking when I checked out. Not that *she* had any room to talk."

"Hey, man, you did great, even if they only cover about half of me. And you know I appreciate it." Morgan raised a forearm to his face and smelled. "They smell pretty, and I only got to wear them long enough to show Anne…uh…Cindy, I'm not a wild man."

The fifteen-minute trip to the junction of Highway 167 was wordless, Reed chain-smoking and Morgan stuffing Days Work into his mouth with nervous fingers. *What if Cindy brought Gary with her?* Reed considered. The thought curdled his stomach. By now he was content that they were not married and that Gary wasn't Kimberly's father. But, what did he care? They were Butch's responsibility now, Cindy, Kimberly, and even Gary

Stockton if he showed up. He'd done his part. Gary was a decent enough guy he supposed, and some day he would be one of the richest men in Garfield. But there was something about Stockton that he didn't like or trust. Cindy could do better.

Kirk had been surprised to see Gary Stockton show up at Cindy's door, and he was even more surprised to see that Stockton wasn't already married. He hadn't given one thought to Stockton since he had plowed the guy's head into the grass at their last football game, but now he was wondering why some girl hadn't snagged the rich bankers' son. He had everything his dad could give him. He tried to think of any of his friends his own age that hadn't bit the dust at least once.

He didn't know, and he didn't care, why Gary Stockton wasn't married, but he didn't have to guess why he hadn't taken the plunge at the altar. He had purposely avoided commitment. While all of his old high school friends were getting married, having kids, and building white picket fences around their starter homes, Reed was working seven days a week, saving his money, and building a cow herd.

He tried to convince himself there would be plenty of time to think about falling in love, marriage, and starting a family after he became the owner of the Homestead Ranch and paid off part of the debt. But, deep down, he knew these weren't the real reasons he avoided commitment; he was nursing a guilt that he could feel clear down to his toes. He knew how the gossip went, and he knew some of it was true.

It had been eleven years since the night of that tragic accident that killed his friend and classmate. And, since that horrible night, Reed had allowed himself only one other chance at dating.

He reluctantly escorted a town girl, Alice Hornby, to the senior prom. Alice was another classmate of Reed's. She obviously considered herself a plain, homely girl, which she was. If her name was mentioned at all by the boys in school, it was a metaphor for unattractiveness.

Alice was a tall, gangling girl, with long, stringy blonde hair, which she allowed to fall over her face when sitting at her desk or when she was shyly moving about the school hallway. Alice had not had a happy childhood or a happy life. She'd lived in a small, clapboard, rental house in the oldest part of town with her three younger sisters, and a mean, drunken father and a cowed, submissive mother. Her dresses, skirts, and blouses were shapeless, stitched-up hand-me-downs from another generation.

Alice did not date, but she was not a complete loner. She attended all the school athletic events, where she sat with two or three other girls, who genuinely liked her, laughed and enjoyed herself. After the games, the other girls would join their boyfriends, and Alice could be seen walking home alone. Reed had never seen her with a boy, at a movie, or at a school or public dance, and, until the day he considered asking her to the prom, he didn't care enough to wonder why.

Reed could have asked any number of popular girls to his senior prom. Just the thought of being there with *any* girl caused his stomach to knot in fear, especially Alice Hornby. And he sure as hell didn't want to attend the prom. But, his mother insisted. After arguing with her every day for two weeks, Reed caved. He would go to the prom, have a lousy time, and embarrass his mother as a bonus. Poor, drab Alice Hornby would be his date to the prom—if she would go. He couldn't remember if he had ever spoken to her, but, somehow, he would find a way to get her to the prom.

Reed was driving home after school. A mischievous grin formed at the corners of his mouth, thinking about his decision to ask Alice Hornby to the prom. He hadn't told anyone. They would just show up.

His thoughts wavered, again. It was still two weeks away— plenty of time to change his mind. He couldn't even dance. Alice Hornby couldn't dance. How could she know how? He'd known her since kindergarten and he'd never seen her on the streets after dark, much less at a dance. Today was Friday. He would have to decide by Monday. Even Alice Hornby needed some time to buy clothes, fix her hair....

Monday came too soon for Reed. He was still debating if he should just go right up to his mother and tell her he definitely wasn't going to the prom or face the music and figure out a way to ask Alice. He finally decided, in the long run, it would be less painful to spend one night in misery than face his mother's scorn for months on end.

Before the first bell in the morning, between classes, and during the noon hour, he searched out Alice and either watched her directly, when she wasn't looking, or out of the corner of his eye. Throughout the day, Reed tormented himself with indecision, and figuring out how to get Alice Hornby alone, though he wasn't sure he wanted to. He didn't know where she lived, but several times he'd seen her walking north from the school building. He'd park his pickup close to the sidewalk, north of the school, wait until she passed, say hello—start a conversation....

At the last bell, Reed rushed through the hallway and went directly to his pickup. He was leaning against the hood, when Alice approached. She was carrying her books clutched to her chest with both hands, her chin tucked under. She was looking neither right nor left—her eyes on the sidewalk. If she saw Reed, she didn't let on. He was afraid she would pass him by, and he would have to chase after her to get her attention. He forced a smile and stepped into her path. "Alice," he said hesitantly.

Startled, she stopped dead still, lifted her chin off her books, and stared at him.

"Yes?"

"Ahh...I know you're in a hurry, but I was just wondering if you have a date for the prom."

"I'm sorry...but I don't understand....Why do you care?"

"Well, I need a date...and I know it's late and all...with the prom being just two weeks away, but if you don't already have a date...."

Alice glanced down at her feet, then raised her head to stare Reed full in the face. Her face flushed. "This is a joke, right?

Well, I'm not laughing, so you can go tell your jock friends it didn't work."

She stepped around him briskly and was half-way across the street before he came to his wits and started after her. He overtook the distraught girl and walked beside her for a minute or two before saying anything.

"Hey…Alice…wait…please, I'm serious," he finally said. "Really, I'm not kidding. I need a date for the prom. I can't dance very good, and I might step on your feet a lot, but I'd sure like to have you go with me."

Alice stopped, still clutching her school books tightly to her chest, as though she expected Reed to grab them and run. Reed waited for her to say something…anything…wondering if it would even happen. Classmates and other students passed by them on their way home, staring curiously, or outright smirking. Alice looked straight ahead.

Finally, Alice turned and looked straight up at him with a look of confusion. "What's this all about, anyway, Reed Carson? You've never even looked my way, let alone spoken to me. Anyway, you have to know I can't dance, so what's the point here?"

Reed laughed. His chest lost some of its tightness.

"Hey—I *really* want to take you to the prom. We'll probably look silly, okay, but if you know how to laugh, it might be fun."

She put on a quick, crooked little smile, then her face turned serious. She stared at him again, but not too long.

"Okay. I'll think about it. Ask me again tomorrow. But, if this is a joke, Reed Carson, I may have to kill you."

Alice walked away, smiling. Reed swung his rubbery legs behind the steering wheel and took a long breath. The adrenaline rush from their conversation almost made him forget his purpose of asking Alice to the prom. She had a nice smile, something he hadn't seen her do before, and who knows, if she bought a dress and fixed her hair….

Two days before the prom, three of Alice's girlfriends took her under their wing, supervised her visit to the hairdresser, and stood by while she tried on and bought the most beautiful gown in the store. Alice Hornby had no money. Her three friends paid for everything.

An hour before Reed was to pick her up, Alice's friends applied makeup and gave out helpful hints on how to walk in her high heels and floor-length dress.

Reed was stunned. He could see the same disbelief on the faces of everyone at the prom. Reed remembered a few dance steps he'd learned as a freshman, but it didn't help much. Alice had not tried to dance even once in her life, but they made do. They stepped on each other's feet, laughed, and exchanged a few dances with other couples.

It didn't surprise Reed that not all of the girls at the prom were captivated with Alice's makeover. It was on their faces, their crafty glances, and seemingly effortless attempts to hide their intentions when they turned their heads to whisper to each other. Reed smiled toward them, thinking he could read their minds: *Poor Alice Hornby, thinking she can be like us! Poor, poor Alice.*

After the dance, they attended an all-night party in the newly-finished basement at Jimmy Doyle's house.

At five o'clock the next morning, couples started to leave. Reed didn't want to see the party end. He especially didn't want to burst the bubble for this unassuming attractive girl by leaving her at the doorstep at the ramshackle house she called home.

He wanted to go some place and park, hold her and kiss her, tell her what a great time he'd had, maybe more. He didn't. Instead, he drove her straight to her house, kissed her lightly on the lips once, then a long hard kiss while holding her body close to his. He thanked her for the evening, and left her staring after him in the doorway.

Reed smiled to himself all the way back to the ranch. He couldn't remember if he'd ever had so much fun. He was euphoric. *Wow, the look on the faces of those two snotty Lambert twins.* He'd call Alice tomorrow, tell her, again, how much fun he'd had, how much he had enjoyed her company, what a perfect date she was.

Reed did call Alice Hornby the next day and told her all the things, and more, that he couldn't bring himself to tell her after the prom. He could feel her blush as he talked. He blushed, too, not realizing that he could utter such words to *anyone.*

One week later, Reed Carson and Alice Hornby graduated high school. During that short week, they often talked in the hallway, and a few hurried moments after school. They did not date again. Alice accepted a job as secretary for the sawmill, and Reed as the new foreman of the Homestead Ranch.

Over a period of six months, Alice and Reed talked on the phone several times. She seemed cheerful, even happy, but it was impossible to tell if her one-night-stand as Cinderella had made a positive difference in her life. He hoped that it had.

One night, toward the end of one of their short telephone conversations, Alice happily revealed her plans to marry a man who owned and operated his own logging truck.

It was four years before Reed saw Alice Hornby again. He had joined a long line at the concession stand to purchase a hot dog and soda pop, before the bareback bronc riding started at the annual Fourth of July Rodeo, when he felt a hand touch his shoulder. He turned to look into the face of a smiling woman, holding the arm of a tall, craggy-faced man, about his own age. The man was holding a small child in his arms. Alice introduced her husband as Tom Richards. "And this is little Tom," she said with a broader smile.

———

While they waited by the roadside waiting for Cindy, Reed bothered himself, again, with thoughts about Cindy and Gary. *There's something wrong there. They don't belong together.* Cindy had a strong will and a certain bearing, like her father. And he could tell right off she wasn't a push-over. He knew Gary from football, and he knew about the Stockton family— rich, country-club-type people. But, Gary had fried his chances of Reed ever looking at him in a friendly manner from the first words the banker's son had ever said to him. 'Hey, half-breed, how's your girlfriend?' Stockton shouted across the line in their last football game. He would never forget it.

He still had the picture framed in his mind of Stockton's seemingly lifeless body being carried off the field on a gurney. Reed had been called 'half-breed,' or just 'breed,' a lot by his high school buddies. That was okay. He was proud of his Indian blood. But, it wasn't okay for Stockton to smear his heritage.

Morgan sat like a boulder, staring straight ahead, his only movement when he raised his arm and used the sleeve to wipe the wetness from his forehead. They'd been parked at the highway intersection since ten-thirty. Reed gave in to the urge, stepped outside the vehicle, lit a cigarette, and checked the tires with Mister.

Reed saw a blue two-door, Chevrolet approach and recognized it immediately, just as she had described it. "That's her," Reed called out. Morgan quickly stepped out of the pickup and stood as straight as a power pole, one hand nervously smoothing his spotless beard.

The car clattered over the metal cattle guard and stopped opposite Reed's pickup. Cindy rolled down her window and smiled up at Reed. He returned her nervous smile. He wanted to keep looking at her. Her gleaming, long brown hair was pulled back from her tan face in a small, smooth ponytail. Without makeup she looked younger, even prettier.

She unbuckled Kimberly's seat belt then glanced up at Reed again. Her smile broadened. The knot in his stomach went away.

Reed glanced over at Kimberly standing in the seat, smiled, and started to say something before Kimberly interrupted him.

"I know you. You're Mister Carson, aren't you?"

Reed's smile widened. "Yes, and I know you, Kimberly Morgan. And I know something else. If you like to ride horses, I have just the one for you. His name is Lurch and I've told him all about you."

Kimberly's face brightened. "Really?"

"Yep, so let's get this show on the road. Old Lurch is expecting you." Cindy's lips parted slightly as she glanced toward her dad, who seemed to be waiting for an invitation to breathe.

Reed opened Cindy's door. She swung her slim, Levi-clad legs around and out of the car in one fluid motion. The ground was slushy with melting snow and Reed noticed she'd worn snow boots for the occasion. She made the practical footwear look as sexy as heels on a runway model, he caught himself thinking.

He reached across the car seat and Kimberly accepted his outstretched arms. "Go ahead, Cindy. Kimberly and I will take Mister for a short walk."

With Kimberly clinging to his neck, Reed walked away from the vehicles, entertaining the excited girl with stories about Lurch, her favorite horse now.

Reed slowly walked about fifty yards before he turned and started back. Mister ran ahead, pushing his nose under the snow and throwing it over his head. Kimberly pointed at the dog and giggled.

Reed was about to speak when father and daughter stopped embracing and turned, revealing their wet faces. Cindy used a sleeve to dry her cheeks and reached for Kimberly. Mother and daughter faced Butch full on for a moment, "Meet your granddaughter, Dad," Cindy said with a wide smile.

Butch stood motionless, grinning, eyes wide with delight. He tried to make his voice soft. "Hi sweetheart, I'm your grandfather."

Kimberly buried her face in Cindy's shoulder. "Mama can we go ride Lurch now?" Cindy flashed an apologetic smile toward her dad and patted Kimberly on the back.

When Cindy started toward her car, carrying Kimberly, Reed moved quickly to hold the car door open while she buckled the tiny girl in her seat belt. "You may want Butch to drive, Cindy. Snow's melting pretty fast and the roads will be muddy. And, it's all uphill."

Cindy straightened up from bending inside the car and smiled at Reed. "That sounds great. Dad was driving the last time I saw roads like this."

TEN

Cindy sat on the bench, arms resting on the small table, her long legs crossed, smiling to herself as she watched the wooden fingers of the two big men nervously putting lunch together. She offered to help, but they would have no part of it. 'No, ma'am, this is going to be our treat,' they insisted.

She wanted to laugh at their comical movements, dodging each other setting out tin plates, silverware, paper towels for napkins, packaged potato salad, and parting the chickens into portions. *What a strange pair,* she mused. Except for Reed's darker skin and coal-black hair, they were enough alike in appearances to be father and son. And it was obvious they had high regard for each other.

And Reed Carson—who was this tall, handsome cowboy, really? She'd heard his name mentioned at coffee breaks, and parties, and always it was about the "accident."

None of the local gossip sounded like the Reed Carson she had come to know the last few days.

Cindy had to admit, she felt a pleasant sense of friendliness the moment she laid eyes on Reed Carson. On her long drive from Garfield today, she smiled to herself as she thought about him blushing and fumbling with his hat at the school. Then, later at her apartment where she trusted her first reaction: He definitely seemed different than any other man she had ever met. But, not just because he was the son of the rich, flamboyant Lucy Carson, or because of his tall, good looks. He had a kind, manly manner that made her feel safe.

She looked forward to having Reed as a close friend. That is all she wanted from any man. She didn't think that Reed would ever push for anything more, not like Gary, but, if he did, he would have to understand—just like she had made Gary understand: she would never, ever, allow a man to get close enough to hurt her again.

Maybe it was everything that he had done these last few days to reunite her and her father, but already she was feeling a close friendship developing with this tall stranger, something even closer than she had ever felt with Gary Stockton.

Poor Gary, knocking himself out, begging her to accept his marriage proposals. Had she been using him the past two years? He was so good to Kimberly. And what about all the dinners, movies, and parties he'd willingly shelled out his hard-earned cash for?

A flush of guilt tightened her chest. No, she finally told herself. She didn't need to feel guilty about Gary. She'd been honest with him and her plans for herself and Kimberly, which didn't include an intimate relationship at this time in her life.

Reed walked to the door and called to Kimberly, "Hey, cowgirl, let's chow down, then we'll see how Lurch feels about giving us a ride."

"Yeaahh!" Kimberly screamed, threw the stick one more time for the dog, grabbed Reed by the leg and stuck her chin in the air. "Are we really going to ride Lurch, Mr. Carson?"

"You bet we are, but you gotta fill that tummy of yours first."

Butch sat on the wooden bench next to Cindy. Kimberly preferred Reed's leg to the wooden chair he had prepared for her with a pillow. Through mouthfuls of chicken, picked from Reed's plate, she ruled the conversation with questions about Lurch.

Cindy looked toward Reed, with a bit of a smile, then bent over and whispered into Kimberly's ear: "How about if I just leave you here today with Mister and Lurch?"

"Great...! Are you serious, Mom?" Kimberly said, through a mouthful of potato salad.

Reed and Kimberly left the meal first, legging it toward the barn. Butch poured two cups of coffee, set out powdered cream, and a small sack of sugar. "First thing I'm gonna do is get that girl a horse. How else can I get her attention?"

"Maybe it's Reed, Dad," Cindy said, with a teasing grin.

Cindy stood in the doorway, watching Reed's practiced hands bridle and saddle the gray gelding. Their eyes met when he glanced over the saddle toward the cabin. They exchanged smiles. Reed looked down at Kimberly and grinned as he watched her tiny hands wrap around a stirrup. "You ready, cowgirl?" he asked, gently lifting her into the saddle. She grabbed the saddle horn with both hands and waited for Reed to swing into the seat behind her.

"Hope you don't mind us leaving you with the dishes," Reed called to Cindy. "We've got cattle to herd. See you in about an hour."

"Be careful. Hold on tight," Cindy cautioned.

It never crossed Reed's mind that taking a little girl horseback riding would be a challenge. But she proved to be all he could handle. Once they rode upon the cows, not a quarter mile from the cabin, Kimberly's mind turned to herding, and unending questions about why the calves had their heads under their mother's legs, why did one big cow have a bag so much larger than the others? Reed had never spent any time around kids, much less a little girl, but he laughed with her, and answered questions the best he could.

Butch and Cindy met them part way on their return to the cabin. Cindy had her arm entwined in Butch's. They were walking just fast enough to maintain their balance.

They'd had a good talk, and a few laughs, especially when Butch explained how he had acquired his new city wardrobe.

"Mama, I herded cows!" Kimberly called out. "Reed said I'm gonna be a real cowgirl!"

Cindy smiled at the two and reached to pull her daughter from the saddle. "That's wonderful, honey, but now it's time we saddle up old Blue and light a trail for home."

"Ah, Mama, can't we stay a little longer? Reed wants to show me his rope tricks."

"Some other time, sweetheart," Cindy said. "I'm sure Reed won't mind if you come back and see him."

They didn't leave immediately. It took a while for Kimberly to relate her riding adventures to Cindy and her granddad. Reed stood to the side, watching with an amused smile.

"Okay, darling, save the rest for show and tell. We *must* go! There's still some slick spots on the roads, and we don't want to drive them after dark."

"Butch's gonna follow you to the highway in my truck," Reed volunteered. "It's all downhill. Just watch for the deep ruts and slick spots."

Butch asked for a hug from his granddaughter. And he got it. Reed kneeled down and Kimberly's arms encircled his neck. He kissed her cheek, sat her in the car, and buckled the seat belt.

Reed was holding the car door open for Cindy, watching Kimberly squirm in the back seat. A hand touched his arm and he turned. Cindy's arms encircled his waist, her head buried in his chest. His face felt warm. He wondered if he was having what women refer to as "a hot flash." He could smell a delicious scent of a light perfume. He had an urge to touch her soft brown hair, just once, but he didn't. "Thank you, Reed," she whispered, then smiled up at him and slid her slim hips under the wheel.

———

The snow had melted fast with the warm sun, causing the roads between the cabin and highway to be slick and muddy. "So this is what *he* calls a road?" Cindy grimaced, pulling the wheel to avoid a football-size boulder in the path. Her dad had driven when they had left the highway, and the roads hadn't seemed rough at all. She thought about the penciled directions Reed had left with her at the apartment. She could be disgusted, or even angry, with anyone else falsely representing a cow trail for a road. She couldn't make herself feel any of these things toward Reed Carson.

Cindy didn't have to force herself to think good things about Reed. After all, he *was* the one responsible for reuniting her with her father. During their short visit, she couldn't stop herself from asking her father questions about Reed's peculiar living accommodations. Butch didn't say much, or didn't know much, except what few details Reed had related to him about the troubles with his mother. What her dad had told her only added to the other things she had heard and made him seem even more mysterious. She knew parts of the other stories were facts, but she wouldn't let herself believe Reed would steal cattle from his own mother.

At the highway, Cindy waved and cast a smile toward her dad as the little Chevy rattled across the rickety cattle guard. Ahead lay miles of undulating hills to the west and the Platte River to the east, with its now leafless, cottonwood trees, paralleling the highway until it divided the town of Riverdale. She would cross the river in Riverdale, then travel forty more miles of mostly the same treeless, rolling hills and sagebrush landscape. She glanced in the rearview mirror and smiled. Kimberly was sound asleep.

Cindy adjusted the radio to KRTO, a country music station. How very different her life was than just two days ago, and how lucky she felt to have a wonderful, caring, loving father. He had promised to change his living habits and become a part of their life.

But she knew it wasn't going to be all that simple. Her dad had his mine to work. She had her job and Kimberly. Then there was her mom...she knew her too well to think even for an instant that she would enjoy the position she'd been put in. From the first day, her mom had accepted that Butch was either dead or gone from her life forever—without shedding a single tear—and went on with her life as if he never existed.

It wasn't going to be easy for her mom, and she suddenly felt sorry for her, mixed with hurt and resentment. But she wasn't going to let anyone stand in her way of getting to know her dad again, and her mom would just have to take it. She wanted him—needed him—in her life. Kimberly needed him. It would all be worth it, and she'd find a way to make it happen, somehow.

Crossing the Platte River Bridge, north of Riverdale, Cindy shuddered at the snow-covered chunks of ice floating on top of the slow moving river. It was all part of the annual April thaw she knew so well as a young girl. She recalled the weekend and evening ice-skating and wiener roast parties with friends under the same bridge, years ago—before her father left.

The ice floating on the river wasn't the only reason Cindy felt a sudden harsh chill between her shoulders. She'd had four months of school left in her sophomore year in Riverdale when the news that her father was a cop killer spread throughout the community. All but one of her friends deserted her. Walking the hallways between classes nearly brought her to tears. In one semester, her grade point average fell from 3.8 to barely passing.

A wave of sadness swept over her as she recalled how her mother had immediately filed for divorce, never doubting her father's guilt. She shuddered, thinking back on her decision to drop out of school, leave Riverdale, and get a job before her mother hastily made plans to marry Harry Bogner, a railroad engineer who lived and worked in Garfield.

———

After Cindy and Kimberly left, the mood was light. The two big men cut strips of tenderloin from a hanging deer carcass and made plans for a festive Saturday evening. Reed reached under his sleeping bag, pulled out a bottle of Johnny Walker Red, and slammed it on the table beside two tin cups. Morgan shouted and almost cut his thumb as he peeled the potatoes. "This is going to be one helluva party, my man," Morgan said, grabbing the bottle and heisting it above his head.

"Can't remember when I had my last sip of good malt whiskey."

"Enjoy it, 'cause that'll be the last good whiskey you'll see around here. Good Scotch ain't something a poor cowboy gets used to," Reed grinned.

Morgan tipped his cup and made a quiet sipping sound.

"Ahh ...that's good stuff. Now back to what you said about being a poor cowboy. Where do you go from here, my friend?"

Morgan continued slicing potatoes during the several moments of silence. Reed didn't know how to answer the big man's question. He hadn't permitted himself to think about what direction his life would take if he could not live it on the Homestead Ranch.

"Don't know. Tomorrow I'll try to contact my mother. Maybe she's had second thoughts about her younger son being a cattle rustler. Anyway, I need to see her. I'm worried. Her spells with depression are getting worse and more frequent. Come to think of it, I haven't seen her during a moment when we could have a normal conversation since I don't know when.

I don't think she talks to other people like she does to me, but when I'm around her she acts like she's been eating locoweed. I know part of it's Bullock's fault. She believes everything he says, and I'm guessing he hasn't put in too many good words for me since I ran him off the North River Ranch."

"How does your brother, Kirk, play into all of this?" Morgan asked.

Reed watched Morgan stir the potatoes and slap the steaks into a frying pan. "Who knows? I used to feel sorry for him, try to protect him. Now I'm not sure how I feel. But if I were a betting man, I'd put my money on him and Bullock putting together some kind of a scheme that involves mom and her money. Bad thing to say about your own brother, but I can't help how I feel."

"You don't think he'd do something to hurt his own mother, do you?"

"I don't know, Butch. What Kirk tried to pull on me the other day was pretty freaky. Hard telling what he might do."

They filled their plates with venison and fried potatoes, refilled their cups, and sat across the table from each other. "I won't get anything like this for awhile," Morgan said.

"I gotta get moving tomorrow," Morgan continued. "But, before I do there's something I want tell you—something that's been eating my guts out for a couple of days."

Reed laughed, starting to feel some affects of the Scotch. "You sound pretty sinister, old fighting partner. What's on your mind?"

Morgan forked a large piece of steak and washed it down with a liberal slug of Johnny Walker. "Well, you have to know how grateful I am about your part in getting Cindy and me back together, and it's been tearing at my guts that I haven't been as fair with you."

Reed leaned back in his chair, drink in one hand, and stared at Morgan. "Whaddaya mean, you probably saved my life, or at least kept me from spending some time in a body cast. I'd say that's a pretty fair exchange."

"That's not what I mean. So, maybe I better come right out and tell you. It ain't the easiest thing I ever did, either, considering your pa and I took an oath of silence the first day he and I met."

"What?" Reed let his chair down hard on all fours and sat his drink on the table. "My dad? What are you mumbling about?"

"After everything you did for me, you deserve to know. And I think Jesse will understand—especially after I explain what you and I've been through."

Reed stared at the older man a full minute in silence. "I knew there was more," he finally found his voice, "from the first night, when you mentioned spending some time with my dad."

"I'd been on the run about two weeks—after I burned my cabin," Morgan started slowly. "I was near starved, and half frozen, moving south away from that scene as fast as I could, when I stumbled on a cave in a hillside. There was fresh boot tracks in the snow, but I was more hungry and cold than I was smart. I walked a piece inside the opening, just to get out of the wind, when I heard footsteps close by. I turned and there's this big Indian, not three feet away, with a rifle pointing straight at my guts."

Morgan laughed and tipped the tin cup to his lips. "Frightened the bejeezus out of me, too. He was one scary

Indian, dressed in beavers just like me, and maybe an inch taller. But to make a long story short, that was the beginning of a friendship that's lasted six years. I told your pa everything, and he never questioned my word once."

"Then my dad was the fellow who supplied you for six years?"

"Yeah, and that ain't all. I told you the truth about my supplier—your pa—having a place on Deadman Hill. But it wasn't just a *place*, like a house or something; it was a mineshaft he'd been living in since leaving your ma when you were just a little britches. And he's still living there in a tunnel he calls a gold mine. He's dead certain there's gold, veins of gold in it, if he can just find it. And you know what, he convinced me enough to bust my tail for two years helping to prove his point.

When I learned, through Jesse's monthly trips into Laramie, that I'd been cleared of murdering that game warden, I filed my own claim, not a half-mile from Jesse's. We're sort of partners, you see. We split fifty-fifty everything scratched out of those godforsaken holes."

Reed laughed, despite Butch's seriousness. He'd heard countless stories of men spending half their lives in the hills and mountains in and around the area of Dead Man Hill. None had found enough gold to buy their way out of town.

"It's no secret around this valley that mom's a little whacked out," Reed said, with a little chuckle, "but I wouldn't have guessed that my dad was crazy, too."

"Ain't nothing wrong with Jesse's head, son. He's a straight shooter. Maybe he just figured he was dealt a bad hand and needed to get away from folks for a while and go for his own grubstake."

"And how much have you split so far?" Reed said, trying to keep a straight face.

Morgan divided what was left of the bottle between his tin cup and Reed's. "A lot more'n you'd guess. Old Jesse and I eat pretty good, and we have a fair-sized savings account at a bank in Laramie. Nothing big, you understand, but it ain't nothing to sneeze at, either."

They sat for a while, without saying anything. Reed could feel the Scotch starting to take its toll. "Butch, do you suppose my dad would want to see me? I mean, he *did* desert us...and after all these years...?"

"Son, you and ol' Kirk is about all he talks about. Course he don't know Kirk turned out like he did. But I reckon he's suffering the same kind of guilt as I was with Cindy. He told me all about why he left, but I'd rather he be the one to tell *you*. Why, I'll bet you my beaver skins that he'll be busting down your door if he hears you want to see him."

Reed coughed and suppressed a grin. He wanted to tell Butch he'd always dreamed of having his own sweat-soaked beaver skins.

"I'd like nothing better than to see him, Butch. Mom told me some pretty wild stories about Dad. I believed her at first. Later I wasn't so sure."

"Will you be here the next few days—just in case I can find your pa?"

"Why sure, but I was hoping you would stick around a while longer. I can't afford a full-time hired man, but I could sure use some help patching the fences around this place. They weren't much before this snow. I don't even want to think about what the blizzard did to them. You could use a few extra bucks. Couldn't you?"

"I don't guess I'm in that big a hurry. And you don't worry none about the hired-man wages. I don't figure we're quite even, yet. But your pa is gonna wonder where I went to."

Reed turned toward Morgan, watched him form a wry smile. Morgan reached for the Days Work in his coat pocket and nearly fell out of his chair.

Mister let out a bark at Morgan's near fall. Morgan righted his chair, glanced at the dog then back to Reed. "To change the subject, there's something *I'm* curious about. What's with that dog riding on the back of your saddle like he'd been born there, fetching your boots for you every morning, and cocking his head when you talk? It's like he understands every word you say."

Reed laughed, then he drained the last bit of Scotch from his cup. "Well, Butch, as you've seen, Mister isn't just any ordinary dog, and sometimes I forget that he *is* just a mutt, with a mutt's brain. I guess he seems strange to you because he doesn't know how to act like other dogs, and maybe that's because he's never been around others of his kind. "I guess he's picked up some of my strange tricks and traits because we've spent three winters together with nothing much to do but feed cattle during the day and follow each other around the house at night, talking to ourselves, or to each other."

There was a long silence. Reed lit another cigarette while Morgan fixed a strange stare in his direction. "You're looking at me like I'm one crazy Indian," Reed said, "Hey, I'm not saying the dog can *talk*. But he listens well and acts like he understands a little bit of what I say."

Morgan finished the last of his Scotch in one long swallow, placed his cup on the table and gave the dog a long, hard look, then back to Reed.

"I never had a dog that understood any more than 'sick'em' and 'sit', and that was a stretch for them. But who knows how much a dog really savvies about life?" Morgan turned to the dog. "I don't care how many words you can understand, old buddy, but I got a notion you understand more'n a dog's supposed to," Morgan said, his words slurring now. Mister wagged his tail and looked up at Morgan. Morgan bent closer to the dog and placed a hand behind his ears. "You did a fine job on that Pratt feller's tail. Just keep up the good work."

ELEVEN

Late Saturday afternoon, less than a half-hour after being fired by Kirk, Justin Bullock parked his green Ford in front of the Pronghorn Bar and swaggered through the door. The place was unusually quiet for that time of day. Two old men he recognized, but couldn't call by name, were sipping beer at one end of the bar. Four long-haired, doper-types were shooting pool in the back. He bellied up to the bar, put one boot on the brass foot railing, and stared at the bartender, wiping shot glasses with a soiled towel.

The barkeep turned his gaze on the man with the scarred, battered face and reached for another glass. "Hey!" Bullock growled. "You work here, or just wash dishes?" The beer drinkers and pool players stopped what they were doing, fixed their eyes on Bullock for a split second, then quickly looked away.

The startled bartender took two steps toward Bullock, still wiping the same glass. "I do both. What can I get you?"

"First, you can wipe that smirk off your face, then you can pour me a double shot of bar whiskey." He was in no mood to have some pint-sized barman making up jokes to pass on to the regulars about his swollen face and broken nose.

"You're Justin Bullock, right?"

Bullock swallowed hard from his drink, sat the glass on the table, and fixed his threatening eyes on the little man. "What about it?"

"Got a box for you. Your boss, Kirk Carson, left it."

"That little dink ain't *my* boss!" Bullock tucked the cardboard box under his arm and slugged down the last of his whisky, then he threw a glance at the barkeep and walked out the door. Bullock backed away from the curb, peeled loose gravel against the side of a parked pickup truck, and turned north toward Riverdale.

He'd check into a motel, clear his head, and allow the swelling in his face to go down, he was thinking. Early tomorrow morning he'd surprise Lucy at the North River Ranch. Sunday morning she'd be home. He'd cured her of that church-going habit. She would probably be sleeping off a double dose of sedatives mixed with a half dozen martinis.

"Double-crossing skunks," he cursed under his breath. They were trying to toss him aside like a worn-out shoe. He didn't blame Lucy for any of this, though. Kirk was the one. Kirk had changed the plans, cutting him out of everything. That little runt probably spiked her Martini or Vodka Collins with a triple dose of Zoloft.

Kirk firing him meant nothing. She'd have to do her own firing. Something she couldn't do. She'd never won a face-off with him. If push came to shove, he'd tell her where the cattle went—and the backhoe. The three dope-heads, Pratt, Rusling, and Dubois, could be bought or scared into backing his charges against Kirk.

———

At nine o'clock the next morning, Bullock slid his old Ford to a stop in the empty driveway of the North River Ranch. Lucy's two brain-dead ranch hands would be on the river bottom feeding cattle, he reasoned. Bullock knew them well. They'd likely be hiding behind the tractor smoking some of the cheap marijuana he'd sold them. The housekeeper could be scared into her bedroom. He could frighten that old cow into whizzing her pants just by looking sideways at her. It would just be Lucy and him, face to face.

———

Reed walked outside the cabin and stretched his large frame. He could tell it was going to be a warm, sunny, spring day. Not all of the snow from the sudden spring snowstorm had melted yet, but if this weather held, it would only be a matter of days now until the grasses would start to come in the creek bottom. It was a good thing too, because he was about out of hay.

After Reed and Butch scattered two loads of hay to the cattle, they had a quick breakfast and started about their plans for the day. Morgan was leading the gray gelding from the corral when Reed emerged from the cabin door, wearing a clean shirt and his work Stetson.

Before mounting the gray horse, Morgan turned toward Reed and said, "Mister and I will make another swing up the creek. If those missing cows and calves are alive they'll be hunting grass by now."

"Sounds good, partner," Reed said. "You might check East Dry Creek, north of the road. Hard telling how far they drifted."

It would be nine o'clock by the time Reed reached the North River Ranch. His mother would be up and around by then. He recalled during her more normal years, before Justin Bullock. She'd be dressing for the ten o'clock services at the Methodist Church in Riverdale.

Mom rarely missed. But even as a tyke, and when he was older, he never understood her demands that they attend Sunday services as a family. She never read the Bible or talked to him about Christianity. It was all about dressing in their Sunday best, smiling, and shaking hands before and after the services, and promises to attend someone's dinner party or picnic.

Reed parked close to the green Ford in Lucy's driveway. He felt a flush of anger race through his body. *What was Bullock doing here so early?* He should be at the South River Ranch feeding cattle. Reed glanced toward the ranch house and saw a man standing in the doorway and the shadow of a woman behind him. Then he stepped out of his truck and heard screams.

Reed crossed the distance to the house in seconds. Bullock turned just as he bounded into the enclosed porch. A woman's scream pierced his ears again. He grabbed Bullock by the shirt and threw him across the porch. Bullock's head smashed against the doorframe with a sickening thud.

Reed was standing not two feet from the housekeeper when she screamed again, "Help, he's going to kill me!"

"What's he done to you, Mrs. Stinson? Where's my mom?"

The housekeeper ran to the kitchen, grabbed the phone and dialed 911, screaming nonsense into the receiver. Reed stood back, trying to calm her. She dropped the phone, and screamed again.

Reed followed her into the kitchen, approached her with forced calmness, and said, "Tell me, where is my mom?"

"She isn't here, I don't know! He's going to kill me if I don't tell him!"

"Please, Mrs. Stinson, you're safe now, just calm down, and tell me where my mom is."

"She's in the hospital—you know that!"

Reed saw the housekeeper look past him, toward the door, heard her scream again, and watched as she fell backwards.

———

At eleven-fifteen Sunday morning, Kirk Carson answered his cell phone on the second ring and listened to a Garfield hospital administrator describe his brother's injuries. "Reed may not live through the day," were the last words he heard the controlled female voice say.

A half-hour later, still trying to control his confused emotions, Kirk dialed the Mineral County sheriff's office. "I can't help you much," Kirk heard the dispassionate voice of the police dispatcher reply to his questions.

"What's your name?" Kirk asked.

"Lewis Dobbs, and I still can't help you, Mister."

"Listen, Dobbs," Kirk said, "I'm a lawyer and the brother of Reed Carson. Now, tell me again that you can't help me!"

"Uh…I'm sorry Mr. Carson, and I'm sorry about your brother too. But all I can tell you for sure is that I dispatched an ambulance and a sheriff's car to the Lucy Carson residence at nine-fifteen this morning. Sheriff Logan returned to the hospital with the ambulance. He's on his way back to the crime scene as we speak. Do you…."

Kirk pushed a button on his cell phone, cutting the dispatcher off in mid-sentence. He fumbled for a cigar in his shirt pocket, wet the cigar with nervous lips, reached for his lighter, and dropped into a leather chair. *It was Bullock*—his mind reeled. That weasel Bullock disregarded his warning and tried to see his mother. Reed had the same idea and Bullock caught him off his guard. It had to have happened that way. Bullock wouldn't stand a chance in a fair fight with Reed. Bullock would go back to prison. But where was he now? What if he wanted revenge from him too? He shuddered.

Kirk pulled himself from the chair, and walked the floor on rubbery knees. He was still walking in circles, massaging his temples, when a sudden brainstorm overtook his thoughts. Maybe this was the big break he needed—Bullock in prison, Reed dead or comatose, and his Power of Attorney for the Carson Ranches.

Even with the bad blood between them, he didn't wish anything like this upon his own brother. But Reed went and got himself in trouble of his own accord. There was no way he could have stopped it, even if he had been with him. With Reed gone, and his mom in a psychiatric ward, what responsible son wouldn't do whatever was necessary to protect the ranches from outsiders taking advantage?

His up-beat, self-congratulatory mood lasted long enough for him to formulate the rest of his plan. The papers to commit his mother to the hospital and the Power of Attorney, with Reed's forged signature, were ready for the judge's review and approval. If Reed lived one more day the papers would be filed and he'd be the sole proprietor to everything. If Reed died tonight, the papers would be worthless.

Meanwhile, he'd take no chances on Bullock finding him. Pack a suitcase and spend the night in Garfield—that was the smart thing to do. He'd talk to the judge and file the papers in the courthouse first thing Monday morning. By noon the papers would be on the shrink's desk, and he would be on his way to Denver.

Kirk found Rusling, Dubois, and Pratt sitting on their beds, sharing a joint and drinking beer. He opened the door to the bunkhouse, kicked aside several beer cans, and met John Pratt's cold stare. Of the three, John Pratt was the most dangerous. Not just because he'd served time for a murder rap, but because he was known to be a cowardly, half-baked little snitch that would shoot you in the back for taking a pack of cigarettes off his bunk. Kirk didn't trust John Pratt more than a stray dog. But Pratt could be bought for the least, and would pull a trigger quicker than the other two.

"John, I need to see you outside," Kirk said, with a shaky voice. It was a request, not an order. Pratt's expression didn't change, but he nodded.

Pratt slowly rose to his feet and sauntered out the door. Kirk stopped at the driver's side of Lucy's El Dorado, opened the door, and removed a brown bag. "I trust you, John, and that's why I've picked you for this important job." He opened the brown envelope, removed a wad of bills, and passed them to Pratt.

Pratt counted the money with a blank face. He rolled his toothpick from one side of his mouth to the other and said, "And...?"

"That's half of what you'll get if you can keep your mouth shut and do as I tell you."

A suspicious scowl lowered Pratt's eyebrows. "So, tell me, what's the hit?"

"Just this, John. You know I fired Bullock, and I think he's hell-bent on getting even. He may come here, try to con you and the others into helping him. You're the only one I trust, John," Kirk said with emphasis, trying to conceal his lie. Pratt cast a glance toward the bunkhouse, spat his toothpick, and focused his eyes on Kirk's red necktie.

"If he shows up," Kirk went on, "play his game with Rusling and Dubois, but don't let him into the house. If he goes into the house or the barn, where we keep our stuff, shoot him. That's breaking and entering, and I'll see that you aren't arrested or charged. I'm leaving for Denver where I'll be working on a case for a few days."

Kirk scribbled a number on a note pad, folded it, and shoved it into Pratt's hand. "That's my cell phone number. I'm leaving my second cell phone with you. Don't use it unless you need to call me. And remember, this deal is just between you and me. Can you do that?"

"Yeah ... I can do that. Just don't forget the money."

———

Kirk stopped at a liquor store for a liter of Scotch before checking into a motel in Garfield. He wanted something stronger—something from his lab in the old barn, but thought better of it at the last minute before leaving the ranch. He ordered pizza delivered to his room and ate slowly while he watched the ten o'clock news. It crossed his mind to call the hospital. If Reed had died, he'd have to return to his office and make up new papers without Reed's signature. He decided to chance it without calling and drank himself to sleep.

———

"I'm sorry to hear about your brother," Dr. Whiting greeted Kirk in a practiced sympathetic tone of voice. "How serious is it?"

"He's in a deep coma, and isn't expected to live. If he makes it, he could be a vegetable the rest of his life. Right now, we're just taking it an hour at a time."

Dr. Whiting scratched something on a note pad then returned his attention to Kirk, who squirmed in the big leather chair. "You know, of course, that your mother's housekeeper is a patient at the hospital. The sheriff of Mineral County has requested they not see each other until he gives the word. I can't explain his motives, but for now we're forced to comply."

The corners of Kirk's mouth suddenly twitched out of control. He pushed himself further into the leather chair and crossed his legs. "Yes, of course doctor, how is Mrs. Stinson?" Kirk struggled to hide his confusion. He didn't give a whit about her condition, but he desperately wanted to know if it had anything to do with Reed's little accident.

The doctor watched Kirk shuffle papers nervously in his briefcase before producing a small stack of papers and handing them over. "I know the strain you've been under these last two days, Mr. Carson. If there's any way I can help....

"Thank you, doctor," Kirk mumbled, "that's very kind of you. If we can finish our business, I'll be getting back to check on my brother's condition."

The doctor stood and extended his hand across the desk. "We're finished here, Mr. Carson. Did you visit your mother before coming to my office?"

"No, I didn't, sir. She needs her rest more than she needs to see me. She's going through a bad time, with Reed's misfortune and everything...."

Dr. Whiting shot Kirk a puzzled look. "Ah ... yes, I'm sure she does. Have a safe trip, Mr. Carson."

Now what was that look meant to convey? Kirk asked himself. Did he say something to blow his cover? *Surely,* someone had told his mother about Reed's accident. What did shrinks know, anyway?

The last thing Kirk wanted was to sit by his mother's bedside and listen to her whimper about Reed, and cry about what a big mistake she'd made in hiring Justin Bullock. 'If only I'd checked his references more thoroughly,' he could hear her whine. He'd see her soon enough. He would be at her side during Reed's final rites, lend a sympathetic shoulder, and offer to find her a reputable manager to run the Teardrop Ranches. When it was all over, he'd drive her back to the hospital and be free to exercise his Power of Attorney.

TWELVE

Reed narrowly opened his eyes to a blurred figure standing at his bedside. He shut them again, turned his head slightly to the side, and blinked at the tube running along his left arm. He heard a quiet, deep voice say, "Somebody got you good this time, Carson."

The man behind the voice pushed a buzzer pinned to the sheet near Reed's hand and lowered his massive weight into a chair. A nurse appeared in the doorway and glanced at Reed, then at the man in the chair. She walked to the bed, checked some tubes attached to a bottle hanging from a metal frame, and glanced at the monitor attached to the wall.

The man in the chair smiled up at the nurse. "I think he's coming out of it."

The nurse ignored his comment as she fussed with the patient's bandages and made some notes on a clipboard. "He'll be okay, but it may be awhile before he's coherent," she said quietly.

"If he can just answer yes or no it could save us a lot of police work. Mrs. Carson's housekeeper was at the scene. She wasn't hurt, but she passed out and is in worse shock than this big guy."

Reed squinted at the white uniform that blocked his view from the man in the chair. He tried to speak. "Ahh ... sheriff?" Reed uttered, in something like a croaking whisper.

"Yeah, Reed?"

Reed moved his lips together several times without speaking. He tried again, "Where's Mom?" His eyes fluttered, and he said, "I'm so tired."

"Can't imagine why, son," Logan whispered under his breath.

The nurse adjusted Reed's head bandages and studied the wall monitor a moment before speaking again. "It's been two days, and he's showing steady improvement. By this time tomorrow he should be wide awake."

"Thanks, nurse. The questions can wait. Can you call my office when he's ready to talk?"

The nurse attached the clipboard to the foot of Reed's bed and smoothed her white uniform. "Yes. I go off duty in one hour, but I'll leave a note with my replacement." Sheriff Logan struggled to his feet and quietly left the room.

Reed squinted at the afternoon sun filtering through the tall window shades. He lay very still, trying to put a thought together. He remembered going to see his mother, just a few moments ago, it seemed. He remembered grabbing Justin Bullock and throwing him across the porch. Butch flashed through his mind, and … Cindy. But they were replaced with a more persistent pain in his head and the realization that he didn't know where he was.

Reed felt a hand lightly touch his forehead. A white uniform occupied his dim view. A nurse carefully raised his head off the pillow with one hand, unwrapping bandages with the other. Reed opened his eyes wider. "Waking up are you, big boy? It's about time. Now you just lay still until I get these bandages changed."

Reed relaxed his eyelids. The nurse finished what she was doing, gently replaced his head on the pillow and wrapped a blood pressure monitor around his upper arm. "Where am I … and … who are *you?*" He asked, without opening his eyes.

"You're in the hospital, and I'm usually a very patient nurse, cowboy. Now you just relax and stay quiet while I get your blood pressure."

"Why am I here?" he said, in barely a whisper.

"You're here because you had an accident. Now, please keep quiet and rest. You're going to be just fine."

"No," Reed whispered, stronger than before. "I want to know how long I've been here."

"You've been here three days and a few hours. Now, just settle down before you tear some of these stitches."

Reed closed his eyes again, a subconscious nagging flooding his mind. Butch! Cindy! Three days! He could feel the nurse fussing with his sheets and adjusting the pillow. "Ma'am, you have to call Butch … uh … Cindy."

The nurse stopped what she was doing. Reed could feel her staring down at him. "Who're Butch and Cindy?"

He hesitated, his lips barely moving. "In my wallet … there's a phone number … Cindy Morgan … lives here."

"Your wallet is under lock and key, honey. I'll try the phone book. What about this Butch fellow?"

Reed's eyes closed. "Please … call Cindy," he murmured before drifting off again.

———

Cindy panicked when she picked up the phone and heard a female voice identify herself as a hospital spokesperson. Reed Carson had been in an accident. They had not been successful in reaching his mother. "Mr. Carson asked a nurse to call you," the voice said.

Cindy immediately called her best friend, Sheryl Becker. Cindy rarely left Kimberly with anyone except her mother, and then only when it was absolutely necessary, and never for an overnight visit. But this was different. She knew that Sheryl would take good care of Kimberly, and she wouldn't ask any questions. She didn't have time to explain Reed Carson to her mother, or for the lecture that was sure to follow.

"I'll be there in a minute, honey," Sheryl called away from the phone, before Cindy could explain her reason for calling. She had to go. Carl was waiting. It was his birthday, and she was taking him out for dinner. She would call back as soon as she got home.

Cindy panicked again. There was no one else she could trust leaving Kimberly with, except her mother. How could she explain to her that she needed to rush to the hospital to be by the bedside of Reed Carson, and she may need to spend the night?

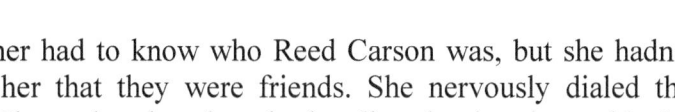

Her mother had to know who Reed Carson was, but she hadn't yet told her that they were friends. She nervously dialed the number. She took a deep breath, dreading the time it would take for the question and answer session.

Julie Bogner answered the phone on the second ring. Of course she would keep Kimberly for the night, but it was almost ten o'clock. "This isn't like you, Cindy. Where, pray tell, could you be going this late ... and to spend the night? Are you in trouble? Because if you are...."

"Mom, I'm not in trouble, but it's personal, and I really need your help this time. A friend of mine has been in a bad accident, and I may want to spend the night at the hospital."

"Who is it, Cindy? Do I know her—him?"

"His name is Reed, and you don't know him. Please, just tell me you'll do it. Just this once ... I'll explain everything tomorrow...Okay?"

At some time during the night, Reed opened his eyes again. The lights in his room were subdued, just bright enough for him to recognize Cindy's worried face, bending low over him, both her palms cupping his left hand. Her hands were soft and gentle. He allowed his eyelids to fall for a moment. He could feel her smile. In his thoughts, he returned her smile before exposing his clouded, bloodstained eyes. "Oh Reed, I'm so sorry," she said, tightening her grip on his hand.

He slowly lifted his right hand to her head and touched a lock of soft brown hair. He studied her face for a moment. "Cindy...I'm so glad you're here."

She squeezed his hand tighter.

Staring into her clouded brown eyes, his memory started to come back. Panic ruled his thoughts. "How long have I been here? How did I get here? Where's Butch ... my cattle ... Mrs. Stinson?"

She leaned closer to his face and spoke softly. "Reed, there's nothing to worry about. Sheriff Logan saw Butch last night. Your cattle are taken care of, and you're going to be up and out of here before you know it."

With his eyes glued to Cindy's forced smile, he tried to put all the pieces of the puzzle together. He remembered getting out of his truck and hearing Mrs. Stinson scream. He remembered throwing Justin Bullock across the porch and watching his head hit the doorframe. The last thing he remembered was the startled look of the housekeeper as she started to fall backwards. "Mrs. Stinson, is she okay?"

"Mrs. Stinson is fine. She can't remember anything that happened, but she didn't get hurt. Now, please, there will be plenty of time to talk about what happened, but for now, let's just get you well."

Reed sensed a wide smile on his lips, but he didn't know if it was real. His mouth hurt something fierce, and he'd felt the bandages covering his head and face. He wanted to know everything, but just knowing that Cindy was there, holding his hand, talking to him, and smiling down at him was enough for the moment. He was starting to feel the bearing returning to his body.

"Cindy...do me a big favor." He struggled with the words. "Find out when I can get out of this awful place."

"Awful place is it?" he heard a slightly familiar voice repeat. "Just for that I'm going to recommend you spend another day in ICU."

Cindy released Reed's hand and stepped aside to allow a short, stocky nurse access to Reed's bedside. The nurse shoved a thermometer into Reed's mouth before carefully wrapping a blood pressure band around his arm. After recording everything into a notebook, she said, "Okay, cowboy, the doctor thinks we can move you to a regular ward tomorrow." She winked at Cindy. "And I'm going to take you up on that dinner date when you're out of the hospital."

Cindy paused with her hand on the doorknob and took a deep breath. She was dreading the questions from her mother about why she had spent the night at the bedside of a man she hardly knew. Reed is just a friend, she had explained when she left Kimberly with her to spend the night. She tried to remember everything she had told her mother. Reed had been in an accident and when they couldn't contact his mother he had asked for her.

Cindy turned the doorknob and entered as quietly as possible. It was early morning—eight o'clock. Her stepfather, Harry Bogner, would be at work, but Kimberly and her mom might still be sleeping.

From the hallway she could see her mother motioning to her from a chair at the kitchen table. "Kimberly is still asleep," Julie whispered over her raised coffee cup. "She was a tired little girl. There's fresh coffee. You look like you could use a cup."

Cindy answered with a tired smile and moved to the counter and poured her own coffee.

"Thanks for keeping Kimberly, Mom," Cindy said, as she sat down across the table. "I'm sorry it was such short notice, but it was a serious accident, and Reed needed someone there. They weren't able to contact either his mother *or* his brother."

"Reed? Reed what?"

"Reed Carson. You probably don't know him, but you've heard of his mother, Lucy ... you know ... the Carson Ranches." Cindy was trying to be casual.

"I know Lucy Carson, and I know as much about Reed Carson as I care to know. He's hardly the type of man I would expect my daughter to be worrying over, even if he is a Carson. Oh, Cindy, I *hope* you aren't involved with him. What is Gary going to think when he hears about you seeing Reed Carson?"

"Mom! I'm not *seeing* anyone! And I don't really care what Gary Stockton thinks. I'm not *seeing* him either."

"I'm sorry, Cindy. We—both Harry and I—just want the best for you. You remember what happened when you got involved with that last creep?"

She suddenly felt sick to her stomach. She remembered everything. How could she forget? Her most vivid memory was sitting between Julie and her stepfather, Harry Bogner, on the couch, the first night she'd told them. That's what she was thinking about now; her mother's red, teary-eyes begging her to get an abortion. It was the same night she graduated high school. Harry would arrange everything, her mother volunteered. There were clinics in Denver.

She remembered that Harry had sat perfectly still, with his hands in his lap, without saying a word. 'No one will have to know,' Julie repeated over and over. 'Think, Cindy! You have friends, you're enrolled in college…think about me and Harry, and all we've tried to do for you. Think of all of your aunts and uncles back in Missouri who will have to know the baby is…well…illegitimate.'

Cindy remembered getting up from the couch and going to her room where she cried most of the night, feeling dirty, unworthy of kindness, and utterly alone. She was still recalling the details of that night, when Julie interrupted her thoughts.
"Anyway, how is the young man?" She asked. "Is he going to be alright?"

Julie pressed hard for all the details of the accident. "And how did you become friends with a Carson?" she persisted. Cindy said she didn't know how it happened. It was a ranch accident. And she and Reed had been friends for some time. Just friends, that's all, Cindy insisted.

She hated lying to her mother. She didn't trust herself not to break down if she told the truth. She had nearly passed out when she first received the call from the hospital, and later, when the doctor told her that Reed had suffered multiple fractures of the skull, several broken ribs, and severe bruises on his back and thighs.

She was not ready to tell her about the meeting with her dad. She almost spilled her coffee when the thought occurred to her that Kimberly could have said something. She let out a heavy sigh when she remembered that her mother had said Kimberly was a 'tired little girl,' meaning that she probably went right to sleep. She had been waiting for the perfect time to tell her mother everything. A time just like this—over a cup of coffee—

is what she had had in mind. *But, this certainly isn't the perfect time,* she thought.

———

The condo was bright and clean, with a flat screen TV, large bedroom, walk-in closet, and a king-sized bed. "Not bad for two grand a month," Kirk mused. And the view overlooking an eighteen-hole golf course wasn't all that shabby either. He could hear rock music coming through the walls from a stereo, and smell meat searing on someone's barbeque grill.

Kirk removed himself from the leather chair, pulled off his blue suit, placed it on a hanger, smoothed it, then folded his red necktie and carefully placed it into a bureau drawer. Wearing shorts and T-shirt, drink in one hand, cigar in the other, he stood on his tiny deck, overlooking a manicured landscape. He set flame to a fresh stogie and smiled.

But, Kirk didn't waste time getting comfortable in his new digs. The morning after checking into his rented condo in Denver, he bought two papers, turned to the real estate section and picked up the phone. *All Country Ranches* caught his eye after his sixth call. "Yes," the salesman replied, "we sell ranches in Wyoming. Our main office is located here in Denver, but we have a branch office in Cheyenne. Where are you now?"

"I'm in Denver. I'm an attorney working on a case here, and since time is of the essence, I would prefer to list my ranches with your Denver office."

"Wonderful, sir. My name is Carl Henson. Can we meet today?"

Today will be perfect." Kirk replied.

"How about lunch at the Brown Palace…say eleven-thirty? I'll meet you in the foyer?"

"That will work for me," Kirk replied. "How will I recognize you?"

"Light blue suit," Henson began, "blonde, late thirties, about five-ten, maybe a few pounds overweight," he laughed.

"I'll find you," Kirk said, declining Henson's invitation to detail his own physical description.

Kirk ordered a Johnny Walker Black Label on the rocks. Henson motioned the waiter to make that two. Sipping his drink before the meal arrived, Kirk elaborated his position to the salesman: "My mother is a very sick woman, who can no longer handle her large ranching empire," Kirk said over his raised Scotch glass. "With due conscience, I can't take time away from my large law practice to manage her three ranches. Therefore, as her lawyer, and Power of Attorney, I have decided to sell everything while the ranches are still profitable. Her entire estate is free from mortgages. All monies realized from the sale will go into a special account to see her financially comfortable the rest of her life."

Henson was busy scribbling on a note pad. "How many acres and what price range are we looking at?"

Kirk raised his glass again, swallowed hard, sat it back on the table and touched his nervous lips with a napkin. "There are three large ranches. Combined, I would say fifty or sixty thousand acres. There has not been an appraisal, but I'm guessing we're looking at a price tag of twenty to twenty-five million dollars, conservatively. The exact acreage can be obtained at the Mineral County Courthouse in Garfield."

Henson's face lit up. "Kirk, you're going to be happy you've chosen All Country Ranches. We have buyers from all over the states, big money men and corporations, calling us every day wanting to get their hands on properties like this."

"How soon can you start showing the properties?"

Henson smiled thinly, trying to control his enthusiasm, as he reached for his briefcase. "I have all the necessary papers right here. The minute we have a signed deal, I'll start organizing a team of appraisers, buyers will be contacted, and in less than three weeks you can expect offers to start coming in."

Kirk finished the last of his drink in one long swallow, motioned to the waiter with the empty glass, and sat back in his chair. "Carl, I want you to move on this as fast as possible. My mother is in no immediate health danger, but if she should have another one of her strokes—God forbid. What I'm saying is, things could get sticky if my mother should pass on and my little brother gets involved…you understand?"

Henson formed a knowing smile at one side of his mouth. "Yes, I do understand. Trust me to give it the highest priority and discretion. This type of situation is not new to us at All Country Ranches."

Henson paid the hefty luncheon tab. The two smiling men shook hands in the foyer, Henson hurrying to his office to report his good fortune and Kirk making haste to the nearest bank to transfer money from his mother's account to his own.

THIRTEEN

Sheriff Logan was Reed's first visitor the day he was moved out of intensive care. Reed was finishing his breakfast of oatmeal, toast, orange juice, and coffee when Logan quietly opened the door and scooted his well-worn boots across the tile floor. Reed recognized the portly sheriff from the corner of his eye. "It's okay sheriff. I'm not dead, and I'm not asleep. Now, make my day and tell me that Bullock is in jail."

The sheriff eased his heavy torso into a chair beside the bed, leaned forward and used both hands to pull one leg over the other. "What I wanna know is when you're going to stop taking up all my police work time, kid?" Reed spooned his last bite of oatmeal and tried to form a scowl on his bruised face. "Just kidding, son," Logan added. "To be honest, I'm just pleased to see you're getting well. I was worried—we all were. You were left for dead."

Reed raised himself on one elbow to face Logan. "I want to know what happened, sheriff. The last thing I remember is Mrs. Stinson's terror-stricken eyes and her starting to fall backwards."

Reed winced at the pain as he tried to lie more fully on his side and remembered the nurse's admonishment. Reed wasn't allowed a mirror during his five days in ICU. The instant he was alone in his new room, he made a painful trek to the bathroom and cringed at the image staring back at him in the mirror.

Above his thick, swollen lips, black eye, and puffy face, his head resembled a radar dome, wrapped in thick white gauze. As he turned to use the toilet, the sharp pain in his side reminded him that he had three broken ribs.

Logan hitched his chair around to face Reed more fully. "Here's what we know: Around nine o'clock on Sunday, it appears Mrs. Stinson dialed 911, then went bonkers and dropped the phone. It was still off the hook when we arrived. Back at my office, I listened to the tapes. There was a loud scream, grunts, cursing from a male voice, and some other sounds, all yet to be sorted out. The 911 monitor identified the call as coming from the North River Ranch. I was on duty at the time. I called for an ambulance and we arrived a half-hour later."

"We found you first," Logan continued, "looking somewhat worse than you do now. I followed Mrs. Stinson's hysterical crying to her bedroom, and I could see right off her injuries weren't physical. While the medics were working to stabilize you, I coaxed her into the patrol car. And believe me, my friend, I earned my pay on that ride back to Garfield. Oh, she loaded easily enough, quiet as a newborn calf. Fifteen minutes after we left the scene, she started screaming and yelling worse than a drunk lunatic. I didn't wanna do it, but I finally stopped the car, coaxed her out and into the back seat, and locked the doors."

"Where is Mrs. Stinson now? Is she okay?"

"I don't know. She was examined here, then transferred to the psycho ward at Cheyenne Mercy Hospital. As far as I know, she's still there. I have a note to myself to call about her today."

There was a long pause, with neither man saying anything, Reed staring at the large clock on the wall above Logan's head. "Has my mother been contacted?" Reed finally broke the silence.

Logan glanced toward the door and lowered his voice to a bare whisper. "I'm glad you waited until now to ask. Your mother was taken to Mercy Hospital a day or two before your troubles with Bullock. The hospital has instructions to keep her and Mrs. Stinson apart. In your mother's state of mind, I thought it best to wait until she's released before telling her anything."

So that's why she hasn't visited me? During the long silence that followed, Reed's expression turned sullen, as he thought about how he had kept a heavy heart during his waking hours in intensive care. Except for Cindy's visits, he had felt alone and neglected. He exhausted his mind the past few days, recalling as a child all the special attention his mother had given him when he stayed home from school with flu, chicken pox, and mumps—

fussing over him, forcing him to eat hot chicken soup and drink extra water.

Reed finally lowered his eyes to the needle mark bruises above the knuckles on his left hand, the product of four days in intensive care. "You did right, sheriff. Thanks. I'm sure she has all she can handle right now."

Reed's brow furrowed. "Cindy said you've seen Butch Morgan. When was that?"

"I didn't actually see him. I sent Billy Schultz; told him not to lay it on too heavy about your injuries, and I returned to the North River Ranch. Morgan sent word back not to worry about the cattle. By the way, do you know who Butch Morgan is—his history?"

Reed's eyelids narrowed. "I know he's one nice guy. Why do you ask?"

Logan rolled his weighty shoulders. "Just wondered. I don't know the guy personally," which Reed recognized as a lie. The sheriff had a file on Morgan that would fill the bed of his pickup truck. For the two years Morgan was a suspect in the game warden's murder. Logan organized and conducted searches for the man on an almost daily basis.

Reed showed Logan a puzzled face, then changed the subject. "You went back to the ranch? Why?"

Logan dropped his mouth, and bent forward. "*Why...?* Fingerprints, cordon off and secure the area, blood samples from the house and from a pool of blood on the porch, a thorough search of the outbuildings...not to mention, we talked to Lucy's two hired hands, Carl Linden and Joe Ward, who swore they hadn't been to the main house and hadn't seen or heard anything. I think they're lying—just a hunch, though."

"What else can you tell me?" Reed asked, in a tired voice.

"Just that the fingerprints taken from the doorknob belonged to Justin Bullock, and the blood on the porch matched his prison DNA. There's a lot we don't know about what happened out there."

"Whadda'ya mean, prison DNA? Is Bullock an ex-con?"

"Yes, he's an ex-con—bad one, too, with a long rap sheet. He busted up one of my deputies pretty much the same way he did you. You didn't know that?"

"How *would* I know, sheriff? But, you knew he was working for the Carson Ranches, and you didn't bother to tell me or Mom about this scumbag."

"Reed, Kirk should'a been the one to tell you and your mom. He was the one who arranged the work release from the pen— Bullock, Pratt, Rusling, and Dubois—all of them."

Reed turned away from the sheriff and rested his head on the pillow again, without saying a word. Morgan waited. There was a long silence before Reed found his voice again. Then he said, more to himself than to the sheriff, "What is Kirk doing? When I get out of this bed people are going to pay."

"Time is up sheriff," a stern female voice broke in.

"Thanks nurse, we're about through here, anyway," Logan said.

The sheriff wriggled his bulk out of the chair and stood by the bed. "No, we haven't found him, yet, to answer your first question. I have all my available men looking, and we have help from some other counties. We'll find him." Logan shuffled toward the doorway, lifted his hat to the side, as to wave, and pulled the door behind him.

———

Reed lay back on his pillow, followed the nurse with his eyes, while complying with instructions to, "open your mouth, move your toes, wiggle your ears."

Wiggle your ears? He managed a smile, then studied the movements of the short, slim, pleasant looking blonde nurse, he judged to be about his own age, and the thought occurred to him that he was returning to normal. He noticed she had good, suntanned, clear skin and soft blue eyes. He sensed her light perfume as she leaned across him to check his bandages, smelled the pleasant presence of lingering shampoo on her short-cropped hair, and thought about Cindy.

The nurse finished her routine, made some notes on a clipboard and smiled down at him. "My name is Susan Wheeler. I will be your day nurse. As you can see, you have a private room. If you need anything, just push the buzzer and one of the nurses on the floor will respond. Do you have any questions?" She managed a tight, clinical smile.

Reed returned her smile, almost feeling well enough to flirt. "Just a couple, Susan. Exactly how long have I been in the hospital, and when can I go home?"

The cute, blonde nurse reached for the clipboard. "I see you were admitted to ICU last Sunday. Today is Friday. As to when you will be released, you'll have to ask Dr. Barela." She dispensed a painkiller into her palm from a small paper cup, placed it into his outstretched hand, and watched him swallow it. She started to move toward the door. He wanted her to stay so he could ask more questions.

Reed elevated his bed, relaxed, turned on the television, scowled at a daytime soap, and switched it off—too much time on his hands—lying in bed, napping during the day, having his meals brought to him on a tray. His mind was restless and disturbed like never before.

It was ten o'clock. Cindy wouldn't be off work for another six hours. He'd come to look forward to her daily visits more than he wanted to admit. She'd slept in the chair beside his bed the night of her first visit, farming Kimberly off with her mother, and missing work the next day. There was something more to her than the smooth, perfect skin, tall, slim, beautiful body, and finely etched facial features. Her sense of humor, quiet dignity, her tone of voice, and the glow in her expression when she spoke of her dad, and Kimberly—and, yes, the way her long, lean body moved in a pair of ladies Levi's intrigued him.

Reed thought about the way Gary Stockton looked at Cindy when he had seen them together at her apartment. He had hailed an insult at him during their last football game and was in love with the only girl he'd given a second look in the past eleven years. Gary would inherit the Stockton fortune, and they would get married and live in that big old brick house on top of the hill. He probably carried a two-carat diamond ring around in his pants pocket, just waiting for the slightest nod from her.

———

At exactly four-fifteen, by the hospital clock, Cindy walked through the door; Kimberly at hand. Reed smiled until his face hurt. Kimberly ran to the bed, leaned over, and gently placed a paper bag on his chest. "I'm sorry you're sick, Mr. Carson," she said, in a small, quiet voice.

"I'm sorry too, sweetheart. I'd rather you and I would be herding cattle on old Lurch."

Kimberly giggled.

Cindy grinned at Reed and said, "She begged to ride Lurch again tomorrow, and I made the mistake of telling her she couldn't because you were in the hospital. She insisted on coming and bringing you some cookies."

Reed chuckled, carefully opened the paper sack, and peeked inside. He passed a cookie to Kimberly, then to Cindy, and took one for himself. He looked at Kimberly and put a finger over his lips. "Shhh, don't tell the nurse." Kimberly giggled as she bit into a cookie.

Reed munched and turned his attention to Cindy. "Have you talked to Butch—your dad?"

Cindy touched his arm, leaving her hand there while she said, "As a matter of fact, we have. I played sick this morning, and Kimberly, Gary, and I visited him."

Reed could feel the blood rushing to his head, but said nothing.

"I figured Dad would need your pickup to haul hay to the cows. After clearing it with Sheriff Logan, we stopped by the North River Ranch and Gary drove the pickup and followed me to the cabin."

"Thank you," Reed said, simply, with genuine appreciation. The blood drained from his upper body and he regained his composure. Then he added, "How *is* Gary?" He was trying to sound casual.

Cindy chuckled. "Gary is just Gary," then quickly added, "I'm sorry Reed. What I mean is, Gary is always just good old Gary. He's a sweet guy and would give anyone the shirt off his back. He's the dearest man. Sometimes I feel sorry for him, though. His father owns the bank you know, which should be a sweet deal, but he insists that Gary should work at every desk until he knows the business inside and out before advancing him to a management position. He's been a cashier for a year and he hates it. Would you believe he wanted to come with us to the hospital? See what I mean?"

Reed didn't *see*, and he didn't want to.

"I wouldn't mind Gary coming, but I'd be jealous," Reed said lightly, as he tossed another cookie into his mouth. It felt good to flirt with Cindy. *And why not,* he reasoned. He wasn't sure he was quite even with old Gary yet.

Cindy moved closer and adjusted Reed's pillow. She ran a gentle finger over his bruised face and softly touched his lips with her fingertip. Then she whispered, "That's okay, I'll make sure you and Gary have plenty of quality time together."

Reed nodded, too enamored with staring into her laughing brown eyes to know what he was agreeing to. The way she touched his face made him feel special. She used the small bedside stool to lift her body and gently place her hips on the edge of his bed, then she stared down at him with a mischievous grin without saying anything. He had an urge to reach up and touch her long brown hair, but before he could work up the courage the spell was broken. Kimberly had spilled a glass of water down the front of her blouse.

FOURTEEN

Butch and Cindy Morgan stood at the foot of Reed's bed. Kimberly was to their left, rehearsing her latest tap dance movements for Reed's benefit. It was Reed Carson's fourteenth day at the hospital, and he was going home. Everyone, except Kimberly, was impatient for Dr. Barela's arrival to sign off on his release. Worst of all, he didn't feel like this was his last day of confinement. Susan Wheeler, his day nurse, warned him at six that morning to stay in bed, decked out in hospital whites until Dr. Barela's final examination.

Reed felt a pressing need to escape the four walls that had contained him the past fourteen days and nights. His mother was still confined to a mental ward in Cheyenne, and he hadn't heard one word from, or about, his brother, Kirk. He needed to drive to Cheyenne to personally check on his mother, fences around his lease needed to be fixed, and he had an overwhelming urge to join the search for Bullock—all the while dreaming that he would be the first to catch him.

Reed glanced at his watch, noted the time and frowned. Nine-fifteen. *Where is Barela?* But he shook off his impatience, and turned his eyes from Kimberly's act to fix his gaze on Butch. He had to stifle a laugh. Butch was standing erect, with a slit of a smile, visibly proud of his new store-bought wardrobe—red and black plaid shirt with sleeves two inches too short, Wrangler jeans, and a wide leather belt around his lean waist.

Reed stared at Morgan for a moment thinking that he'd seen Denver Bronco linemen under full pads with less bulk than Butch Morgan. The new-leather smell from Morgan's size fourteen, JC Penney high top work boots overpowered the antiseptic odor of the hospital. A barber had left his hair well above his ears and trimmed his beard to a Rabbi's respectability.

Kimberly finished her dance act and skipped to Reed's bedside. She wrapped her delicate fingers around his forearm and looked him squarely in the eyes. "Mr. Carson, can we ride Lurch when you get home today?" she asked in a little girl's pleading voice. Reed tilted his head toward Cindy and their eyes met. Cindy bit her lip. Butch coughed.

Reed laughed, as if laughing was what he did best. He pulled himself to a full sitting position, placed his hands under Kimberly's armpits, and gently sat her on the bed. She turned to give him her full attention. He placed one hand softly behind her head, tussled her delicate brown hair, and spoke quietly. "You know, sweetheart, I've been asking myself that same question. Maybe Lurch is wondering that himself. It may be a few days before I get back in the saddle again, but I know your grandpa will be more than happy to have some company herding cows." Butch was nodding, showing a broad smile.

Kimberly studied his face for a moment, then she giggled. "Can Grandpa *really* ride Lurch?"

Reed's face got serious. "I'd say your grandpa can ride Lurch even better than I can."

"Is that right, Grandpa?"

"You know Reed don't lie," Butch answered.

Cindy had taken Reed's clothes home in a black garbage bag, cleaned them by hand in cold water to remove the blood, then washed them with her other laundry at the Laundromat. The bloodstains didn't wash out. The day before Reed's release from the hospital, she drove to the cabin with his hospital clothes and exchanged them for a clean but rumpled shirt and pants. She ironed the shirt, smoothed the Levi's cowboy style, and placed them on Reed's bed the day of his release. This thoughtful act, like so many others, was in the back of Reed's mind as he chatted while waiting for Dr. Barela.

Dr. Adam Barela entered the room without ceremony, looked in Reed's ears, and shined a light into each eye. "You'll have to be careful about butting heads with any more cows," Dr. Barela said directly to Reed. "Your stitches can't hold your head together any more, and some of the bone fragments aren't quite healed. You'll be fine though. Just rest as much as you can, and see me in my office in a week. The nurse will give you some written instructions on caring for your wounds, and here's a prescription for pain. You've been a good patient." He shook Reed's hand, turned, and moved toward the door.

Reed was dressed, anxious to duck through the door of the small room for the last time, when Cindy placed her hand on his arm and turned to face him. Her face flushed as she tilted her head to meet his eyes. "Reed, I've been thinking, and please don't be angry. Dad and I have been talking…the ranch…it's so far from the doctor, and your bandages need changed every other day." She paused, without taking her eyes away from his. "Would …would you consider staying with Kimberly and me for a few days, just until your bandages come off for good? You can sleep in Kimberly's bed and she can sleep with me—she'd love that."

Reed almost gasped at the invitation. He smiled down at her, and his thoughts went soft. "Cindy, you've done so much for me already. And Butch—he's been like a father. Those first few days were hell, and having you there kept me going. I can't impose on you more. I don't know if I can ever repay your kindness, but I have to stand on my own two feet now."

Her eyes burned. "I understand," she whispered. "I know how anxious you are to get back to your place … to feel free again. That man, Bullock, is still out there, somewhere, and I'm just scared you'll start taking chances before you should."

They faced each other for a minute without saying anything. "Time to go, cowboy," Nurse Wheeler interrupted, pushing a wheelchair into the room.

Reed chuckled. "Who's the buggy for?"

Nurse Wheeler parked the wheelchair, set the brake, and smiled up at Reed. "Guess," she said, with a wink toward Cindy.

Reed closed his eyes in disbelief and shook his head. "Oh, no you don't!

"Hospital policy," the little nurse replied. "Now sit, unless you want to spend the rest of your life in this little room."

Reed scowled, balanced his gray Stetson on top of his bandaged head, lowered his tall frame into the wheelchair, and muttered, "Get 'um up."

Butch chuckled. "Mister's waiting in the truck. He's gonna fall down laughing when he sees you in that carriage."

———

"Ahh ..." Lucy gave out a low moan. "What time is it?"

"It's three in the morning. too late for you to be thrashing around in bed. Go back to sleep now," the nurse said, in a soothing voice. "Dr. Whiting will be here early, and you need to be rested."

Lucy groaned, looking away from the strapping nurse, trying to recall parts of her nightmares. The nurse recovered sheets and blankets from the floor and covered her again. Lucy turned over and stared at a street lamp which haloed through the thick curtains. *How long have I been here? When am I going home?* She'd been through all this before, but this was different. She knew she wasn't getting any better. Mind-numbing depression set upon her. Sleep. That's what she needed. She'd see Dr. Whiting in the morning, check herself out, and call Kirk to come and pick her up.

———

"You're looking better," Dr. Whiting greeted Lucy cheerfully. Lucy returned his smile and sat her empty coffee cup on the nightstand.

"I feel wonderful," she replied. "I left a message on Kirk's answering machine to pick me up today."

Dr. Whiting recorded Lucy's blood pressure, checked her ears and mouth, and placed his stethoscope on several areas of her body. Finished with the examination, he seated himself in a chair, barely above her eye level, and placed both hands on his knees. He looked squarely into her questioning eyes for a full minute before speaking. "Lucy, you're not going home today," he said, simply.

"What are you talking about? I'm the one who decides when I come and when I go!"

"I'm sorry, Lucy, but that isn't the case this time."

"What? If you think you can keep me here, *you're* the one that's sick!"

"I'm sorry, Lucy, but that's the way it is," Dr. Whiting said.

"Just where did you get your new authority? My son is a lawyer. Just try and keep me here, and I'll own you and this hospital!"

The doctor winced. Lucy was out of control. She jumped out of bed, waving her arms, looking for her street clothes, murmuring obscenities under her breath. Two orderlies appeared and stood just inside her doorway. "Lucy, won't you please settle down and let me explain?" Dr. Whiting said.

Lucy threw her leather handbag at the doctor.

Dr. Whiting looked toward the orderlies and nodded.

She gave the beefy attendants all they wanted before her arms and legs were pinned to the mattress. Dr. Whiting moved as close to the bed as he dared and spoke in a calm voice. "Lucy, I'm not the one who's keeping you here. For your own good, your sons, Kirk and Reed, signed papers, which were approved by a judge, to have you committed until we can diagnose your illness and treat you. Do you understand what I just said?"

Two more orderlies joined the melee, immobilizing Lucy's arms and legs as she lay on her back, shaking her head in a rapid, rhythmic motion, damming her sons, Dr. Whiting, the hospital staff, and the rest of the world, for the ears of everyone on the floor. Dr. Whiting called for a nurse, ordered a strong sedative, and left the room.

———

Reed and Butch left the hospital to drive directly to the ranch. Cindy would stop at Safeway, get what she needed for Reed's homecoming dinner, and be along later. Her dinner was planned in stages over the past five days. It had to be special. She'd rummaged through Reed's pots, pans, and skillets on her last visit to the cabin, just to be sure there were enough utensils to cook a meal for four people. There weren't. Before going to the hospital that morning, she boxed frying pans, pots, silverware, glasses, and several other items and hid them in the trunk of her car. Wine would be nice, but Reed was still on antibiotics and she wasn't sure he should be drinking alcohol.

Butch stopped the pickup at the wire gate entrance to Reed's property. The gate was open. Reed scowled. "What fool would leave a man's gate open?"

"That's twice in a week," Morgan said.

"What...?"

Butch was stroking his beard, as if trying to think his way through a maze. "The night I returned from my first visit to the hospital....about eleven o'clock it was. I was getting ready to roll in, when Mister jumped onto your bunk and started barking his head off...that was about the time I heard a motor running.

I let Mister out while I grabbed my rifle and flashlight. Then I stood inside the door listening to the sound of his barking disappear down the road. No sooner did I see the lights when the fool slammed on his brakes and skidded into a u-turn, almost running over Mister."

Reed's eyes narrowed. "Did you get a good look at the pickup or whatever it was?"

"Yes and no. I could see it was an older model pickup. Too dark to tell the color, but it sounded like a Ford, gas engine. Guess I'd had a better look, 'cept I was sure Mister was run over, and I was eyeballing him while he was getting out of my sight."

"Probably some dumb hunter poaching deer. But what's that got to do with the gate?" Reed asked.

"He was in a big hurry, peeled gravel everywhere. Figured he was up to no account. So, I got my rifle and Mister, and I followed him in the pickup, all the way to the gate, which he didn't bother to close."

"Lots of old Ford pickups in the country. Don't guess you could tell if it was green?"

"Could've been green or any dark color," Butch went on. But it wasn't white or another light color. There was some moonlight. White or another light color would've shown."

Reed pulled his door handle. "Let's check for tracks."

The road was dry, but areas around the gatepost, where snow had drifted from the big storm were still damp. Boot prints, about his size, Reed guessed, were plainly outlined near the gate. All-weather tires had left vague marks in the shallow ruts on the road. "Not much to go on," Reed said. "It doesn't matter, there's a lot of deer in this country, if that's what he was after."

The cabin door was wide open when the truck rolled to a stop. "What...I padlocked that door before I left this morning," Butch said. "I bought the thing special after our strange visitor the other night." Lurch nickered from the corral. Mister leaped from the pickup bed to nip at his heels.

Panic raced through Reed's mind. Everything he owned was stored in that little building—rifles, pistols, clothes, saddles.

Everything.

Neither man noticed that Cindy had coasted to a stop behind the pickup. Reed stepped out of the truck and started for the cabin when Kimberly grabbed his fingers and held tight. Cindy touched his shoulder. No one spoke. Together they approached the little building. Morgan followed close behind.

Reed stood slightly left of the opening, placed his hand on the door jamb and peered into the darkened cabin. Cindy dropped her eyes to the steps, grabbed Reed's arm, and choked back a shriek. Reed scooped Kimberly up with one arm, wrapped another strong arm around Cindy's waist, and steered them toward the barn.

Butch sprinted to the door and glanced inside. "Oh no..."

FIFTEEN

For Kimberly's sake, Reed did his best to make light of his quick actions. He smiled at the tiny girl, hoisted her into the air, and sat her on a bale of hay, close to the corral. Kneeling in front of her, he said, "You and your mama can feed Lurch some hay while your grandpa and I clean that old dirty cabin." Reed turned, slowly walking toward Butch, who was standing a few feet away from the building, staring at the ground.

"What a mess," Reed said to Morgan as the two men stood inside the cabin, looking at the strewn contents of the room. The stove and table were overturned, ashes scattered about, the little wooden cabinet pulled off the wall. Everything of value was gone, including his rifles, bedroll, boots, work hat, and his toolbox.

Their eyes met—neither wanting to face the truth of the moment. "I'm sorry, partner," Butch finally said, laying a hand on Reed's shoulder.

Reed's face muscles relaxed. He slowly kicked aside an old mesh cap with a broken strap and a broken board from one of his wall cabinets, tilted his head, and fixed a gaze on Butch. "If we expect to get any supper, we better get started and get a fire going."

Thirty minutes later, Reed smiled, doffed his hat at the door and introduced Cindy and Kimberly to a clean, but nearly empty, one-room cabin.

"You guys can entertain Lurch and Mister for awhile," Cindy said. "Kimberly and I have cooking to do."

Reed started for the truck, talking to Morgan as he went. "Guess you noticed those tire tracks going past the cabin. What say we check 'em out?"

Reed fired the engine, eased the gearshift into low range, and slowly idled the truck toward the creek bottom. Neither man spoke. Morgan stared straight ahead, straining to catch sight of anything moving.

Already, Reed knew what he would find. He could feel his anger and rage building. Sharp streaks of pain ran down the back of his neck. Whoever ravaged his cabin was a madman, and he was deadly certain that the madman wouldn't be satisfied with just the cabin.

Reed spotted the first dead cow as they topped the crest of the hill. Droplets of cold sweat trickled down between his shoulders as he idled the truck closer to the animal. "Gut shot with a high powered rifle," Reed said, almost to himself. They were standing, looking down at the swollen carcass. Butch pointed toward a lone calf, not far away, making the deep lowing sounds of a hungry animal.

They drove upon four more cows near the creek bottom, all gut shot, with abandoned calves near the bodies. A hind quarter had been taken from one of the cows.

Morgan looked to the side and spat hard. "I'm gonna get the man that did this."

Reed searched Morgan's scowling face for a moment before he dropped his head to watch a puddle of blood find its way into the loose soil. Reed turned and slowly walked toward the truck, and mouthed the words, "Not if I get him first."

Morgan opened the truck door and sat down hard. "Reckon we better keep all of this to ourselves for a while. I think the cabin is about all Cindy can handle for now."

It was a solemn meal. Kimberly hadn't noticed the wrecked cabin and not a word was mentioned about the break-in, but there was little else on their minds.

Reed forked a bite of lettuce and leaned his head toward Kimberly. "Best meal I ever ate. Did you make the salad?"

Kimberly giggled. "No, but Mama let me set the table and fold the napkins."

———

Justin Bullock was helping himself to the amply stocked liquor cabinet, baking potatoes in the tiny vacation cottage oven, frying round steak in an iron skillet, and rejoicing at his good fortune. *Rich city people leaving a nice place like this for a smoke-filled high rise—serves them right,* he was saying to himself. He had to break into three places before finding one that suited his tastes. This one did. Snuggled against a hillside, good roads—but not good enough to attract outside traffic—and just two miles, as the crow flies, from Reed Carson's tasty beef herd.

He refilled his glass with rum, lit a cigarette, and watched his steaks sizzle in the pan. Reed didn't die after all. What did it take to kill a half-breed Indian? He was satisfied that Carson was dead before those last two whacks to his ugly head. If that high and mighty Carson isn't dead now, he's gonna be, and his little brother will look real proper in his pretty red necktie, lying there beside him.

Bullock refilled his glass, cut his steak in a dozen pieces, and gingerly removed the hot potato from the oven. He was in a good mood, partly influenced by the half-empty rum bottle. Boy that Carson beef tastes good! He felt a smile crease his lips. Fat old heifer just popped like a big red circus balloon when that bullet went through her belly.

He'd lay low, he thought—two, three weeks, maybe longer, and grow a beard. Let those dumb cops run around looking for him in Florida or California. When the heat was off, he'd make his move against the high and mighty Carson brothers...and sweet little, conniving Lucy would get hers, too.

———

Sheriff Jim Logan arrived within an hour after Cindy left. He listened with a serious face to what Reed and Butch had to say, took notes, and asked if there was anything in the cabin that hadn't been touched by someone other than the intruders. "Fingerprints would be helpful," he scowled. He snapped pictures of the dead cows and warned Reed not to touch another thing until fingerprint and ballistic experts could do their jobs. Logan questioned Morgan about the suspicious pickup from several nights ago, folded his notebook, and made his way toward the patrol car. Reed and Butch followed close behind.

"Are you thinking what I'm thinking, sheriff?" Reed asked.

"Could be, but without his fingerprints we have nothing. We don't have one solid lead on Bullock's whereabouts. About everyone except me believes he's left the state. But he *could* be sunning himself in Florida for all I know—that's where he's from."

"Let's be realistic, sheriff. We both know he's not in Florida. He's hid out around here some place."

"What makes you so sure about that?"

Reed torched a cigarette and slowly shook flame out of the match while he studied Logan's face. He sensed the sheriff was baiting him. "I know what you know, and maybe a little more, that's all."

"And what's that?" Logan asked, waddling toward his car.

"Maybe what Bullock did to me didn't sit well with Kirk. Maybe that wasn't it, I don't know, but something happened between the two of them, and Bullock got kicked out in the cold, broke and pissed off. What happened to me has been all over the news, so he's gotta know he didn't kill me. It's a cinch he'd like to finish the job, and if he had a run-in with Kirk he's bound to want a piece of him too. So I'm thinking he wants revenge from Kirk and me, and he wants Mom's money, or as much of it as he can get."

Logan stopped and turned to face Reed. "I've been wanting to question Kirk, but nobody knows where he is. I'd sure like to see his face when I tell him his drinking buddy is a suspect in all of this. It would be a stretch to think that Kirk is involved in any of Bullock's work, but it's been working on me a little thinking about Kirk not visiting you in the hospital. And I know he didn't because I checked the visitor register. Kirk's name wasn't on the list. Doesn't that strike you as being a little strange?"

"Not at all, sheriff." Reed let it go at that.

Logan rested his bulk in the well-worn car seat and looked toward Reed. "We'll get this guy, Reed, I'll promise you that much. Meanwhile, I'm asking you to let me and my deputies handle the case. And, you might want to watch your back a little closer."

***

With Morgan behind the wheel, Reed and Butch followed the sheriff to the highway, then sped ahead of him, towards Garfield. Long shadows were settling across the cool, serene valley of the Platte River, and they had no sleeping bags or food in the cabin. Cindy had left the cooking utensils she had brought with her to cook Reed's homecoming meal. Wal-Mart would be open and the Co-Op. They would get their supplies and return directly to the cabin. Bullock, or whoever robbed them, was still out there, somewhere, and they weren't taking any chances.

***

"Half of this tab is on me," Butch insisted, grabbing for his leather pouch as they waited in a short line at Wal-Mart.

"Not on your life," Reed protested. "Everything that skunk stole was mine, except your greasy beaver skins."

"My Winchester was taken, and the new one in that cart looks just like it."

"Sure does," Reed allowed, "but this one is on me. It's *me* he's after, not you. If you hadn't married my problems, you'd still be in your warm beaver skins, sipping on some fine coffee with my dad."

"Ain't no worse coffee than Jesse makes, and those skins were sure as hell ready to be buried."

Mister greeted the two big men from the bed of the pickup, huffing, wagging his tail furiously, and sniffing at each box, as they unloaded the three carts.

They were well on their way home before Butch stopped growling about not paying his half of the tab, then for a while, neither of them spoke.

Finally, Reed glanced toward Morgan, and took note of the big man's sullen expression. He cracked his window and touched a match to a cigarette before speaking. "Hey, pal, you aren't still mad at me, are you?"

"Naw, I never was mad," Morgan said, without changing his expression. "I should've just wrestled you down and did what was right, though."

"There's something else on your mind," Reed said. It was more of a statement than a question.

"You're right, son, there's a lot on my mind, catching that crook that took our stuff not being the least. But the hanging can come later; there's something else that bothers me more."

Reed knew the robbery was eating at his guts, and he was just as sure that this was the first time anyone dared steal anything from Butch Morgan, but his curiosity peaked. Neither man spoke for several more minutes, while Reed's impatience grew. "Well, are you going to tell me or keep me guessing all night?"

"First off, what are your plans for the next week or two?" Butch asked.

Reed glanced at the older man, who was steering with both hands on the wheel as if it were a big effort to keep the truck on the road. "Tomorrow I've got to catch those baby calves that lost their mothers, and take them to Wisner's dairy. The dairy has extra milk and each of those calves are worth about a hundred dollars. Then I'm going to call the hospital and see if my mother is in any condition to talk. If she goes home with Bullock still on the loose, she could be in real danger. There's fence to be fixed, and there's a dirty rotten crook just waiting for me to get my hands on him. Is that enough?"

"About what I thought you'd say. I got a plan I want you to chew on, but first of all, the fences are fixed. I took care of that days ago."

"Thanks," Reed said simply.

Butch stared into the headlights. "Tomorrow, I'll rope the calves and haul them to the dairy, then I hope you'll let me borrow Brownie and Lurch for a spell."

"Why, yes, but you don't have to ask a question like that. I won't even ask where you're going."

"Don't have to ask. I'll tell you—after I tell you what's bothering me the most."

Reed curiosity was getting the best of him, and he could feel his brow furrow. "Okay, Morgan, what's this mysterious thing that's bothering you?"

"What's bothering me is, you're still wearing that rag around your head that the doctor calls a bandage, your ribs ain't healed, and in your mind you think you're good as new. Fact is, you ain't even half new, and you're all hell-bent on doing what you always did—not to mention your cockamamie notion of forming a one-man posse and going after Bullock. Now tell me if I ain't right?"

"You're right again, partner. Now tell me you would do things differently if someone bashed your brains in with a steel pipe."

"Don't reckon that matters. I ain't the one wearing a sheet on my head. Reed, you gotta listen to some sense. Sure, you need to see your mother, warn her if you can, or hire a bodyguard if need be. That's all good and doesn't take a big toll on your body. And, yeah, we can do the Bullock thing...and I got a plan if you're interested."

"I'm interested."

"After I get those calves delivered tomorrow, I'm gonna saddle Lurch and that bay gelding and go hunt up your pa."

"My dad...?"

"That's right, son. Old Jesse's the best scout and tracker in the country. I wanna bring him back here, to meet you, and to help us track Bullock. He's one, big, mean Indian when he's riled, and what Bullock did to you is sure to get his dander stirred proper."

"He'd do that—I mean, help us find Bullock?"

"That'd be the most fun he's ever had, especially after what that skunk did to you. But you gotta promise me you're not gonna run off and do some fool thing on your own."

Reed chuckled. "You got it, Partner."

"How's your head this morning?" Dr. Whiting asked. Lucy was sitting on her bed, brushing furiously at her long, wet hair, straight from the shower.

"Better, but I'm still not speaking to you. So if you don't mind ...." she answered with ice in her voice. It had been four days since she'd bruised her forehead on the headboard while being subdued by hospital orderlies—two days on sedatives and two days of intense counseling by hospital staff doctors. None of the counseling was performed by Dr. Whiting. She had refused to see him. Even with counseling, she still didn't understand why she was committed. Dr. Whiting left word that he would explain everything if she agreed to allow him a visit.

"I can understand why you are not in a very good mood, Lucy. However, my staff told me that you would see me today. You don't have to talk to me. But, we can't help you to get well until you understand why you are kept here against your will, and unless you are willing to accept our treatment."

Lucy ignored the doctor and continued pulling at her hair with the brush.

The doctor turned and moved toward the door. "Very well, Lucy. Call me if you have a change of mind."

Lucy threw the hairbrush hard to the floor and stood on her feet. "Okay, I'll do it. I think it's a waste of time, but if it will satisfy your curiosity, sit down and tell me about my loving sons, who've convinced you their mother is loony."

The doctor smiled thinly, and dropped his plump torso into a chair at her bedside, seemingly oblivious to the coldness of her invitation.

Lucy retrieved her hairbrush from the floor and began working it through her wet hair again, refusing to meet the doctor's gaze.

Measuring his words, the doctor said, "Lucy, I don't need to remind you how many times you've checked yourself into and out of this hospital, never allowing me time to diagnose and properly treat your condition."

Lucy inhaled a deep breath, and pushed it out. "Who needs your reminders? And for that matter, who needs the rest of your bullshit?

"I can understand that you don't want to hear this, and I don't blame you, but you're not getting any better—we both know that, don't we, Lucy? For fifteen years I've treated your symptoms—not the cause. You're not loony, as you put it, but you *are* very sick, and getting worse. Your sons love you and want the best for you. That is why they agreed to have you committed."

Lucy whirled the hairbrush across the room and threw herself face down across the bed, a pillow muffling her loud sobs. The doctor waited patiently, hands in his lap. After several minutes, she regained her composure, sat up in bed, and covered her face with both hands.

"I must look terrible. I'm sorry, doctor; I just can't take any more. Why is all this happening to me? I have two loving boys, friends who would lay down their life for me, a healthy bank account, and three beautiful ranches. I'm the luckiest woman in the world, and I'm always too nervous to enjoy any of it. Can you really help me, Doctor Whiting?"

The doctor leaned on her bedside and gently held her hands. "Lucy, I can safely say that your condition is treatable. With your help, we can have you stabilized and on your way home in a very short while."

SIXTEEN

"Reckon I'll see you when I see you," Morgan called out, putting a heel to Lurch's side, and keeping a firm grip on the halter rope of Brownie, the big bay gelding. "Don't figure it's gonna take more'n a day or two to round up that Pa of yours, but don't hold your breath if it takes longer."

"Take care, and keep your eyes open in that thick timber," Reed warned.

Reed was totally alone for the first time since before his run-in with Bullock. "Aaah, the freedom," he whispered to the cloudless sky. From the time he started his sophomore year in high school, Reed knew he was a loner. Most of his high school buddies, living on isolated ranches throughout the valley, spent their entire summer thinking ahead to their next trip to town, to visit with other friends, to see their girlfriends on a Saturday night. Reed wasn't one of them. He reveled in his isolation on the ranch during summer vacations, doing what he enjoyed the most ... irrigating, calving, trailing cattle to summer pasture, or just sitting on the corral fence right after sundown, listening to the symphony of strange sounds coming from the creek bottom behind the barn — master of his own little world.

Lately he hadn't realized how much he'd missed his privacy—not that he didn't enjoy having Butch Morgan around. How different his life might be if Butch *hadn't* barged into his little world out of nowhere, he thought.

With Mister padding along beside him, Reed slowly walked west of the cabin, to the crest of the hill overlooking Dry Creek. He inhaled deep breaths of cool, spring, mountain air, feasted his eyes on snowcapped Bridger Peak, and felt a wave of exhilaration fill his chest cavity.

He'd found a temporary home for himself and for his cattle, free from the pressures his mother had imposed upon. He was free to be his own man for a while — his own boss. And, best of all, he had met Butch, Cindy, and little Kimberly—true friends if there ever were any.

He thought about Cindy, about the days and nights she had worried by his bedside, soothing him with words of encouragement and hope. And he thought about his special bond with Kimberly. He pictured how her eyes lit up as she waited to be scooped into his arms, and her delight in sharing a saddle with him on Lurch.

He wished they were both here right now, Kimberly running ahead of them with Mister, and he and Cindy walking hand-in-hand, enjoying the cool mountain air. They had become the best of friends. He trusted her completely, and he imagined she trusted him and that those feelings wouldn't change.

He smiled to himself as he reached down to pick up a rock to throw for the dog to chase. "Woolgathering dreams," he said quietly, as he watched Mister retrieve the rock.

His dreamy thoughts about Cindy were suddenly replaced by feelings of intense guilt. He needed to be spending his time thinking how he could help his poor sick mother. And where was Kirk?

For two hours Reed stayed on the hilltop, sometimes lying on his back staring at the blue sky and chasing occasional jet streams. Other times sitting with his knees pulled up to his chest, throwing pebbles for the dog to chase. Once, he walked downhill to Dry Creek, and inspected the coyote-ravaged bones of his once frozen cattle.

It was noon before he realized how hungry and tired he was. The nurses had warned him about overdoing physical activity. He had only laughed. While using all of his strength to return to the cabin, Morgan's words kept coming back to him. "You ain't half new." He was glad Morgan wasn't around to see him struggle a quarter of a mile, consciously placing one foot in front of the other to keep from falling.

Reed stretched out on his bunk, exhausted and hungry—too tired to open a can of beans to quiet his nervous stomach. He lay on his back, one hand over the side, stroking the dog behind the ears. A temporary thing, he told himself. In a few days, he'd be as strong as ever. He'd drive to Cheyenne, visit his mother, and make plans with Butch and his father to catch the scumbag who did this to him.

Reed fought drowsiness and sleep. Today, tomorrow, or the next, he would see his dad. The word seemed strange to him. He'd never called anyone "Dad." He rolled the word "father" over his tongue. He tried the word again, quietly speaking it several times. Mister raised his head, perked his ears, and stared at Reed, as if questioning his master's sanity.

Mister barked once and ran to the door, jerking Reed out of a deep sleep. Reed found a burst of energy, reached for his new hunting rifle from the wall, and yanked on his boots. *I won't be caught off guard this time,* were his first thoughts.

He could hear the uncertain sounding motor before Cadwaller's old faded, tan pickup came into view. He waited in the doorway, his self-confidence rattled at the surge of adrenalin that tightened his chest at the sound of a motor vehicle. He was inwardly embarrassed, recalling the words of his grandpa: 'Reed ain't scared of nothing—that boy would fight a bear with a switch.'

Standing in the doorway, Reed watched Mabel Cadwaller bend her plump form over the pickup bed, grasp a cardboard box, and hand it to her husband. With an arthritic limp, Claude hobbled toward the cabin, holding the box in front of him with both hands. Reed met the pair halfway.

"The missus thought you could do with some home-cooked grub," Claude offered, pushing the box toward Reed.

Reed raised a flap and peeked into the box. His mouth fell open at the sight of homemade apple pie, baked potatoes, glazed ham, and biscuits—all still warm from Mabel's oven. The combined aroma of cooked food seeping from the box nearly overwhelmed him. "Wow," he whistled at the sky. Reed carried the box as if he'd been gifted with a king's jewel case, carefully placed it on the barren table, stood back, and placed a hand over his empty stomach.

"Claude and I've already ate," Mabel murmured. "There's enough for you and Mr. Morgan both, if he's still here."

"Thank you," Reed said, unable to quell his urge to dig into his prize with both hands. "Butch will be away for a day or two, but if you don't mind, I haven't eaten since breakfast. I was just thinking about opening a can of pork and beans when you drove up."

"Sure, son," Claude said, "that's why we brought it up here. You gotta eat to get well."

Reed quietly turned to stoke the stove and add more wood. "Bet you folks could use a cup of coffee."

"Coffee wouldn't taste all that bad," Cadwaller said.

The old couple shared a wooden bench across the table from Reed and sipped coffee while he gorged himself on Mabel's cooking. "Mrs. Cadwaller," Reed said, wiping his face with a paper towel, "I can't tell you how delicious that was." He refilled their coffee cups, and dropped into his chair.

No one said anything for several minutes, all three sipping coffee, thinking their own thoughts. "You gave the missus and me a good scare, son," Claude broke the silence, without looking up from his coffee cup. "We've come to think of you almost like another son. Shame they ain't caught that feller and strung him up."

"Bullock will get his," Reed said. "There's a whole posse of lawmen looking for him, and I'll be joining them in a few days."

Claude raised his chin and met Reed's eyes. "The missus and I've been talking. We don't know all that's happened between you and your ma, but have you thought about getting a little piece of ground you can call your own?"

"I got everything I can afford right here, Claude. We've agreed on a three-year lease, and who knows what will happen after that."

"That's what we've been talking about—the missus and I."

Reed struck a match under the table, put the flame to a cigarette, and blew a cloud of smoke to the side. "You've done more for me than anyone in my family. I don't know what else you could do. Soon as I get over being a cripple, I'll put some elbow grease to this place, and you won't recognize your old homestead."

Cadwaller set his coffee cup down, put both elbows on the table and looked Reed squarely in the face. "No need of beating around the bush about it with you, son. The missus and I've been wondering if you'd like to buy these six sections, maybe build you a house, and get a forest permit for your cattle...make a regular place out of it. Thirty eight hundred and forty acres ain't much of a cattle ranch, but it's a start. It's pretty good grass country, should handle eighty to a hundred pairs year 'round, with a little hay thrown in on bad years."

Reed took a deep breath and let it out slowly. Just today, standing alone with Mister, absorbing the splendor of this beautiful piece of land, he'd wished there was some way it could be his own. His chances of returning home seemed slimmer every day, and he had to start over somewhere. "I don't know how to answer you, Claude," Reed said quietly, his eyes darting from one to the other. "I'd give my right arm to own this place— who wouldn't? I have a little money saved, but no more than enough to see me through a year or two, and losing part of my herd in the storm didn't help any."

Cadwaller sipped once on his coffee, slowly sat the cup back on the table and looked across the table at Reed again. "We bought this place in the late sixties, hoping our only son, Mark, would want to be a cattleman. He didn't. But he always talked about it, that is, until he married that city girl from back east."

"Mark could change his mind," Reed said, "Maybe he'll get tired of fighting the smog and all the stress most city folks have to live with."

The determined couple shook their heads in unison. "Not a chance," Claude said, still shaking his head. "That little gal's got

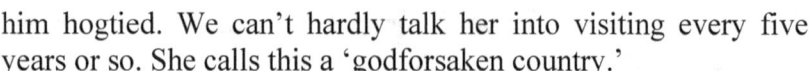

him hogtied. We can't hardly talk her into visiting every five years or so. She calls this a 'godforsaken country.'

"As I said, folks, I'd give anything to slap my brand on this place, but I can't even think about it right now. Who knows, though, if cattle prices hold up and we have some good grass years, I could talk serious with you in a year or two."

The old couple glanced at each other, then focused their eyes on Reed again. "It's no secret that the missus and I are getting on in years," Claude said, with a little trace of sadness in his voice. "If Mark gets his hands on this place it'll be sold to some city folks who'll scatter summer homes all across our land. We can't let that happen. We never lived on the place, but that don't mean we don't love it. You can't love something and have it ruined just because you die."

Reed's brow furrowed. He walked to the stove, and chunked his cigarette through the coal grate. "I see your point, but all the love of land in the world doesn't help my situation any."

"We want you to have this land, Reed," the old man said, simply. "You'll treat it the way we have for more'n thirty years. The price would be right, and we don't want much money down. We have some money saved, and the missus and I both get social security checks."

Lost for words, Reed studied their sincere faces across the table, his mind reeling with astonishment. He drew in a short breath and pushed it out, as if winded. "I don't know what to say. You can't know how grateful I'd be if we could work something out, but I would want both of us to think about it for a spell before we sit down and talk seriously."

"We can talk now, if you got the time," Claude offered, then turned toward his wife. "You got them papers old Jim Peters drew up for us when we was visiting Reed the other day, Mabel?"

Mabel scrambled through a dog-eared, black purse and handed Reed a large brown envelope. "Mr. Peters gave us the same papers, so you can keep these," she said sweetly. Reed glanced at the envelope for a minute, without opening, and slowly placed it on the table to his left.

"Folks, I've been out of my head for so long I couldn't tell you if I have two quarters to rub together. Then there's the hospital bill ... Sure, I have insurance, but they may not cover all of it."

"Told you we don't want much down," Claude countered.

"Tell you what, let's both give it some thought for a couple of weeks. Meanwhile, I'll read the papers, count my pennies, and it will give you time to discuss it with your son."

"No need to discuss it with Mark," Claude said, "that wife of his wears the pants in *that* family. And we know what *she* wants!"

Reed waved as the Cadwallers slowly eased out of the driveway. They'd been there less than an hour, but it seemed much longer. He watched the old Ford rattle over the hill before moving his tired body back to the bunk. He felt his sore ribs, and wondered if a pain pill would help his elephant-sized head.

SEVENTEEN

Reed couldn't will his mind to sleep, feeling a ridiculous sense of unease, and cursing his body for not responding to his needs. Tomorrow, he told himself. Tomorrow he'd read the papers in the brown envelope, call his mother—maybe Butch would be back with his dad.

His thoughts turned to the Cadwallers. He'd known the old couple all of his life, but he never really *knew* them. In this world, kindly people like them didn't exist, except in fairy tale books he'd read as a child. With all these thoughts going through his head, he slipped out of his boots, stretched full length on the cot, and closed his eyes.

Slits of sunlight were shining through the cracks in the walls and through the tiny windows before Reed woke to the sounds of Mister's relentless whining. He raised his head and shoulders off the pillow with one elbow, just as the dog jumped full-force onto the foot of his bed and barked loudly. He couldn't remember removing his pants and shirt and crawling into the sleeping bag to ward off the night chill. He felt a dull pain above his ears and carefully rolled out of bed at an angle to protect his ribs, still tightly wrapped in elastic-like material.

He slowly gathered kindling, set fire to the dry wood, and added fresh coffee to the old grounds, before he eased into a chair at the table. He stared at the brown envelope, while rubbing sleep out of his eyes. Later, he thought. Coffee, fried eggs, and a peanut-butter-and-jelly sandwich would clear the sleep out of his head.

Reed refilled his cup with hot coffee, sat at the table, and slowly opened the brown envelope left by the Cadwallers, bracing himself for disappointment. Right off, he could see the typewritten pages were prepared with legal skill. Not a word misspelled, not a period or a comma was out of place. He slowly and very carefully read each page a second time. He took a deep breath and leaned back in the chair until his bruised ribs stopped him.

From memory, Reed recalled all the important words and numbers in the documents: one thousand dollars down payment on thirty-eight-hundred and forty acres, selling price to be fifty dollars per acre, total selling price to be one hundred ninety two thousand dollars. No payments for three years, then five thousand dollars a year at three percent interest for fifteen years. Remaining principal to be paid in full or guaranteed financing at same rates for an additional fifteen years, balloon payment at the end of thirty years.

He lit another cigarette and neatly placed the pages back into the envelope. There was a mistake. The land was worth three times that much for grazing purposes alone, and who knows how much to some millionaire in Denver for recreation or subdividing into forty-acre plots. The place would be a steal at fifty dollars an acre. He'd return the papers to the Cadwallers, and tell them about the mistake—a simple typo error—a one was omitted before the fifty. He drank the rest of his warm coffee in a long swallow and went for another walk.

Buying the Cadwaller lease would either make his world or break it, and he couldn't decide which would be worse: Try to make a go of it on six sections of grazing land or take a chance on returning to the Teardrop Ranch and be a slave to his mother's whims. She would never, ever allow him back on the ranch if he bought the lease—grazing land that had been a part of the Carson Ranches longer than even she could remember.

And what if he did buy the lease? It would be nothing more than a start, and it would be years before he could be an independent rancher. He was wishing he didn't have to think about any of it. He missed his mother, his home, the ranch, and he couldn't bring himself to think he would ever live anywhere else. Yet he needed to secure a place for his cattle, his future, either on the Teardrop or maybe here on the lease.

There was no hurry, he decided. He would think about it, after the old couple corrected the pricing error and countered with something he could live with. Meanwhile, he'd talk to his mom, because, if she wouldn't drop the cattle stealing charges, he didn't have a future, anywhere.

It had been one week since Bullock broke into a vacation cabin, depleted the liquor supply, and ate all the dried food and canned goods—a week of boredom, frustration, anger, and impatience. He would be as wacko as old Lucy Carson in another week of this, much less two or three weeks, as he'd planned. Not to mention, he was out of cigarettes, grass, booze, and food.

His revenge on those Carsons could wait. He needed money, and he needed it now. The senoritas were waiting. Better to take less money now than stay here and risk some flatfoot sneaking up on him in the dead of the night.

At three in the morning, on a moonless night, Bullock parked his pickup a mile from Kirk's house, on a deserted road. He walked across a field and crept to the bunkhouse, cracked the door and shined his flashlight on three stoned ranch hands, lying on their bunks, fully clothed, mouths gaping.

"Wake up and keep quiet," Bullock said, in a hushed voice. No one stirred. It was all of a half-hour before one of the hired hands was sitting on his bunk, oblivious to everything but his bursting head, and Bullock's flashlight in his face.

"Hey, Pratt, is Kirk in the house?" Bullock, demanded. The hired man groaned. Bullock bristled. "Listen, I'm gonna blow your head off if you don't answer me … right now!"

"Kirk ain't here," Pratt murmured, head down, running a hand over his matted hair. "And you shouldn't be either. You're gonna get us all back in the slammer."

Bullock shoved the Colt .45 he'd stolen from Reed hard against Pratt's temple. "Shut up, and just listen. Where is Kirk, and when is he coming back?" The other two stirred, but didn't move from their bunks.

Pratt placed both hands on his knees, raised his head, and squinted at Bullock. "I don't know, I swear. He left two or three, maybe four weeks ago. Said he had a case in Denver. Left a couple of messages on the cell phone he gave me, but I ain't talked to him, honest."

"You mean, there ain't nobody living in that big ol' house?"

"No. No one is there. We just feed the cattle, eat our meals at the Pronghorn Bar, and stay the hell out of his house. That's what he told us to do."

Daylight was breaking before Bullock could bring the other two hired men out of their drug-induced coma and make himself at home in Kirk's big ranch house.

Reed recognized the unmistakable sound of the little Chevy motor and became instantly awake, even before Mister sounded a friendly whuff. He roused himself from a light sleep and glanced at his watch. "Eleven-thirty," he mused, with a smile. He checked himself in the tiny mirror on the wall while tucking his shirttail under his belt. He reached for his Stetson, remembered his bandaged head, and returned it to the wooden peg.

Reed walked outside as Cindy drove up. She swung her long legs out of the car and smiled at him across the way. She looked radiant and refreshed. Her hair was pulled away from her face in a ponytail, and she was wearing a jean jacket and ladies' Levi's.

Cindy had just flipped the lid of the trunk open when Reed stepped up behind her. She turned and put her hand on his forearm while giving his head and face the once-over, as if examining a child before sending him off to school. Reed scowled, wondering if he'd passed inspection. She gave his arm a friendly squeeze and grinned, with a twinkle in her eyes. "Reed..."

"Don't say it. I didn't change my laundry because it's coming off tomorrow."

"I was going to tell you how handsome you look, but now that you mention it, you *could* use a clean bandage." She leaned over and lifted a Styrofoam cooler out of the trunk. "Here, you

can show me how strong you are. Our picnic lunch is in there, so be careful with it."

Reed carried the cooler from her car into the cabin and sat it on the table. He was cracking the lid to steal a peek when Cindy placed her hand on his and gently forced the lid closed. "Not so fast, cowboy, first we take a look at those bandages."

"You'd deny a poor bachelor a peek at real food?"

"Don't poor bachelor me, you big crybaby. Word gets around. Now sit and let me have a look at that gorgeous head of yours." Blood rushed to Reed's face. He pulled a chair from under the table and promptly seated himself without another word.

Reed winched as Cindy pulled away blood-dried gauze from areas where surgeons had cut deep into scalp to allow bone to refasten to bone. She wadded the old wrappings and bent over to get a plastic bag and her first-aid supplies out of the cooler. Reed reached for a mirror.

When Cindy turned from the cooler with a plastic bag in one hand, her eyes fell on Reed's horror-stricken face as he stared at his bald, black and blue, distended head. Reed scowled and said, "It looks just like it feels." Reed gathered himself and choked off a wave of self-pity. A wry smile played across his face. "Okay doctor, do I have permission to ask a personal question."

"Only if it's within the boundaries of doctor-patient relationships," she said.

"Is it okay if I flirt with the doctor while she changes my bandages?"

"You can flirt, but no touching, young man. Now, clean up your mind and behave yourself long enough for me to change these bandages."

"You're hardcore. If you were wearing a funny little hat, I'd swear you were Nurse Wheeler."

"And you're a funny man, Reed Carson. Susan Wheeler has a big thing for you. You were her favorite patient."

"Really! Now you tell me," he said, with exaggerated glee.

"She wasn't the only one, either, you silly boy. I didn't tell you because I didn't think your head could swell any more. Now, will you hold still for five minutes?"

He sat perfectly still, winced when the hydrogen peroxide touched his scars, and listened to Cindy talk. "You know that you and Lurch have made quite an impression on a little four-year-old girl, don't you? I didn't dare tell her that I was coming here when I left her at the nursery. But don't get a swelled head over it; Lurch is still her favorite in the whole world. Okay, you're pretty again. Now, let's have a look at those ribs."

"Oh, no you don't. I don't take my clothes off for lady doctors."

A playful grin formed on Reed's face as he stood.

"You know the rules, either you take them off or we take them off for you."

Reed raised his hands to the sky. "I'm all yours, doctor."

Cindy slowly unbuttoned his shirt and pulled it out from his belt. Reed lowered his arms and she gently pulled the sleeves off one arm, then the other. She held the palm of her hand against the injured area, feeling for heat on his wide muscled chest. She looked into his eyes, smiled mischievously, and said, "Sometimes doctors take certain privileges." She reattached the Velcro elastic bandage around his chest, then playfully helped his arms into the shirt. "You're in good shape and you're in good hands, Mr. Carson. Now, for that picnic I promised you...."

"I've got blankets. Let's take the pickup and eat under the trees on Dry Creek. It'll be cool, but the snow is melted and it's dry."

"Is Dad going to join us?" Cindy asked.

Reed turned toward the stove, shook the grate.

"Butch took Lurch and Brownie and rode to his cabin. Said he'd be back in a day or two," Reed barely mumbled, without looking toward Cindy.

"When did he leave?"

"A couple of days ago," Reed replied. "Guess he figured he needed a little time to himself."

It was a beautiful afternoon. Marshmallow clouds drifted across an incredibly blue sky, and it was just cool enough for a light jacket. It was perfect. Reed spread the blanket a few feet from the creek, placed the cooler to the side, and watched Cindy set out paper plates, bread, sliced ham, potato salad, pickles, and tomatoes.

Cindy hardly touched her food, while Reed binged on the Safeway Deli items. A slight breeze rustled through the willow trees. Cindy shivered. "When I get rich, I'm moving some place where it doesn't snow in April."

Reed reached for the extra blanket and wrapped her shoulders, then he moved closer, their bodies almost touching. The minutes and hours passed with hardly a notice while they talked.

Cindy told Reed things she'd never told anyone: how all her friends deserted her when her father was accused of murder and her lonely life during her pregnancy with Kimberly. "I was seventeen," Cindy said, "he was twenty-one, working as a framer on a housing project in Garfield. We dated three months. He said he loved me and wanted to marry me. I believed him. He left town the very day I told him I was pregnant. But the worst hell was the night I told Mom and Harry. That same night, I promised myself I would never trust another man again—ever." She looked into Reed's face and offered a happy smile. "I'm so thankful for my precious Kimberly. That scumbag will never know what a beautiful daughter he left."

Cindy was sitting with her hands in her lap looking toward the beaver pond. Reed sprawled out beside her, resting on an elbow.

He had thought about it all week. Each day his mind became more restless to tell Cindy his side of the story—all of it. He knew what the gossip was, and he was just as sure that she had already heard at least part of what he wanted to tell her. But it wasn't just about the accident he wanted her to know about.

Aside from Butch, he now considered Cindy to be his best friend, and he didn't want her thinking he was pretending anything. It wasn't pretty, and he wouldn't make excuses for his actions. But, at least she would know the truth, which would be a better version than the gossip she'd heard.

If he ever had the guts to tell her, tell her the truth about what really happened, and why he was living in a one-room cabin, this was the perfect opportunity. He would start, and see how it went. He moved to sit even closer and pulled part of the blanket around his shoulders.

Reed started with the problems with his mother from the time he was a teenager when he first noticed her mood swings. He told her about being charged with cattle rustling, and how there was a chance he could go to jail. He told her he was considering buying the little Cadwaller lease, even though it could mean losing a share of the Carson Ranches. She listened silently.

When he finished, she glanced at him and smiled, and they were quiet for several minutes, just listening to the breeze rattle small limbs on the cottonwood trees. His stomach knotted, thinking about how he would tell her the rest. Cindy, Butch, Kimberly—they had become his best friends. As fearful as he was that she would reject him, she had to know the truth about that terrible night he destroyed a persons' life.

"Cindy," he started again. "There are a lot of things that you don't know about me, bad things. I've never revealed anything personal to anyone before, not the things that you're going to hear. But, as much as it's going to hurt, I have to tell you—tell you so that we can be friends without you thinking I'm something that I'm not."

"You don't have to tell me anything you're uncomfortable with, Reed. You and I are friends, and friends don't have to tell each other *everything*."

"You told me about your past—and Kimberly. That had to be hard for you. You deserve as much from me."

"I want to know *everything* about you, Reed. But whatever you tell me, I want you to feel good about it, and know that I will understand."

He didn't know how to prepare her for what she was going to hear. *Just start,* he told himself. "It was my sixteenth birthday, June third. I had finished my freshman year in high school just two weeks earlier. Some of my buddies—about six of them got together and bought a keg and stashed it near the river bottom on the old Carl Chapman place. They all had a date, and told me I'd better show up with one, and to bring a blanket. They said this was going to be one of 'those kind of parties.'" Reed took a deep breath and paused for a moment.

"I'd never had an honest-to-goodness date before, except for at a chaperoned school party, and I didn't figure that counted. I picked up my drivers' license that very day and was feeling pretty good about myself. Good enough to ask the most popular girl in school, Shirley Watson, if she wanted to go on a real beer bust. I almost fell down when she said, "Yes.""

Reed stopped again and looked toward Cindy, still staring straight ahead. Without looking his way, she reached over and gave his hand a slight squeeze.

Reed turned his face away from Cindy and took a long breath. "Mom let me use her Cadillac. She knew where the party would be, but I told her there would be no alcohol, and even if there was, I wouldn't be drinking. That was the first time I could remember actually telling my mom a big lie. I did drink at the party, maybe five or six paper cups. I don't remember how many exactly, but it seemed like most of it was foam. As the night wore on, Shirley and I wrapped up in a blanket and sat by the fire for awhile. The others grabbed their blankets and wandered off into the trees."

Mister was stretched out on the ground, facing the couple. Reed lit a cigarette and stroked the dog behind his ears. "We huddled by the fire, held hands, and kissed a few times, until Shirley said she was getting cold. She wanted to go home.

"She lived with her folks who owned a dairy farm about five miles west of Riverdale," Reed continued, "The Chapman place is about ten miles south of Riverdale—so, her home was maybe a twenty minute drive from where we were. I was feeling good, a little dizzy, but I didn't think about the beer causing it. Anyway, we topped the hill above the Bitter Creek Bridge, and there they were, fifteen or twenty Angus cows right in the middle of the road." He pulled a handkerchief from his hip pocket and wiped his brow.

"Reed," Cindy said, "are you sure you want to go on with all the details. Or maybe some other time would be better?"

Reed continued on, as if he didn't hear her. "I don't know how fast I was going—seventy—eighty, or maybe faster, it was a big car. And like I said, I was feeling good. I swerved, dodged a couple of the cows, then I hit one on my left front bumper, and the car went out of control. The highway patrolman said, later, the car rolled four times before hitting the creek bottom, and came to rest on its back in the creek bottom."

"I was in the hospital for observation and treatment for two days. I have no words to describe my feelings, or the scene, before I was released—except to say, there was my mom, her minister from Riverdale, some lawyer I had never seen before, several cops, and others asking questions that I couldn't answer.

"When I could speak clearly enough to be understood, all I could tell anyone is I didn't remember anything after I hit the second cow, waking up in the hospital with a terrible headache, and being told I had a concussion with some cuts and bruises. The last, and only words I heard from mom's lawyer, who I remember saying, 'Just get some rest, and from now on, don't answer questions from anyone except me.'

"Even to this day, I remember repeatedly asking, 'Where's Shirley?' The answer I received was a practiced: 'Just get some rest, and we will explain everything when you're feeling better.' I wasn't 'feeling better' until an hour before I checked out of the hospital, when I was told by mom's minister, a male hospital representative, and mom's attorney that Shirley died at the scene from a broken neck and other injuries."

"I've asked myself over and over—why not me? All I got was a concussion and a few bruises. Shirley was an only child. Her folks sold the dairy farm and moved away. Nobody knows where. I didn't even get a chance to talk to them, before or after the funeral. They avoided my glances. None of the family would even approach me. I didn't blame them. I killed her."

Cindy turned to Reed and placed her hands over his. "I'm so sorry, Reed, I don't understand any better than anyone else why such things happen. They just happen—things that kill people and destroy the lives of countless others. It doesn't make sense. But, Reed, you weren't charged with anything, were you?"

"I deserved to be, but I wasn't. Mom got the best attorney she could find, Jake McIntosh, from Denver. McIntosh asked me two questions before the preliminary hearing: was I drinking and did I know what the Miranda Rule was? I told him I drank, maybe, four or five cups of beer from a keg before the accident, and that I couldn't remember if the patrolman had read me anything."

———

I went before Judge Ledbetter the next week. The rookie patrolman admitted that he didn't read me my rights because it was a day after the accident, and he thought someone else had. I received a warning from the judge and no charges were ever filed.

"To be honest with you, at the time, I didn't know if I wanted the charges dropped. I knew my life was over, and I wanted to die, but I didn't want to die in prison with a bunch of lowlifes. I've considered suicide, even made a feeble attempt at it one time, but didn't have the guts to go through with it."

"Reed, it won't make you feel any better, but I've heard most of what you've told me at least a dozen times. This is a small valley, and people love to gossip about tragedies. I guess it's human nature. But thank you for telling me the true story. I wish there was something I could say to take away your pain and anguish."

Cindy sat up straight and looked directly into Reed's eyes. "My heart goes out for you, Reed. But I wouldn't be your friend if I didn't tell you what else I'm thinking. You can't do anything about the past—it's gone. You can either continue to wallow in self-pity, hating yourself and believing you're an undesirable human being, or you can start living. You can't be happy yourself or hope to make anyone else happy in your present state of mind. I'm sorry, Reed, if you think I'm hard-core, maybe I am. You've punished yourself enough. It's time for you to start walking tall again and start living. Think about it."

Reed turned toward Cindy and moved his lips as if trying to speak when she started again. "Reed, there's just one other question I want to ask. Then, unless there's more you want to tell me, I hope we never discuss it again — fair enough?"

"Fair enough," he said in a near whisper.

"How ... how did your mother react to everything?"

"Mom and I attended the funeral together. I don't believe either of us lifted our head above the toes of our shoes. She didn't visit with Shirley's parents, before or after the services. We drove home that day in total silence, and we haven't said one word to each other about the incident in eleven years. She didn't chew me out about drinking, destroying her new Cadillac—anything. It was like it didn't happen. She totally blocked it out. So, to answer your question, she didn't react. Her regular spells of depression came and went as usual. I can't know what was happening inside her head, but if I had to guess, I would say, nothing."

"Reed, it's too bizarre. I mean, the poor woman. Everything is still there, internalized, just like with you. The only difference being, if it ever comes out with Lucy Carson, it will take more than one ambulance crew to contain her."

Reed touched Mister behind the ears and started to stand. Cindy glanced at her watch. "Oh, my gosh, it's three-thirty, I've got to go," she gasped. "Mom is picking Kimberly up from the nursery, and she warned me to be home before her bridge club party at seven."

Reed walked Cindy to the car and opened her door. After a friendly embrace, she pushed herself away, slid behind the wheel, smiled, and turned the key on the little Chevy.

Reed followed Cindy to the highway in his pickup. She stopped at the cattle-guard, stepped out of the car, and waited for him to approach. She took both of his hands in hers and looked at the ground for a moment before she lifted her head and stared into his blank face. "Reed, we've all made mistakes in our lives. We're human. I wasn't proud of myself when I got pregnant as a single girl. But I'm not going to let my mind crawl around in the sewer and ruin my daughter's life and everyone else's around me." She released her grip on his hands and turned away.

EIGHTEEN

Saturday morning, Lucy was in high spirits. She would meet Dr. Whiting in the hospital conference room, three floors down, on the first floor. This would be the first time he had allowed counseling outside her private room. She was getting better—she could feel it—the doctor would see it. Cautiously, she began thinking that commitment to this hellhole had been a good thing. She desperately wanted to leave, though, and return to a life on the ranch. "Maybe today," she whispered to the mirror, as she pulled the comb through her hair. Just hearing the words caused her mood to brighten.

Her days and hours at the hospital were filled with staff doctors, nurses, reading material, sleeping, and eating. Television was allowed. She'd pace the floor, with the remote in her hand, turning it on and off a dozen times a day. Soaps were trash and her attention span wouldn't hold for her to watch a movie. She missed the ranch, Justin Bullock, and Kirk. She'd refused calls from Reed. What could she possibly say to a son—her own child—whom she had accused of cattle theft, and threw him out of the only home he'd ever known? As soon as she was out of this miserable place maybe she would find the strength to talk to him again. Neither Kirk nor Justin had called, and messages she'd left on their answering machines went unreturned.

Today, Lucy was allowed to wear her street clothes, walk down a short hallway to the elevator, and find Dr. Whiting's office without the shadow of a clinic orderly. She dressed in the only clothes in her closets—the ones she came in with: wrangler jeans, a red cotton blouse, and a pair of house slippers. No socks.

The doctor greeted Lucy with a broad smile, his bald pate reflecting light from sunshine filtering through thin, white curtains. He walked around his desk and shook her hand. "I see you're tired of whites, frankly, so am I." Lucy returned his smile.

She eased herself into a comfortable leather chair and faced the doctor. He folded his hands on top of the desk and leaned slightly forward. "I commend you for being such an excellent patient. Without your cooperation, we could not have come this far."

"And just how far have we come, doctor?" Her voice trembled a little, but she forced a smile.

"Five days ago my staff and I were sure of a positive diagnosis. We took away the antidepressants and started you on medications to control paranoia—and we can see that it's working."

"Paranoia." The word repulsed her. "So, in a nice way, you're telling me I'm a basket case?"

"Not at all, Lucy. There are degrees of paranoia, mild to severe. We believe you have mild paranoia, which is a form of schizophrenia, and can easily be controlled by medication. Had you allowed us time to properly diagnose you fifteen years ago, we wouldn't be having this conversation."

Lucy swallowed hard, her eyes clouded. "Schizophrenia?" she whispered, as if to herself. She knew the meaning of the word. She'd heard about schizophrenics killing people, even themselves. "I'm not crazy!" she exploded.

"Lucy, please," Dr. Whiting said calmly. "You're not crazy, you're not insane, and you're not a basket case. You're just Lucy Carson, who has problems controlling her emotions under stress. I would venture to say that most of us have your same problem, to one degree or another. The secret is to recognize when we need help, and get it."

Lucy was crushed inside. How would she ever face her cattlemen friends when the word gets out that she suffers from a mental illness? She'd rather be dead. What would Kirk and Justin think? It won't matter what Reed thinks, she allowed; he would never speak to her again, anyway. "How…. how many people have to know about this?" she asked, her voice wavering.

The doctor formed a tight smile. "In ranch language, just you, me, and the gate post. In our language, your hospital records are sealed to anyone except me, your two sons, and our staff doctors who are working with you as a patient. If it makes you more comfortable, you can purchase your medications from the hospital pharmacy."

Lucy seethed inwardly. What did she do to deserve a mental illness, if that's what she had? She just knew someone from the valley would find out, then it would be all over the state: Lucy Carson was a certified fruitcake. She'd play their game, take the medicine, but if the secret were leaked, she'd own this hospital. She'd play along with the good doctor, gain his release, and get out of this psycho ward. Lucy smiled. "Your medication must be working, doctor, I've felt so much better this past week."

The doctor leaned forward in his chair, cupped his hands and rested his elbows on the desk. "You've heard the good news, Lucy. You're going to get better, feel normal again. You will be going home soon. However, I can't release you until I observe your health after I tell you some news affecting your immediate family."

Lucy's mouth dropped. She sucked in a quick breath. "Don't tell me something has happened to one of my children, doctor!"

"Reed and Kirk are just fine ... *now*. But you need to know that Reed was near death for several days as a result of a severe beating at your ranch."

"No!" Lucy gasped. "Where is he? Is he okay? Who beat him?"

"Reed is doing well. Your county sheriff, Logan I believe, called me personally a few days ago. Reed has been released from the hospital and recuperating at his home."

"Thank God," Lucy sighed. A split second later she took a quick breath and held back a gasp. *Home? Reed doesn't have a home!* Could he be calling that rat-infested Cadwaller cabin a home? Oh, Lord, what've I done. I have to get out of here!

"As for your second question," Dr. Whiting said, "I understand the police have only one suspect—your former ranch manager."

"Justin Bullock," she said quietly. "I should have known." She wanted to run to the bathroom, but she couldn't let on her weakness to the doctor.

"That's the name I've been hearing," he answered.

"Is…is Mr. Bullock in jail?"

"That, I don't know."

The doctor's brow furrowed. "Lucy, there's one more thing I must tell you before our session is over today."

Lucy closed her eyes, placed a hand on her forehead. "Oh, no, it can't be any worse—can it doctor?"

"Your housekeeper, Shirley Stinson, witnessed the injuries your son suffered. She went into shock, and she's being treated here. I'm happy to say she's getting better and will be released within a day or two."

"Poor Shirley…she is so sensitive. The poor dear," she said, pursing her lips in concern. "Can I see her, doctor?"

"I'm afraid not—Sheriff Logan's orders. He wants to question her before she leaves the hospital without any influence from an outside party. Exactly what that means, I don't know."

She turned to the doctor with a pleading look. "Doctor, I must go home, right away, please—to see Reed, to get my life back in order."

"I understand your concern for your son, and your other affairs, but it wouldn't be fair to you until your medications are adjusted to the severity of your condition. Give us a few days, maybe a week, call your son, and settle yourself down. Call me at any time if you need to talk. Meanwhile, I'll schedule our next session for tomorrow for ten o'clock, in my office."

The doctor rose from his chair, motioned to an orderly, and together, they walked with Lucy to the elevator and back to her room.

NINETEEN

It had been five days since Reed watched Cindy's little blue car disappear on her way back to Garfield. Six days since Butch rode away on Lurch. He welcomed the time to himself—time to heal his wounds, to think, and plan—but he was consumed with worry about Butch's whereabouts, and how to get his hands on Justin Bullock—all the while with Cindy's words dancing in his head, *You can't do anything about the past—it's gone.*

Had he really been wallowing in self-pity for eleven years?

Deep down, he knew the answer. It was the natural reaction at sixteen, or even seventeen, he reasoned, then it had become a way of life—his whole life. It was like being encased in a block of ice. He could not express it, but all these years the very fact of his emptiness meant something to him. He did not deny or let go of the guilt, and so in that way, he mourned her loss. Even his torturous memories were meaningless, as futile as his silent outbursts of anger that knotted his stomach. No reparation could balance the loss, not even suicide. She was gone, her parents heartbroken.

Cindy couldn't know what he'd been through, but she was right in everything that she had said. Either he could start living, or he would poison the rest of his life, and the lives of anyone around him.

Today was Sunday; Cindy and Kimberly would be coming. Tomorrow he would see Dr. Barela and get his bandages removed, he hoped. Tomorrow he would feel well enough to drive again. He'd return the sales contract to the Cadwallers, explain the error, tell them he was definitely interested in buying the place, and ask them for a new offer. Then he'd drive to Cheyenne and try to visit his mother. The past six days he had used his cell phone to call her room at the hospital, always getting the same answer: 'Yes, she's here,' the crisp voice would say, 'but she's sleeping and can't be disturbed.' He didn't believe any of it. Tomorrow he would get to the bottom of it.

Today, he would rest his healing body, just as he had done the past six days. His days had become routine: feed cattle early, rest on his bunk two hours, lunch, walk to Dry Creek and back with Mister, back on his bunk another hour, another walk to Dry Creek …. It was paying off. He could feel his body getting stronger, less fatigue at the end of the day, and the pain from his head and ribs was nearly gone.

Reed was returning to the cabin from Dry Creek after spreading his second load of hay to the cattle. The sunlight reflecting off a vehicle windshield caught his eye as he topped the hill. He glanced at his watch…ten o'clock. She was early. For five days Reed had relived those painful few moments it had taken him to tell her about the accident. He was glad he had finally told somebody—Cindy—but he hadn't really expected her to come back, as she had said.

Now, watching the little Chevy stop at his cabin, he thought about her words again and wondered if he could really stop hating himself for something that happened so long ago. Even before Cindy so plainly told him, he knew that he would have to change if he were ever to have a normal life. But, until she entered the picture, he was comfortable just fighting demons of the past, and wallowing in his own misery, like a pig in a mud hole without the mud.

Another time, another place, and under different circumstances, and he might have thought seriously about giving Gary some real competition. But, this wasn't the time. They each had problems, which neither had come to terms with. Cindy with her thing about not trusting men…He almost chuckled when he thought of his own wheelbarrow full of problems.

He had problems too serious to think about getting a woman involved in his life. She had a permanent residence, a good office job, and friends. She didn't need his troubles to complicate her life. She'd been hurt enough.

But he had to wonder how things might have gone for him and Cindy had they met two years ago—before Gary Stockton and before Justin Bullock. He was settled on the Homestead Ranch, one of the finest ranches in the valley, building a cow herd and looking forward to the day when his mom would fulfill her promise and sell him the ranch.

A few weeks after Justin Bullock entered the scene, everything changed. His last two years on the Homestead Ranch had been an anxious hell. He was always wondering what her next shenanigan would be. Now, he had almost nothing, save a few head of cattle, a little money in the bank, and a three-year lease on six sections of grazing land with a one-room cabin. But, maybe it was a blessing that things turned out this way. He was now in a better position to talk to his mother, reason with her, help her to see that Bullock was up to no good, and to convince her to accept help from her doctors.

He saw Kimberly first, breaking away from her mother, racing toward the pickup. Reed laughed. "How's my cowgirl?" he asked, gathering her into his arms. "Did you come by yourself?"

"Nooo…I can't drive, silly."

"You can drive this pickup, I'll betcha," Reed said, standing her in his lap behind the wheel. "Just keep it straight and I'll give it the gas."

Kimberly giggled.

"I wouldn't want to meet you two on the freeway," Cindy said. Reed gently lifted Kimberly out of the seat, hoisted her high into the air, and placed her feet-first on the ground. Kimberly skipped toward the horse corral, singing some unintelligible nursery rhyme.

Their eyes followed Kimberly for a moment, before Cindy turned to Reed, and said, "Hey, you look great—must be from the house call."

"Well, yeah, it could be that. She was a beautiful doctor, but she wouldn't let me fool around any. Just left me to think about it."

Cindy's face turned serious. "I know you were just joking." She hesitated. "But, just in case you weren't …."

Reed chuckled, and raised his hand, stopping her in mid-sentence. "Hey, I was just trying to be funny. But, to be honest, they were the best thoughts I've had since I can remember."

"I'm glad."

"You remember what you told me about living in the past? Well, I've been thinking about that a lot, too."

"Really, Reed?"

"Yeah, really. Maybe I'll wake up in the morning and be my old self again, but I've felt better about everything since you left. Like, maybe it *is* possible to start looking at the world differently." Cindy touched his hand and smiled.

They moved apart slightly at the sound of Kimberly running toward them, as though a mountain lion was closing in on her. Cindy grinned. "Can you read her mind at this distance, Reed?"

"Sure can, 'Where is Lurch?'"

Kimberly grabbed Reed's pant leg. Breathlessly, she tried to stare into his face. "Where's Lurch and Brownie?"

"Your grandpa took Lurch and Brownie for a ride a few days ago. He'll be back soon—maybe today."

"I miss Lurch. Do you think he misses me?" Kimberly asked.

"Of course he does," Reed said.

Kimberly grabbed Reed's hand and led him toward the cabin. Cindy was glad for the moment to be alone with her thoughts. She watched the two of them and smiled. Kimberly was pulling on Reed, trying to get him to walk faster, and he was stumbling along as if he couldn't keep up.

Cindy loved these mountains and the promise of freedom the endless view incited in her. She felt a quickening in her chest when she thought about how warm and cozy Reed's little cabin made her feel. It would be so easy to just let her feelings go with Reed, allow a deeper friendship to evolve. But, these kind of thoughts disturbed her, left her with feelings of fear and inadequacy, wondering which realization was worse—allow a man to get close enough to hurt her again, or believing she didn't have enough left to give to someone like Reed, or to anyone for that matter.

Her thoughts turned to Gary Stockton—how much she had valued his friendship these past two years, and how tender and caring he had been when she just needed to unload her troubles. Now, she had another true friend in Reed Carson, but there was no way to compare the two. Reed looked and acted in symphony with everything around him. He was as much a part of this rugged land as the willows that grew in the bottom and the sagebrush that dotted the hillsides.

Gary was a businessman, wore suits and ties, and had been told almost every day of his life that he was being groomed to replace his father as president of the bank. She admired both of them for separate reasons. And, they were both wonderful with Kimberly, if not in a different way. Reed's attentions seemed so true and genuine. But, she always harbored a troubling suspicion that it was Gary's slavish need to please, to demonstrate the perfect father figure, that drove him to kindness with Kimberly.

She cleared her mind of serious thoughts, threw her head back, tossed her hair in the breeze, and marveled at how wonderful she felt just to be here, staring at the snow-capped mountains, and breathing deeply of the fresh mountain air. She was wishing she had all day just to do this. She glanced toward the cabin just as Mister burst through the door with a loud yelp. Kimberly was in pursuit, swinging a rope above her head. The dog ran to Cindy and hunkered down behind her.

"Kimberly, what on earth are you doing? You're scaring Mister half to death!" Cindy called out.

"Reed gave me this rope. He said I could rope Mister if I could catch him."

"He doesn't want to be caught. And he's scared. Look at him. He's shaking. Now, you put the rope down, go pet him, and tell him you're sorry."

Reed was having himself a good laugh as he approached the pair. "I'm ashamed of you, Mister—a big, brave dog like you running from a little girl."

"And I'm ashamed of both of you," Cindy said. "Look at that poor little thing, afraid to leave my legs. Next time, Mister goes with me. You two can just rope each other."

Cindy brought Safeway deli items for a picnic lunch and a list of food and supplies Reed needed from town. They were unloading the trunk of Cindy's car when a strong blast of wind rocked the car and rattled tin on the barn. "Our picnic wasn't meant to be," Reed called to Cindy, struggling to stay on her feet with an armload of groceries.

While they listened to the wind blow and feasted on their indoor picnic lunch, Cindy talked about her week at work. How the other girls in the office were teasing her about taking advantage of a certain handsome, injured cowboy. Where was she spending all the sick days she'd been taking?

Reed explained his new routine to get his body back in shape and told her about his planned trip to see his mother on Monday.

"When are you going to tell me where my errant father really ran off to?" she said, behind a mischievous grin.

"I was just about to get to that. *Your* dad went to find *my* dad," he whispered.

"What? Are you putting me on?"

Reed flushed. "I'm glad you're sitting down for this one. I meant to tell you before, but there wasn't a good time."

Reed told Cindy what little information he knew about his father. "Butch says Jesse, my father, saved his life—took him in when he was almost dead. For two years they batched it out in Jesse's mineshaft, digging for gold. When Butch found out he was no longer a murder suspect, he filed his own claim, near Jesse's. They split everything mined from the two claims."

Cindy laughed. "I'm sorry, Reed, I can't help it. I'm picturing two grizzly bears sharing cooking and housekeeping duties for two years in a dark cave. It's a wonder they didn't kill each other."

Reed joined her laughter. "As big as they are, they could kill someone by accidentally falling on them."

"My father is bringing your dad here just to see you? How sweet of him! Dad looks so mean and ferocious. Who would ever guess he's just a pussycat?"

Reed was anxious to change the subject before Cindy suspected he'd told her a half-truth. There was an aching in his center to tell Cindy everything, but he didn't want to burden her with the whole truth of why Butch hand gone to fetch Jesse. "Your dad and I shared this tiny space for several days. If anyone knows him it's me, and I can tell you he has a heart as big as a mountain. But I wouldn't want to get on his bad side."

"If the three of you are planning to sleep in this cabin, you'll *really* get to know each other!" Cindy laughed heartily, covering her face with both hands. "Let's see," she went on, glancing around the tiny room, "that will give each of you about three inches of space apiece. When do you expect them back? I mean, could they be here today?"

Reed's face went somber. "To be honest, I expected them three days ago. I'm worried." He dug in his pants pocket and retrieved a wadded half sheet of white paper. "Butch left this sketchy map of his claim. I got a notion to head in that direction tomorrow. I know some back roads that will get me close to that area. I can walk the rest of the way."

"Reed, you can't! They're big enough to take care of themselves. Please wait until you see your doctor on Monday. At least get the bandages off your head first. I'm sure there's a good reason why they haven't returned yet."

Reed gave Cindy a sullen expression and looked out the open doorway. "Tomorrow is another day. Who can tell?" he said, in such a soft tone that Cindy strained to hear the words.

Although Reed had looked away, she put her hand on his arm and continued to study his face. She was not used to giving advice to a man and felt uncomfortable with her feeble efforts. She could see right off that her gentle caring had not favorably impressed him. Reed wouldn't be swayed by coddling from anyone. She searched for something to lighten the impact of her statement. "Okay, cowboy," she said, "you ride off with that turban bandage on your head and some redneck rancher will shoot you for a foreign agent. Anyway, how are you going to recognize your father if he's not with Butch?"

Reed's face brightened with an amused smile. "Well, if you can believe it coming from your own father, Jesse is nearly as tall as a house, with shoulders wide enough to carry a mule on each side, and room left over to roost a couple of magpies. And, you'd easily recognize him as a full-blooded redskin. His eyes are as black and fierce as a grizzly's, and his long, black hair, tied in a ponytail, makes him a spitting image of Geronimo. He's as good natured and patient as Grandma Moses, but you better be in another state if he finds out you've lied or stolen from him."

Cindy laughed until tears came to her eyes, and she finally gained her composure enough to speak. "Sounds like a regular guy to me, someone who wouldn't seem out of place at all walking the streets with my dad. Seriously, Reed, I think I'm more excited to meet him than you are."

TWENTY

Cindy was preparing for the long trip back to Garfield when the sound of hooves echoed through the cabin. Kimberly rushed to the doorway and shouted, "Grandpa is here and there's someone with him!"

The two, tall men dismounted, and Kimberly raced to be hoisted into the air by her grandpa. "Lurch is all wet, Grandpa, did he go swimming?"

"Naw, honey, Lurch just got all excited about coming home and seeing you and worked himself into a sweat."

Reed's eyes focused on the tall stranger. He felt like smiling. Aside from his clothing, he was nearly as Butch described him—tall, long, black pony tail, dark skin, clean shaven, and shoulders wider than the horse he straddled. He was wearing Levi's, a plaid flannel shirt, and cleated, leather work boots. Above his long dark face sat a flat-brimmed, black hat pulled low over his eyes. The hat brim had a greasy and fatty surface. Reed's mind flashed back to the brief sighting of his father as a small boy and wondered if this could be the same hat he wore that day as he sat in his old truck in front of their yard.

Butch tossed Lurch's bridle reins to the other man, and he carried Kimberly toward the cabin. He handed her off to Reed's waiting arms and met Cindy's welcome embrace. "Daddy, I've been so worried. It's so good to *see* you!'"

"I missed you too, sweetheart."

The stranger walked the horses to the corral, removed the saddles to a fence rail, and threw them a few flakes of hay. He turned toward the cabin and met the others, anxiously waiting to greet him. "Jesse, you recognize this tall guy, of course, but you haven't met my daughter, Cindy, and all of our pride and joy, Kimberly."

Without a word, Jesse shook Cindy's hand and knelt to offer a bear-sized paw to Kimberly. Butch lifted Kimberly into his arms and motioned Cindy to follow him to the cabin, leaving father and son staring at each other. Jesse moved first, extending his hand to Reed. Reed accepted his firm handshake. "Shall we join them?" Jesse said, placing a hand on Reed's shoulder.

"Yeah, I'll bet you guys are hungry," Reed said. They started toward the house. Reed turned toward Jesse and said, "Hey, I'm glad you're here."

"You guys look starved. It'll just be a minute." Cindy handed paper cups to Kimberly to put on the table. "We just finished eating, but I brought plenty of food. And guess what, I brought wine." She raised a tall bottle of Woodbridge into the air. "We can have a toast."

"We were worried; figured you got lost in the dark timber," Reed put in, with a glance toward Butch.

"Naw, I didn't get lost, but old Jesse threw me a curve, though. He'd traipsed off to Cheyenne right after the big storm. Left me a note saying he'd be back, but didn't say when. I waited four days before he comes skidding into the yard, grinning like a cat that just swallowed grandma's parakeet. Come to find out...."

"Butch, you still got that chaw on you that I bought in Cheyenne?" Jesse interrupted. "A chunk of that would taste pretty good right now." Jesse ducked out the door, with a nod toward Butch.

Butch trailed Jesse outside. Cindy and Reed could hear the two men conversing in low voices, but their words were unintelligible. Cindy raised her eyelids and shot a puzzled expression toward Reed. Reed answered with a shrug.

Cindy stepped out the door and called to the two men, "Dad, Jesse, the wine is poured."

Butch and Jesse choose the two wooden chairs. Reed and Cindy sat together on the bench. Kimberly scrambled between them, clutching a glass of Seven-up in the air. They touched their glasses, each searching the other's eyes, waiting for someone to speak. Cindy smiled and raised her glass in the air, "To our family."

Butch lifted his glass and repeated the toast. Then he added, "Yep, Jesse and I've been family so long I'm beginning to smell like him. But, now, thanks to the blizzard, and Reed, we have a real family."

Kimberly lifted her head toward Reed, "Can we ride Lurch now? Please."

Butch stood and lifted his granddaughter into his arms. "Reed's gonna be busy for a while. You're gonna herd cattle with Grandpa today. But how 'bout we give your old pal about another half-hour to chew some hay. He's had a long ride. Lurch is a tired old horse, but that hay will get him going again."

"Okay," Kimberly said, "can I throw some sticks for Mister?"

"You can throw the whole woodpile, sweetheart, but stay close to the house," Butch said, standing Kimberly on her feet near the door.

The wind had died to a gentle breeze. Cindy was busy cleaning the table for the second time. An uncomfortable silence fell upon the cabin. Reed moved to stand near the door. "Butch, how does that grass look in the bottoms? Reckon it would hurt to toss a load of hay out today? Keep 'em from grubbing off that new grass that's trying to come."

"I checked it yesterday. Snowdrifts've been melted for a couple of weeks, but the nights are still too cold for the grass to come along real good. What say Jesse and I load up the pickup with hay bales and you and him can scatter it in the creek bottom?"

"Sounds good," Reed said.

Jesse hadn't said ten words since his arrival. At first, Reed was just curious, thinking he was naturally quiet, same as all the Indians he had read about in books and seen in movies.

He'd always known that sooner or later his dad would show up. And how many times had he wondered what that meeting would be like? Now, glancing at his dad from across the room, he even imagined how it might go. Thanks to wise old Morgan, they were going to scatter hay together. They would have that long talk. He was already framing the questions in his mind.

For the first few minutes they worked in silence, two men accustomed to the routine of feeding cattle out of the back of a truck. Jesse kicked the last bale of hay off the tailgate and called for Reed to stop the truck. He squeezed his towering frame into the pickup, glanced over at Reed, and cleared his throat. "What say we park this thing, have a chew, and chat a while?"

Reed killed the engine and padded his shirt pockets for a cigarette pack. "Got some Days Work here," Jesse offered.

"Thanks, but I got enough bad habits without starting another one."

Cows brushed the sides of the pickup with their flanks, rushing toward the fresh feed. Reed found a pack of Marlboro's, struck a match under the dashboard, and lit up. "Fine looking bunch of cows you have here, son," Jesse broke the silence. "Don't see many grade Herefords showing this much breeding. They could easily pass for a registered herd." Jesse glanced toward Reed, then back to the cows.

Reed said, "Thanks." He wanted to say, thanks Dad, but the word was too awkward. "I guess we could talk cattle all day," he continued, "but we've got more important things to discuss, and I wish it were easier."

"You want to start first?" Jesse offered.

"I think so," Reed said, still staring into the windshield. "But you can probably guess most of what I'm going to ask."

Jesse turned slightly in his seat toward Reed. "Maybe, but I want to hear it from you."

"Why did you leave, Dad?" Reed said in one burst. There...the word was out.

Jesse turned his face away from Reed and stared at the dashboard. "It's a long story, but I'll make it as short as possible."

Reed flipped a cigarette butt out the window into a dying snow bank. "The short version will do, for now." Reed noticed Jesse's words had been slow in coming, wondering if he really was just like all the Indians he had seen in movies, or if he hadn't talked for so long that it took a while to put the words together just right.

"Your mom and I started dating in high school; I was a senior and she was a sophomore. I was a sports hero," he said with a little chuckle. "I was credited with helping carry the Lions to two state basketball and football championships. Lucy was a beautiful, bouncy little cheerleader—you getting the picture? Even then, I didn't figure she had much passion for me, but she was the queen, and just couldn't see any other girl dating the biggest jock in school. I figured it was all over when I graduated from high school and started to college…"

"You went to college?"

Jesse laughed again. "Full-ride football scholarship—University of Wyoming—four years," Jesse said, in a matter-of-fact tone.

"I guess Mom just forget to tell me about it. But, come to think of it, she didn't mention dating you in high school, either."

"My first two years in college I dated other girls, and Lucy dated other guys, although she denied it. Your grandpa had season tickets, and he and Lucy attended all our home games. But I still wasn't convinced either of them gave a hoot about me as a person. I guess it meant something to them for their friends to know that Lucy's boyfriend was the star defensive tackle for the Wyoming Cowboys."

"You know what…? I was going to say that I can't believe that Mom didn't tell me any of this. But, I guess it's easy enough to believe, since she didn't want me to think any decent thoughts about you."

"There's a lot more," Jesse went on. "I was a junior, majoring in Animal Production, when your mother started college. Lucy majored in Home Economics. By then we were talking seriously about getting married after she finished school.

What a natural match, I thought—with her home economics and my agriculture degree, she would be the perfect housekeeper, cook and mother, and I'd see to the cattle raising. It almost turned out the other way around."

"What did Grandpa think of all this?"

"He treated me decent—considering."

"Considering what?"

"He never came out and told me directly how he felt, but in other ways he kept my self-esteem in check by letting me know where I stood. By that, I mean he always allowed that no Arapahoe Indian boy, born and raised on an Indian reservation, was even close to being good enough for his daughter. He mellowed a little before his death though, and he stopped treating me like a dumb kid right off the reservation."

Reed removed his hat and ran his fingers through his thick, black hair, astonishment showing in every line of his face. "Lander, Wyoming, is a far piece from Riverdale. How did all of that happen?"

"My folks were poor, but not dirt poor. Dad worked at the Indian Nation doing odd jobs and ferrying big shots back and forth to the airport...and there was a little oil money from the Nation. I lived with my three brothers, four sisters, my mom, and Dad until finishing the eighth grade at the Indian school. My three older brothers quit school after finishing the eighth grade, and it broke Dad's heart. Dad had almost no education, but he could see that the only way out, of what he judged to be a dead-end existence, was education, and he wanted that for all his kids."

Jesse was silent for a while before he went on. "My four sisters all got pregnant and married Indian boys before finishing the tenth grade. I was his only hope left, and he was bent on one of his kids finishing high school. To wrap up a long story, Dad wanted me off the reservation, out of Lander, and away from 'a bunch of drunken Indians,' as he put it. Through some Christian organization, he arranged for my board and room with a preacher and his wife in Riverdale. You pretty much know the rest of it."

"Shoot, I don't know *any* of it! Mom just told us you were a good-for-nothing, drunken Indian, and that's really all I know about you…or thought I knew."

Jesse bellowed with laughter.

"Considering the circumstances, that part would have been easy. Fact is, while I was married to your mother, becoming a drunk crossed my mind more times than I care to admit. Seriously, though, Lucy and I got on pretty good until your grandpa died. Things were never perfect, understand…they didn't include me in making any serious decisions, but I always figured that would change once I got the hang of their operations.

"Well, as I said, after old John passed on, your mother suddenly turned into a ring-tailed she-devil. It was like she didn't know me at all. She took her wedding ring off, wouldn't introduce me to her new friends, and stopped speaking to me. She issued all the work orders to our hired men, ran off to the Cheyenne sale without me, and bought and sold cattle like I didn't exist."

"If it'll make you feel any better, that's how she's treated me the last two years," Reed said.

"After about two months of not speaking, I agreed to what she called a 'trial separation.' I got a job in the mill, a motel room in Riverdale, and she got a restraining order against me—next came the divorce papers. She had me arrested twice. I pounded a few cops, and spent more time in jail. Then I gave it up. Living under the white man's set of rules just wasn't going to get it for me I decided. I quit my job, drew my pay, and headed for the hills."

"Didn't you ever try to see Kirk and me again?" Reed asked, with a snap of bitterness in his voice.

"Yeah, I did—one time. You were about five or six, I guess. You see, she had a permanent restraining order against me, but I thought she'd matured some after four years. Anyway, I called her, but she hung up before I could say a dozen words. I got pissed, got in my pickup, and drove to the place. You and Kirk were playing outside. I was about to get out and say something when she came to the door and called you in. I sat a while longer, or until the cops came and ran me off. I wanted to bust some heads right there, but decided against it at the last moment .... when I remembered jail wasn't a fun place to be."

"I watched you from the window. Did you see me?"

"No, I didn't, son. I mostly just stared straight ahead, fighting the urge to go in there and wring her ornery neck. After that, I never went back."

"Dad, I had no idea you waded through so much wooly-headed junk."

"Yeah, well, I'm just real glad I didn't lose it, and do something to cause you and Kirk more hardship."

"Maybe you'd rather not answer my next question, but I have to ask," Reed said.

"Go ahead, son," Jesse squirmed, "but I already know what it is."

"Okay," Reed said, "I'm twenty-seven-years old. That means I've been a legal adult for nine years, and you apparently haven't made a dimes' worth of effort to contact me. Why?"

"Good question, and I wish I had a good answer to it. All I can tell you is my heart has ached for over twenty-years to see both you boys. I knew your mother had brainwashed you most of your lives, and I just didn't figure you would want to see me. My only hope was that some day I would get a chance to tell my side of the story. To sum it all up, I was ashamed to show myself, and the longer I waited the harder it got."

"Shame we wasted all those years," Reed said. "You can't know how many times I just needed a father....to see me play football and basketball, watch me graduate. Not to mention, I should've had someone to drop-kick my tail clear to Oklahoma a time or two. I turned down a football scholarship to the University of Wyoming because I had this bad attitude toward myself about the time I graduated. Plus, Mom said she needed me on the ranch. Hard telling what my life would be had you been there. Not to say it would have been better—just a lot different."

"I'm proud of you, son. Can't say I could've done a better job of raising you. And I haven't been sitting around all these years blaming your mother for what happened. It takes two, you know, and we both failed miserably."

"Don't bust the buttons on your shirt. There's lots of things in my past that *I'm* not very proud of."

Jesse's brow furrowed. He rolled down the window and discharged a stream of brown juice. "Reed … what's this thing between you and Kirk? Butch tells me there's some hard feelings there."

"How much did Butch tell you?"

"Not much. Mostly about what happened when you and him were digging your cows out of the snow after the blizzard. And bout him and his hoodlum, hired men giving you some problems when they should've been helping. Butch isn't real high on Kirk."

"I can't say as I'm all that proud of him right now, either. It's a long story, but Kirk and I have never had a real brotherly relationship. Since I can remember, Kirk has hated himself, Mom, me, everything and everybody in the whole world. When he was in school, I mostly felt sorry for him and tried to help him. Kids would tease and make up little chants about him. I can't even count the number of heads I busted in school over him. Kirk would laugh while the principal dragged me into his office."

"You telling me that Kirk couldn't fight his own battles?"

"He either couldn't, or he wouldn't. He just let the whole school run all over him—never tried to fight back. Kirk was always small for his age and different in a lot of other ways."

"Different? Whaddya mean?"

Reed lit another cigarette while taking his time to answer.

"I'm not sure what I meant. I don't wanna make it sound like I'm busting on old Kirk just because I'm mad at him right now. But I'll tell you he was always mean to Mom, and to everyone else. He just tried to be the most obnoxious person you'd ever want to meet. He never cared much how he looked either, even in high school. Used to embarrass Mom something fierce, and I always figured he was acting that way just to piss her off. He didn't clean himself up much until he got into law school. Now, you'll never see him without a clean-pressed blue suit, a red necktie, and a pair of two-thousand dollar Lucchese boots. You figure it out."

Jesse frowned and twisted in his seat. "I've a feeling you've told me everything you're comfortable with. I'm not gonna push you for the rest. Do you suppose Kirk would welcome a visit from *me*?"

"Two years ago, my answer would be—maybe. But even then, we didn't talk about anything much. I don't recall you being mentioned more than once or twice. Mom wouldn't allow your name to be spoken around the house. Today, your guess is as good as mine. Kirk is acting flaky—even for him. I think he's tied in with Justin Bullock, Mom's foreman, or ex-foreman. It's just a gut feeling, but I think they're cooking up some scheme involving money—Mom's money. Bullock is the one that put me in the hospital. He's an ex-con. The sheriff says he has a rap sheet a mile long."

Neither man said anything for a moment or two. "We can talk about Kirk later, or maybe I'll have a chance to see him. Right now, I'm more interested in what you see as your future."

Reed crushed his cigarette in an already full ashtray. "You're looking at it...but don't get me wrong, I'm glad to have it. Until a few weeks ago, I couldn't even bring myself to think that I could live anywhere except on the Homestead Ranch. From the day I graduated high school, Mom promised to sell the ranch to me. I lived for that day. Now, I know she never intended any such thing. Mom will go into a rage when she learns I have control over her summer pasture. I'll be surprised if she even allows me to visit the ranch again."

"There's nothing wrong with this little spread, son. But don't be surprised if she changes her mind and asks you to come home."

"I won't be surprised at anything Mom does. But, it doesn't matter. There's something pretty wrong with her head right now, and I'm not sticking my neck out again until she agrees to get some help for whatever it is."

"This little place won't make me a living," Reed said, "but I can work for some neighboring ranchers to take up the slack. Yes—I want to go back to the ranch. That's where I belong and want to spend the rest of my life. But, I have security here. The bottom line is, I'd rather starve to death on this little place than be under Mom's beck and call again. And, believe me, I never thought I'd be saying that."

Jesse sat back in his seat, with a satisfied grin. "I admire your grit, son. And I ain't worrying about you starving to death."

From the corner of his eye, Jesse could see Butch and Kimberly urging Lurch off the hill toward the creek. Kimberly was smiling and waving. Jesse laughed. "Old Butch hasn't ridden for years. He's got sores on his ass big as dollar bills from that ride off the mountain. But he'd bleed to death before denying his granddaughter a moment of pleasure."

Reed turned the key, shifted to low gear and let the truck idle toward the cabin. "We got a lot more talking to do," Reed said. "You're not heading out of here any time soon are you?"

"I'm not going anywhere until the coward that put you in the hospital is behind bars. We'll get together with Butch later today and talk about it. By the way, Butch told me all about the part you played in getting them back together. He's pretty high on you." Jesse paused with a grin. "And I didn't miss the way that pretty little gal looked at you, either."

Reed gave out a little chuckle. "She always has that friendly look about her. She's a nice gal. Got a good head on her shoulders—not to mention she's kind of easy to be around. I owe her a bunch, too. She hardly left my bedside the first few days after Bullock worked me over. But, you can wipe that little grin off your face. She already has a boyfriend."

"Butch tells me you have a mining claim. How's that going?" Reed wanted to change the subject.

Jesse grinned. "Old Butch and I worked side-by-side in that hole for two years, him laughing at me all the while. Then, when he finds out he isn't going to be hanged, he goes and files a claim on his own. Now, I'm laughing at him. To be honest with you, I never figured on hitting the mother lode, but I needed to get out of Dodge, so to speak, and that was about as far out as I could get. But to answer your question, it's going better than I ever dreamed. I'm anxious to tell you all about it when we have more time."

Reed lit another cigarette and pushed a cloud of blue smoke out the window.

"How much did Butch tell you about what's been happening in my life?"

"He told me a little about how you happen to be living in a one-room cabin, a little bit about Kirk, and a lot about Justin Bullock. In time, I want to hear it all from you."

Reed glanced at his watch. "It's four o'clock. Cindy will be anxious to get on her way. And, I'm getting hungry. What say we check on the cook?"

TWENTY-ONE

If anyone had told her two months ago that she would be spending the day with her dad, cooking supper for someone by the name of Reed Carson and his father in a one-room cabin, she would have referred them to the nearest psycho ward. But that is exactly what she had done and loved every minute of it. Now, adjusting her cruise control, just two miles from the cattle guard where she had said goodbye to her grinning father, she felt herself smiling—anxious to relive the day in her thoughts.

Cindy glanced over at Kimberly, securely fastened in her seat belt, looking very tired. When she turned to the road again, a green Ford pickup, parked by the side of the road, caught her eye. *A motorist with a flat tire*, she thought. She slowly braked to a stop, cautiously pulled off the pavement, and rolled down the window. A smiling cowboy, she judged to be in his early forties, kicked a rock across the road and slowly approached the car. "Sorry to bother you ma'am, but I got a low front tire and no jack. I'd be obliged if I could use yours. It won't take me a minute to get that thing in the air and change tires."

Cindy sized the man up. She believed he was just a local rancher with a flat tire. He looked friendly enough, and she had her cell phone—just in case. "I don't think my little jack will raise that pickup, sir, but you can try," she replied, opening her car door with her cell phone in one hand. She moved to the rear of the car and unlocked the trunk. Shuffling various items around, she searched for a jack she'd never used.

The stranger silently opened the door of Cindy's car. "Hey, you're a pretty little girl. What's your name?" he said through a wicked grin, as he unbuckled Kimberly's seat belt and lifted her into his arms.

"Hey!" Cindy yelled. "What are you doing? Put her down!"

Cindy fumbled to take her cell phone off the lock position.

The stranger waved a switchblade in one hand, holding Kimberly with the other. "Drop the phone or I cut the brat's throat. Now just calm down and nobody will get hurt. I'm Justin Bullock. If you ain't heard the name, ask your high and mighty boyfriend. He'll tell you all about me."

Cindy dropped the phone, held out both arms toward her daughter, with a pleading motion. "Please....mister....mister Bullock, just give my baby to me, and let us go."

Bullock coughed out an evil laugh. "Let you go, you say? Hell, no."

Kimberly started to cry. "Mama, make him let me go! Please!"

"Put her down, now, or Reed's going to kill you....he will!"

"Oh—feisty aren't you? Well, let me tell you something, I've been watching you and your half-breed lover boy. I parked my pickup in the trees, walked to the top of the hill, made myself real comfortable behind that big tall Ponderosa, not two-hundred yards from your little love nest."

"I'm sorry, Mr. Bullock, I don't understand what you want with us. Please just let us go!"

"I'll tell you what you'll do, and you better do it *now,* or I spill the kid's blood all over your nice car. I'm taking the brat with me, and you're gonna follow us in your car. Stay close, and no signaling with your headlights, or the brat dies. Savvy?" Bullock grabbed the cell phone off the ground and turned toward his pickup, carrying a screaming little girl like a sack of potatoes.

Cindy followed the man carrying her daughter as closely as she dared. He still had the knife in one hand, horsing Kimberly along on his hip. He shoved the little girl across the seat, slammed the door, turned the key, and glanced at Cindy. "Time's a wasting, get moving."

"Don't worry, honey, I'll be right behind you! Please don't hurt her, Mr. Bullock!" Bullock slipped the clutch in the old Ford and threw gravel against her car windshield.

Reed lay in bed wondering when he would hear the wind scatter what was left of his small barn across the hillside. Even a raging blizzard, he thought, wouldn't be much worse than this howling, drying wind that drove his cattle into the creek bottom where the grass was overgrazed and trampled. Many more days of this and he would be hauling bales to restock his dwindling hay pile. Reed glanced at the two bedraggled giants, still grumpy with sleep, seated across the table.

"No need for you guys to haul more hay to the bottom today," Reed said, while sipping on his third cup of black coffee. "If this wind keeps up, you could dump another load to them tomorrow morning. After that, they'll have to hustle for themselves, because that's the last of it."

"Don't worry," Butch said. "It's the middle of April. Those cattle can dig for roots a couple of weeks if they have to."

"Think your mother will see you today?" Jesse asked.

"She'll either see me or I'll take up residency there," Reed said, without a trace of humor in his voice.

"When do you figure on being back?" Morgan asked.

"Can't say for sure—maybe tonight, maybe some time tomorrow. Depends on how lucky I get. But first I've got to return this contract to the Cadwallers and see old Doc Barela about getting these rags off my head."

"Don't worry about this place, son," Jesse said, in his easy way of speaking. "Butch and I will catch up Brownie and Lurch, check on the cattle, and maybe cut some trail over by Saw Mill Road. Bullock can't be far from here, and I'm guessing he's closer than we think. There's enough old mineshafts, caves, and vacation cabins in that area to hide a whole cavalry. The cops think he's left the country, and anyway, you won't catch a self-respecting lawman crawling on his hands and knees in a stinking mineshaft when he can be arresting some ten-year-old kid for shoplifting a fifty-cent candy bar."

"Dad, you have to know, this Bullock character is cunning, he's tough, and he's got nothing to lose," Reed said. "He's out on parole and he knows he'll go back to prison for a long time if he's caught. I'm just saying, be careful…and save a piece of him for me."

———

Reed knocked twice before Mabel Cadwaller opened the door and greeted him with a smile. "Come in, son, we've been wondering when you would be paying us a visit. The Mister and I just finished breakfast. I'll clear the table and get you something going in no time."

"Thanks, Mrs. Cadwaller. I had a bite to eat before leaving the cabin, but that coffee sure smells good."

"Reed, good to see you," Claude called out. He was sitting at the table, his hands wrapped around a coffee mug.

Cadwaller extended an arthritic hand toward Reed without getting up. Reed scraped a chair back from the table, sat down, and placed the large brown envelope between him and the old man.

While sipping on a cup of steaming coffee, Reed answered questions from the old couple concerning how he was feeling, how his cattle were holding up under the terrible windstorm, and yes, Mr. Morgan was doing fine. Reed turned to look directly at Claude, feeling pressed for time. "I read the contract last night, and there seems to be a mistake."

"A mistake?"

Reed fumbled through the twelve-page document, found the page he wanted, and placed the others on the oilcloth table covering. He handed a single sheet of paper to Cadwaller. "I believe you'll find the secretary left out one important number on this page," Reed said, putting a finger on the 'fifty dollars per acre' line.

Mabel went to the living room to search for Claude's reading glasses while he squinted at the contract. "Mabel, just find me the magnifying glass. Forget the spectacles!" Cadwaller called through the doorway.

"Here they are, honey, but don't get your blood pressure up. I'm sure it's just a simple mistake. The poor dear was working after hours to finish typing our papers — remember?"

Claude stared at the single piece of paper a full five minutes. Reed sipped his coffee and studied the image of a flower vase on the smooth oilcloth table covering. "Mabel, do you see anything wrong here? I can't tell."

Mabel studied the document a few minutes. "I don't see anything wrong at all," the old lady murmured, offering the paper to Reed. "I ain't as good as I used to be at reading legal papers and all, maybe you can just point to the mistake, son."

"I had to read it twice, myself, but it says you're selling me the property for fifty-dollars an acre," Reed pulled a pen out of his shirt pocket and neatly underlined the figure.

The old couple exchanged confused looks. "Well—that's sure the truth," Claude said, scraping his chair around to face Reed. "Don't see no mistake there."

"Have you had an appraiser look at the place?" Reed asked. "Other places are selling for a lot more than fifty dollars an acre."

"Could be," Claude put in, "but that's what we want for it….that is, if you're interested. Ain't nobody else gonna buy it for that price, though. The fences, corrals, and barns are falling down, and there ain't much of a place to bed down, either. We'd be happy if you'd take it and make it into something we could all be proud of."

Reed didn't answer right off. Why would they want to sell the place for less than half of market value? What had he ever done to deserve special treatment? He barely knew them until a few weeks ago. Maybe they were so totally pissed at their son and his eastern-bred wife that they wanted to sell him the place at a ridiculous price out of spite. No, they weren't that kind of people. They knew the value of the place, and for whatever reason, they wanted him to have it. It was settled.

"I'll do my best," Reed said, mindlessly rearranging the papers in order. "Looks like we have a deal, folks. Your signatures are notarized. I'll give you a check and have my part fixed legal today in Garfield."

"Can't wait to see the face of Mark's greedy little wife when she learns we sold her gold mine," the old man said, showing a toothy smile.

"Now, Claude, you be nice," Mabel said.

Reed wanted to stay and visit for a spell, tell them all about finding his father. Another time, when he could do justice to the story, he decided. "Thank you," Reed said, as he handed a check to Claude. "This will make a world of difference in my life."

———

Reed was twenty miles north of Riverdale before he contained his excitement enough to think about the rest of the day. Next stop, Dr. Barela's office. Then, if there was enough time, he would drop by the school and talk to Cindy a minute.

It was nine o'clock. He wanted to be at the hospital in Cheyenne no later than one o'clock—time enough for an hour or two of visiting with his mother and be back at the cabin by dark. He'd buy a bottle of Scotch to celebrate the Cadwaller deal with his dad and Butch.

Reed stepped into Dr. Barela's office a few minutes before ten o'clock, signed the register, and searched the crowded waiting room for an empty chair. At ten-thirty he was pacing the floor when he heard the petite receptionist call his name.

He followed a white uniform down a corridor, ducked into a cubicle behind the hurried figure, and impatiently watched while a middle-aged nurse went through the blood pressure, temperature, and eye and ear inspection routine. She made the last entry to her clipboard, stepped to the door, and turned. "The doctor will be with you shortly." Thirty-five long minutes later, a knock sounded at the door. Before Reed could answer, Dr. Barela entered, with the same nurse who didn't know what the word 'shortly' meant.

Ten minutes later, minus the bandages and chest elastic, Reed was hurrying toward his pickup. He glanced at his watch again—almost eleven-thirty. It was not enough time to go by the school. In his present state of mind, it was probably best, anyway. He'd call her on his cell phone. Then he remembered the new principal had declared a 'no personal calls allowed during working hours' policy. Better to call her after work, anyway, he concluded, now speeding east on Interstate 80 toward Cheyenne.

The sky was cloudless, but it wasn't a particularly bright day, the sun being partially obscured by fine dust particles carried along by a forceful wind from the north. Large semi-trailer trucks fighting to stay upright from shifting crosswinds reminded Reed of that morning's view of his devastated barn. He listened to the wind whistle through invisible cracks in the pickup windows and doors. He wondered how much of his barn was left standing and pictured Butch and his dad checking the cows, cutting for sign, against all odds that Bullock would leave a telltale trail.

Through a low-grade headache, he worried about how to approach his mother. How much should he tell her about the changes in his life since she threw him off the ranch?

He would have to tell her about Bullock, but not about meeting his father or buying the Cadwaller lease. She could handle the shock of his recent injuries; he wasn't sure about the other events.

Inking the contract on the Cadwaller place seemed like a dream. He almost laughed aloud at the thought because nothing in his life, since being evicted from the Homestead Ranch, seemed quite real. His worst nightmares, and some of his lifetime dreams, had all come true in less than two months. So many unreal things had happened; he felt prepared to deal with anything his mother could throw at him.

As Reed fought to keep control of the Dodge from strong blasts of wind, his mood turned sullen, thinking about his mother's reaction when he would finally tell her about buying the Cadwaller lease. He didn't doubt for one minute that he had just driven the last nail in the coffin that sealed any chance that he could ever return to his old way of life.

His heart ached to sleep in his old bed, catch Brownie and lead him out of the old familiar corrals, ride the meadows he'd spent countless days irrigating, cutting, and picking up hay. But, as much as he wanted to resume his old way of life, he would not let on to his mother. If ever it happened, she would have to come to him, explain her actions, and ask him to return with a signed legal contract, naming him as manager with a definite date that he could purchase the ranch. It was a big order—one he was sure would never be filled.

———

Lucy Carson had spent the weekend reading, avoiding conversation with her personal nurse, and planning ways to outsmart Dr. Whiting. "A week or two, yeah right," she mused. "I'm getting out of here!" Today, she would insist upon reviewing the document that had kept her imprisoned for so many weeks. She'd get a copy for her newly hired lawyer, Burt Rosenberg, to review, and find loopholes, if necessary. The fat little toad should be good for something, she thought, with all that money she was paying him.

Today, she would see Dr. Whiting again, in his private office. "What a privilege," she said to herself. She could buy him a hundred times over, and he was allowing *her* the privilege of visiting *him* in his office. Today, he will find out just how good his medicine is working. What was it her daddy used to say? 'If you can't dazzle them with brilliance, baffle them with bullshit,' or something like that. That's what she would do.

———

"You're looking spry today, young lady, tell me you've had a good weekend," Dr. Whiting greeted Lucy.

"I swear, doctor, how you do flatter a girl," Lucy replied with a slight drawl. *That ought to get the old sucker going.* She stifled a giggle at her own cleverness.

"Well, well, you really are back to your old self," the doctor added with a broad smile.

"My old self enough to walk out of this prison today a free woman, doctor?"

"Maybe not today, but it won't be long if your progress continues."

Lucy frowned, her eyes cold.

"Lucy, I can't give you the exact date that you will be well enough to function without the psychological support we're offering here. But I can assure you I won't keep you a day longer than I feel is necessary for your own good."

Cool it, she told herself. *Baffle him with bullshit and keep this session going my way.* "Doctor, I don't know what would have become of me, acting and feeling as I was, without the help from you and your staff. I don't even recognize myself." She smiled brightly.

"I'm very pleased to hear you admit that you have a problem, Lucy. That is always the first step in healing. You've reached the first rung on the ladder, of which there are many. Working together, we will see you looking down from the top rung of that ladder in a very short period of time."

"Thank you, doctor, I feel so fortunate. Now, if you could find the time this morning, I would like a copy of the order confining me to this hospital. Until now, I've accepted your word, and the word of your staff, that I was legally committed. My attorney, Burt Rosenberg, will be here at two o'clock today to review all of the legal formalities of that order. I told him everything was legal and all, but you know how lawyers are. I knew you wouldn't mind," she said sweetly.

"Why, of course, Lucy," Dr. Whiting, said. "I would have insisted from early on, but your thoughts and actions seemed distant to the legal technicalities of your stay with us. I'll have the papers sent to your room immediately."

"You *will* see that I get them before two o'clock, won't you doctor?"

"Oh, yes, you can be sure. Now, Lucy, I'm going to cut our meeting short today. I marvel at your improvement, and I'm very pleased. By the way, you are well enough to take your meals in the cafeteria, if you prefer that to eating alone in your room."

Lucy rose from the chair, tilted her chin, and said, "Thank you, doctor, you're so encouraging." She smiled sweetly, turned, and walked toward the door. In the elevator, she scowled. *Eat with the other inmates in the cafeteria! Indeed!* How could he possibly think she would enjoy waiting in a food line watching a bunch of slobbering morons.

TWENTY-TWO

Reed removed his Stetson as he approached the receptionist counter. It was one-thirty. "My name is Reed Carson," he said to a slender girl about his age. "My mother, Lucy Carson, is staying here, and I would like to visit her."

The girl behind the counter punched some letters on the computer keyboard. "Lucy Carson isn't allowed visitors without special permission," she said, lifting her head above the computer screen. "Do you have a permission slip from her doctor?"

"No, I don't, but I'm sure the doctor wouldn't object to a visit from her son."

The girl studied Reed's frustrated expression for a moment before a pleasant smile formed on her face. "I'm sure you're right. Who is her doctor?"

"Dr. Whiting, I believe."

She pushed a button on her desk and spoke into the telephone receiver. "Would Dr. Whiting be available to speak with a Mr. Reed Carson for a few minutes?" A long silence followed, while the girl fingered the keyboard on the computer. Finally, she looked up, and said, "Dr. Whiting's office is room one-twenty-two, down the hall to your right, second door on the left."

"Reed, it's good to see you again," Dr. Whiting said, standing behind his desk, extending his hand. "You've come at an opportune time. I have a note to call you today. You've had a terrible ordeal. Your brother, Kirk, was quite distraught when I saw him last. He was sure you wouldn't make it through the night. How good it is to see you looking so well."

"How's Mom doing?" Reed asked.

"Better, but not as well as she would try to make me believe."

"What does that mean, doctor?"

"She *is* doing better, but she isn't well enough to be dismissed. We have diagnosed her with mild paranoia, and she's on a new medication, which seems to be helping. As I explained to your brother, if you had not committed her against her will she could have gone *another* fifteen years without being properly diagnosed."

Reed's forehead furrowed. He leaned forward in his chair. "I don't understand what you just said, doctor. Kirk didn't have the authority to commit my mother without my knowledge."

The doctor's eyes narrowed. He sat straight up in his chair and glared at Reed. "Maybe I'm the one who doesn't understand, Mr. Carson. Your signature is on the papers that had your mother committed. Now, you're telling me you didn't do it. Am I right?"

"I'm telling you my brother and I haven't exchanged a civil word in months, much less agreed to have my mother committed to a mental hospital. Now, I want to see those papers, immediately."

Dr. Whiting sat back in his chair for a full moment, rolling a pencil between his thumb and forefinger with both hands. Reed sat quietly, staring at the doctor's anxious expression. Dr. Whiting pulled himself forward and pushed a button on the intercom box. "Martha, I want you to stop whatever you're doing, call the hospital admissions office, and bring me Lucy Carson's latest admission records. Do you understand?"

Ten minutes later, there was a knock at the door. Martha entered and gave him a large manila envelope. "Now we'll get to the bottom of this," he murmured, as if to himself. He found the paper he was looking for, inspected it for a moment, cleared his throat, smiled, and shoved it toward Reed. "Is this your signature, Mr. Carson?"

Reed inspected the signature for less than five seconds before responding. "No, that is not my signature. But I can tell you who forged it," he said in a matter-of-fact tone.

Dr. Whiting closed his eyes in seeming disbelief. His smile disappeared. "Mr. Carson, this is very serious. Are you *positive* that is not your signature?"

"Of course it's not my signature. Kirk forged it. This isn't the first time, but I'll do my damnedest to make it the last."

The psychiatrist leaned over, squinting like he was looking into sun glare. He put his palms together, pushed them between his knees, frowning now. "I don't know how to tell Mrs. Carson, and I don't know how all this will affect her emotionally, but I'm sorry to say, I must place the hospital liability above her health considerations at this moment."

Reed stared at the anxious, overweight doctor, not caring that he was suffering, and suppressed a smile. "Dr. Whiting, my mother is stronger than you give her credit for, and you can be sure she'll make you pay, one way or the other. She's ill-tempered, conniving, shrewd, and a regular 'ring-tailed she-devil'—as my dad would put it—but on her good days, she's also one of the sweetest women in the world. Now, let's go take her temperature."

Dr. Whiting pushed the intercom button again. "Martha, cancel my appointments for the rest of the day."

Dr. Whiting paused at room three-sixty-nine long enough to draw a deep breath, then he knocked and pushed the door open without waiting for an invitation to enter. Reed's eyes went immediately to his mother who was seated at a small, paper-littered table with a bushy-haired man.

Lucy gasped, "Oh my Gosh … Reed!" She put a hand to her face, started to rise, and then slowly lowered her body back into the chair. The man with the bushy hairpiece and wild black eyebrows slowly turned in the chair and stared at the two men, without changing his expression.

"Don't get up, Mom," Reed said, as he slowly approached the table.

Lucy pushed her body out of the chair, anyway, and held her arms out toward Reed. She burst into tears and buried her head in his chest. "Oh, my son, what have I done to you? I've been so worried!"

"It's okay, Mom," Reed said, while lightly patting her behind the shoulders. "I've been worried about you, too."

Lucy stepped back and stared into Reed's eyes through her mascara-streaked face. "What are you doing here, Reed? Are you okay, should you be in bed?"

"I'm fine, Mom. The question is ... how are *you*?"

Without answering, she glanced toward Dr. Whiting, then to the man still sitting at the little table. "I'm sorry," Lucy said, with a hoarse voice. "Mr. Rosenberg, this is my son, Reed. Reed this is Burt Rosenberg, my new attorney. And Burt, you haven't met my doctor, Doctor Harold Whiting." Dr. Whiting stepped forward, shook the attorney's hand, backed away two steps, and folded his hands in front of him.

Even before Lucy made introductions, Reed had pegged the plump little man with the black cauliflower hairpiece, expensive leather briefcase, and unapproachable expression as a lawyer. She hadn't used anyone but Kirk since he graduated from law school. *What's going on here?* Reed asked himself.

"Mrs. Carson, our business is finished here, I'll see you in two or three days, maybe sooner," the lawyer said, arranging papers on the table.

"Thank you so much, Burt. Don't hesitate to call me the minute you find something."

Lucy took Reed by the hand. "Let's sit on the couch where it's comfortable. Darling, you can't believe how wonderful it is to see you. I only learned yesterday what that terrible Justin Bullock did to you. I hope they keep him in jail the rest of his life."

Seated on opposite ends of the small sofa, they turned to face each other, Lucy holding onto Reed's hand. Dr. Whiting was clutching the brown envelope in one hand and shifting his weight from one foot to the other.

"Mom, Bullock is not in jail."

"What?"

"After Bullock hit me from behind with a metal pipe, or something similar to that, he fled in the Ford pickup you helped him buy. A few days later, he ransacked my cabin, shot some of my cows, and fled again."

"Reed, honey, I had no idea Justin was capable of doing something like that."

"*Mom*....you don't know Bullock at all. You hired him right out of prison. He was an ex-convict, Mom. He was serving time for nearly killing a cop. He left the poor guy for dead, just like he did me."

"Reed, this can't be. He had a reference...some rancher in Gillette. I can't remember his name. He said Justin was a good worker, very reliable. You remember me telling you that."

"Mom listen, Kirk pulled some strings to get Bullock out of prison on a work release program. The reference you had was probably written by Kirk himself. I wasn't going to lay all this on you today, but for your own protection, you have to know that Kirk is acting as sleazy as Bullock. They, the two of them, are up to no good."

"How do you know that, Reed? Kirk has treated me better recently than he has in his whole life."

"I don't *know it*, but I have good reason to suspect it. Mom....I don't want to go into all of the details. Now isn't the time."

"Okay, baby, I understand you're upset, but please don't blame your brother for everything that's happened to you."

Dr. Whiting was still wavering, ignored. Finally, he cleared his throat. "Mrs. Carson, I have something important to discuss with you, then I'll leave you two alone to visit." Sweat beaded his furrowed brow.

Lucy looked up, surprised, as if the doctor had just entered the room. "Why, yes, of course, doctor. I'm sorry, won't you sit down." She waved her hand toward a chair.

"Thank you, Mrs. Carson, but I'll stand. Before I go on, I want you to think about your stay here at the hospital and how much your health has improved as a result of our diagnosis and treatment, and...."

"Yes, doctor, we've already discussed all of that. Is there something else I need to know about my treatment?"

"No ... no .... it's not about your treatment. The doctor paused. Lucy, this is just as hard for me as it will be for you, and there's no easy way to tell you." He cleared his throat again.

"Well, what is it?" Lucy sat back, but her eyes remained glued to the doctor's face.

"Please hear me out, Lucy, before you react." He took a deep breath. "Just a few minutes ago, I learned that your stay here may have been imposed through duplicitous representation by one party."

Lucy rose to her feet with narrowed eyelids. "What....? What are you talking about? Duplicitous...."

The doctor paused for a short moment, and swallowed hard.

"I'm sorry. I'll be more specific. Before coming to your room, Reed and I had a long conversation, during which he swore to me that he did not participate with Kirk to commit you. He said that he did not sign the papers, and he did not go before the judge with Kirk. If that is true, and for the moment I have to believe that it is, we have held you here under a fraudulent order—simple as that." The doctor fished for a handkerchief in his pants pocket and swiped his brow.

Reed had moved to stand beside his mother. She turned and stared into his face with fire raging in her speckled green eyes. "I want to hear it from you, Reed. Is that true?"

"Mom, settle down, please. Yes, it's true. Kirk committed you while I was snowbound for three days in my cabin on the Cadwaller lease. I didn't know you were here until a few days before I left the hospital. Kirk forged my name on all of the papers."

Lucy drew a deep breath and held it while her eyes bulged and her lips tightened. Then, like a punctured tire, she exploded. "No! No! No!

"Wait, Mom," Reed pleaded, again, "It's not Dr. Whiting or the hospital's fault. They had no way of knowing my signature

was forged. Even old Judge Ledbetter was duped. He signed the order—maybe you should punch him out, for starters."

Lucy dropped hard to her knees, buried her face in the couch, and sobbed uncontrollably. "You animals! Keeping me in this nut house weeks on end, treating me like a mad, hair-brained idiot! I'm going to drain your rotten blood! All of you!"

The two men watched without moving or saying a word. Several moments later, she pulled herself to her feet and stumbled toward the bathroom. A minute or two later, she returned holding a mascara-soiled towel to her face.

She hurled the towel toward the doctor before grabbing Reed by the arm, steadying herself. "Reed, take me home. Now! Please!"

Reed cast a questioning glance toward Dr. Whiting. The doctor nodded. "Yes, Mom, I'll take you home. How do I go about checking her out?" he said to the doctor.

Dr. Whiting moved to leave, "They'll help you at the desk." To Lucy he said, "If there's ever anything we can…."

"Get out of here, you quack, and I don't *ever* want to see your despicable face again!"

The ride from Cheyenne to the North River Ranch was not one Reed would beg to take again. Lucy never recovered from her foul temper, complaining about her treatment at the hospital, questioning if Kirk was really responsible for the forgery, and how could her best friend, Justin, turn so savage in such a short period of time? Why hadn't Kirk been to visit her at the hospital? "Nobody must know about me being in that awful place, Reed! *Nobody*! I'll kill that doctor if somebody finds out!"

She got quiet for awhile, yawning continuously. Reed thought about the pills. Finally, she sunk down in the seat. Reed glanced over at her and thought he could hear her heavy breathing over the noise of the diesel engine. He had almost said no when he saw her shaking the pills into her hand as they left the hospital parking lot. He hated drugs, and he especially hated to see his own mother addicted to them. But, today he didn't feel like playing 'the-good-son.' Maybe the pills would calm her down.

The sun was low, casting long shadows ahead of the truck, when Reed turned off Highway 167 onto North River Ranch property. A shiny vehicle parked in front of the ranch house was visible from a distant half-mile. "You have company, Mom," Reed said, with a glance at Lucy's bedraggled face and sleepy eyes.

Through a long yawn, Lucy said, "Mrs. Stinson was released from the hospital yesterday. Maybe it's her."

A minute or two later, Reed could make out a green Lincoln Continental with a Colorado license plate. But, he didn't recognize either of the two men who were leaning over its hood.

TWENTY-THREE

It lasted less than a half-hour. It seemed like forever, and it was a nightmare. Cindy hunched over the wheel as she drove, trying to keep the car straight on the road, just the right distance from Bullock's taillights, while trying to control the worst fright of her lifetime. Her only child was in the hands of a madman. Tears streamed down her cheeks. She wanted to scream to release the pressure in her throat and chest, but this wasn't the time for hysteria. She must remain calm and allow herself to think. What could Bullock possibly want with her and Kimberly? To get revenge on Reed, of course—and money.

When the brake lights from Bullock's pickup came on, Cindy pulled to a stop and watched him approach, carrying her sobbing daughter under one arm. "Turn those lights off and follow me, but not too close!" he ordered.

Even in the limited light of the stars, the house loomed large, menacing, and ominous. Using a flashlight, Bullock unlocked the front door, wordlessly walked through what Cindy guessed to be a large living room, and sat Kimberly on her feet inside a dark room. Bullock fished in his pocket for Cindy's cell phone and forced her to leave a message on Reed's phone. He warned her what would happen if she tried to escape, and walked away, locking the door behind him. The room was dark and quiet. Cindy groped her way to a light switch, checked the lock again on the door, and cautiously inspected every nook and cranny of the spacious bedroom.

After securing his prisoners with a padlock on a newly installed hasp, Bullock went to see Pratt in the bunkhouse. He told Pratt to follow him to the old barn on the banks of the Platte River. Bullock parked the pickup inside the barn and pulled a canvas over it. "Where you hiding the good stuff now?" Bullock asked.

"Same place, in the old tack room, behind the boards. But I don't know how much is left. Rusling and Dubois have been hitting it pretty hard."

Bullock was prying off loose boards in the tack room to get at a small, hidden compartment in the wall. "Hey, Bullock, whatcha gonna do with the girl and the kid after we get our money?" Pratt asked with a wistful smile.

Bullock stopped what he was doing, let his crowbar rest in his hand, and turned toward Pratt.

"What the hell do you care?"

"We was just wondering, the others and me…if you're gonna put her down anyway, why…maybe we could just all have at her first. Wouldn't do no harm."

Bullock stared menacingly at the little ex-con for a long time before speaking. "Pratt, if I see you even look sideways at that broad, I'll skin you and pour salt over your carcus—and that's just for starters. And you can tell the others, that goes for them too. Do you *understand me?*"

Pratt backed up a step and chuckled nervously. "Oh, sure, boss, I was just funning, anyway."

Bullock pried another board loose, scowling. "You're so damn stupid."

———

The room was large and comfortably furnished, with a king-sized bed, leather rocker with a matching couch, a small oak roll-top desk, and a large, full-sized bathroom. The two closets were full of identical blue suits, each with a red necktie neatly folded over the shoulder. On the floor of one of the closets were several pairs of expensive looking boots. A man's room, Cindy ventured, without really caring. The large picture window was boarded with plywood and nailed shut from the inside.

Kimberly followed her mother about the spacious room, tightly gripping her hand and whimpering: "Mama, why did that man do that to us? Are they going to let us out? Mama, I want to go home!"

Cindy dropped to her knees, pulled Kimberly to her, and squeezed her gently. "Darling, we have to be strong, do you understand?" she whispered. "The man who kidnapped us is bad, but Grandpa and Reed are going to rescue us. You can be sure of that, honey. Can you be a big girl and help your mama be strong, too?"

"Yes, Mama, but I'm scared. Can I sleep with you tonight?"

"Yes, baby, we will both sleep in that big bed. Remember, we have to be really brave. Okay? We're safe here until your grandpa and Reed come to get us."

They had nothing to eat Sunday night. Early Monday morning, while Cindy was washing Kimberly, she heard the lock turn on the door. She locked Kimberly inside the bathroom and crept to steal a glance at a craggy, sandy-haired man as he pushed a bag inside the door. She watched him close the door and waited until the outside lock clacked.

After she finished dressing Kimberly, they inspected the contents of the bag. "Food," Cindy said. She managed a smile of relief, hoping to give a moment of cheer to her daughter. "Look, Kimberly. There's orange juice, coffee, scrambled eggs, and toast." It was restaurant food. She was sure of that. Probably from the Pronghorn Bar and Grill they had passed near the river bridge before turning south onto the dirt road that led to the house.

In late afternoon, the door latch turned again, another man— older, dirtier, and more frightening than the last—dropped a bag of food inside the door and left without a word or a glance in their direction.

———

Two men, in casual city dress, leaning over the hood, writing on tablets, looked up when Reed braked to a stop. Reed and his mother walked side-by-side as they approached the two smiling strangers. Reed noted the sign on the car door: *All Country Ranches-Nationwide.* "Carl Henson," the man said, extending his hand to Reed. "My appraiser, Les Wadley." He motioned toward a tall, slim man, offering his hand.

"I'm Reed Carson. This is my mother, Lucy Carson." A surprised look creased the faces of the two men. No one said anything for a full minute, while Reed fished in his shirt pocket for a cigarette and struck a match. "What are you fellows doing here?" Reed asked, pushing a cloud of smoke their way.

"Uh, I'm a salesman for All Country Ranches and Mr. Wadley is an independent land appraiser. Kirk Carson has listed the three Carson Ranches with my company, and I'm happy to say we have buyers ready with offers as soon as Mr. Wadley finishes his appraisal."

"What?" Lucy shouted, suddenly awakening from a half-sleep.

"Hold on, Mom," Reed put in. "Will it hurt your feelings if I tell you Kirk doesn't own the Carson Ranches?"

"We're aware of that, sir, but he, Kirk Carson, has Power of Attorney for them. I have it right here," Henson said, pulling a handful of papers out of his briefcase.

Reed read the paper and handed it to Lucy. "At least the signature doesn't look forged." Reed almost laughed at his own words.

"What the...." Lucy turned red and puffed up like a poisoned toad. "I want you to get off my property....*now!*"

Reed gently took hold of Lucy's arm. "Let me handle this Mom." To the two men, he said, "Okay, gentlemen, the show's over. You can leave now. We'll keep the Power of Attorney, and it will be in your best interest not to show up here again under the same pretenses."

"But, Mr. Carson, Kirk is...."

"Mr. Henson," Reed said, "Kirk is going to jail, and if you don't want to be his cellmate, you'd better pack your bags and go—right now."

"Mom, you have to do something about Kirk...before he ruins you," Reed said, unlocking the door to the ranch house.

"Nonsense, Kirk wouldn't do anything to hurt me. I don't know what those two idiots were doing here, but Kirk didn't send them."

Lucy found glasses, rummaged through the liquor cabinet, and stepped to the refrigerator for ice and Coke. "I'm having a rum and Coke, care to join me, or would you prefer your usual?"

"I'll have my usual," Reed replied, reaching for a bottle with a Johnny Walker label.

How could he impress upon her that she could be in serious trouble? Reed thought, as he poured his drink and fetched more ice. Was she beyond comprehending that Kirk was out to have it all—everything she owned?

"Mom, whether you want to admit it or not, you're in a crisis situation. Kirk has a Power of Attorney over your entire estate—your property, your bank accounts, and everything else you own. Can you understand that he could wipe you out and leave the country with you sitting here flat broke without a roof over your head?"

Lucy gave out a cocktail party laugh. "Reed, darling, that head injury must have scrambled your brain. I know my Kirk. He wouldn't think of doing something like that to his own mother. Now, why don't you just have your drink and relax while I open a can of soup. I'm just too tired to cook anything. Oh, I wish Shirley was here."

Reed sighed, dropped into a kitchen chair, and took a long swallow from his glass. "Did you understand from our conversation at the hospital that Justin Bullock is out there somewhere, and that he's dangerous?"

"Of course, Reed," Lucy answered, above the whirr of the can opener, "I'm not deaf and I'm certainly not crazy, in case you didn't know. It's *you* Justin wants to hurt, not *me*. It's a small wonder he lashed out, though, the way you treated him. No matter, I certainly don't approve of what he did to you. Don't worry, son, he won't be coming around here. He doesn't want to deal with me after what he did to you."

"I'm wasting my breath," Reed said, quietly. He'd stay the night, alert the banks in the morning, just in case Kirk decided to clean out her accounts with his bogus Power of Attorney. It would give him a chance to relax and call Cindy from a real telephone. Maybe he could talk some sense into his mother in the morning after she settled down a bit.

"Think I'll spend the night," Reed said, between spoonfuls of beef noodle soup.

"That would be wonderful, son. It's been so long since we've had any time to visit. Anyway, I haven't told you, I'm calling that old fool, Tim Barkley, tomorrow morning and dropping that ridiculous charge against you. I don't know what got into me, honey. Maybe I really *was* a little cuckoo. Any more I just do things, then wonder why I've done them. Can you understand what I mean, son?"

"Yes, Mom, I understand." Actually, he didn't have a dime's worth of understanding why she did anything. Never did. He didn't understand why his father wasn't allowed to see him ever, or why, even after he became an adult, he had to obtain her permission to buy a saddle horse, pickup or any other personal property. *No, mother, I don't understand,* he wanted to shout, but he didn't. Instead, he said, "I'm really tired, Mom. Think I'll make a couple of phone calls and turn in."

"I'm tired too, Reed. Get me up before you leave, and I'll fix you a nice breakfast. Shirley keeps the guest room made up, and there'll be clean towels in the hall closet. Good night, honey."

Reed lifted the telephone and glanced at the answering machine blinking with what he imagined was a thousand unheard messages. He started to dial, then remembered turning off his cell phone before entering the hospital. He placed the phone back in the cradle with the thought that maybe Cindy had tried to call him. He checked his cell phone and smiled. There was one message, with Cindy's cell phone number as the caller. Reed smiled, thinking about her deep, throaty voice. He wanted to tell her about purchasing the Cadwaller place. Tomorrow evening he would take her to a nice place for dinner—if she would go.

He punched the numbers on the cell phone to receive the message.

"Reed…this is Cindy. Please don't worry—"

"Cut the lovesick sap and give him the message!" A man's voice in the background said. Stunned, Reed pushed the phone tighter to his ear.

"Reed," she said, between gasps, "Kimberly and I have been kidnapped by Justin Bullock, and…."

"That's enough," the male voice cut in, again. "Listen, and listen closely, Carson. Don't try anything and your sweetie won't get hurt. You know who this is, and you know better than to screw around with me. Don't call the cops, and don't tell those two gorillas living in your cabin. Don't do anything until I contact you again. If the cops come, they both die. Understand? Just sit and wait until you hear from me again. After all the trouble you've caused me, I want to see all you Carson's suffer."

Reed was too stunned to move—to think. He sat, watching the light blink on his mother's answering machine, suddenly feeling frail and nauseated, shock waves shooting through his body. Several moments later, he collected himself enough to start feeling guilt and regret about dismissing her at the gate with a wave of the hand.

He tried to imagine what kind of hell Cindy and Kimberly were going through. He cursed himself for not following her home and searching her apartment before she entered.

Reed pushed his body out of the chair and went for the liquor cabinet. He rakishly poured more Scotch over the fading ice cubes, studied the amber liquid as he sloshed it around the glass, took a step, and poured it in the sink. He put flame to a cigarette and paced the floor, trying to answer all of his own questions.

Pull yourself together! Whatever Bullock wanted, he'd get for him, somehow. It had to be money. He's broke and wants a ticket out of the country. He's gotta know I'll kill him if he hurts the girls. I'll play along, he thought, give him money, anything, until I get them away from him, then that dirt-bag is going to pay.

Reed dropped in the chair by the phone and stared at the blinking light again. "Could one of those messages be from Cindy's mother?" She didn't have his cell phone number and wouldn't be able to get it from information. She would naturally call his mother and ask for his number. If he only knew when Bullock had kidnapped her. Maybe Cindy's mother had already called the police and reported her missing. Bullock would hear the news on TV or radio and think he reported it. Bullock said he would be contacted again. Bullock's words rang in his mind. "They both die."

No way was he going to sit by and be at that lowlife's beck and call. With Cindy and Kimberly to watch over, Bullock wouldn't be showing his face at his mother's house. He could safely leave her...for the night, anyway.

Try to find out when she was kidnapped—that would be the first thing to do, he reasoned. He started through the names listed on the caller I.D. "Harry Bogner, Harry Bogner," he repeated, aloud, flipping through the names. "That's it! Someone called at 9:30 this morning. He pushed the button, afraid of what he would hear.

"Mrs. Carson, this is Julie Bogner, Cindy Morgan's mother. Cindy is a friend of your son, Reed. Cindy went to visit him yesterday and hasn't returned. Reed's home number has been disconnected. Could you please get a message to him to call me as soon as possible? It's urgent. Thank you so much." Reed jotted down the number on the machine and stuck it in his shirt pocket. He prayed she hadn't called the cops.

Reed stood by the door of his mother's room. "Mom, are you in bed?" he called.

"Be there in a minute, son." Reed could hear ice jingling in her glass as she walked toward the door. "What is it, Reed? I thought you'd gone to bed."

"Uh....Mom, I've decided to return to the cabin tonight. Forgot I was out of hay to feed the cattle tomorrow. Sorry."

"That's okay, son, we'll have our little talk some other time. Call me tomorrow after you feed your cattle."

It was still early evening—eight o'clock. Cindy's mother had to be told. She would be worried sick. If she called the cops, the news would be all over the radio. The thought sickened him. If she hadn't already notified the police, he would have to chance that she would trust him enough to handle it his way. He sped out of the driveway and dialed the Bogner number as the tires screamed onto the pavement. "Mrs. Bogner, this is Reed Carson…"

"Reed, we're so worried about Cindy. Is she with you?"

"Uh…no…Mrs. Bogner, she isn't, but I know where she is, and she's fine. Mrs. Bogner, if you're going to be home, I'd like to stop by and visit with you for a few minutes."

"Is Cindy with you? Just tell me, please, where is she?"

"No, Mrs. Bogner, she's not with me, but she's fine. I just need to visit with you a few minutes."

"Something is wrong. I just know there is! Please tell me what's wrong!"

"Mrs. Bogner, I'm on my way to your house. I'll be there in less than an hour. Can you give me your address?"

"Three-twenty-four Gilpin Street. Please hurry."

When his feet touched the asphalt, he took a long drag from his cigarette, dropped the butt, and ground it with the sole of his boot. He glanced over the cab of his truck and caught the glow of light from an opened doorway.

A stocky man, Reed hastily judged to be in his late forties, with thinning, gray hair, was holding the door open as Reed approached. "I'm Harry Bogner," the serious-faced man introduced himself, offering a hasty handshake while standing aside for Reed to enter the doorway.

Julie Bogner was standing in the middle of the small, carpeted living room, her facial expression wrought with anxiety and dried tears. Even in her panic-stricken condition, it was easy to tell this attractive woman was Cindy's mother, with her tall, slim, angular body, and finely sculptured nose and chin. "Mrs.

Bogner, I'm Reed Carson," he introduced himself. "Can we please sit down and talk for a few minutes?"

"Where is Cindy?" She said with a trembling voice.

"Please, give me time to explain," Reed said.

Julie motioned him toward a chair without another word. The couple sat on the edge of the couch. Reed eased his tall frame into a straight-back chair. He sensed he couldn't beat around the bush. Anything he could say preparing them for the shock would only build their tension. "Folks, Cindy and Kimberly have been kidnapped," he said in one breath.

Julie gasped and covered her face. "Oh! Oh my God! Oh God, this can't be!" she prayed aloud.

Bogner stared squarely at Reed. "How do you know that?"

"I'll tell you everything I know," Reed said, returning Bogner's fierce stare. "But first let me tell you that I'm sure Cindy and Kimberly are *not* hurt."

"Have you called the police?" Bogner asked. At that, Julie removed her hands away from her face, and they both stared at Reed as though waiting for a full police report.

"No, I haven't, and it's important that we don't...not right now, anyway."

" I'm calling the cops!" Bogner said, reaching for the phone.

"No, you're not." Reed said, as he quickly moved from the chair and placed his hand over the phone. "Please, hear me out. After I tell you everything I know about this, you're free to do whatever you think is right. But, right now, it's important that you just listen."

"All right, Carson," Bogner said, "but don't try to stop me again from calling the cops."

Julie staggered to the bathroom and returned in less than two minutes, wiping her face and blowing into a large towel. She sat on the couch, leaning forward, holding onto one of Bogner's legs with both hands. He placed an arm around her shoulders, then looked up at Reed, frowning.

Reed sucked in a breath and started from the time his mother hired Justin Bullock, telling them everything he thought they needed to know about a ruthless man. He finished with, "I haven't called the police because I'm scared to death that Bullock will get revenge by hurting her if he thinks I put the law on him. This man is dangerous. You have to know that. I believe he needs money to buy his way out of the country. If he gets what he wants, I believe he'll release Cindy and Kimberly unharmed."

Julie sobbed uncontrollably into the towel. Bogner pulled her closer, trying to comfort her with consoling words that Reed couldn't understand. Reed waited, looked at the floor, and wished he could smoke. "If you aren't going to call the police, how do you plan to get our daughter back safely?" Bogner said.

"I don't have a plan, Mr. Bogner. As I've told you, Bullock said he would contact me again. When he does, I expect there will be demands for money. One way or the other, I will meet those demands, and I will give him what he asks for, provided he delivers the girls to me safe and sound. I don't trust that our local police have the training to handle something like this. Once they know about the kidnapping, it's out of our hands, and I'm afraid of what might happen."

Julie raised her head from the towel. "Cindy is my only child. I would die if something happened to her…and precious little Kimberly…the police should handle this. How can I trust you when you hardly know her, and you're not a policeman!"

Reed leaned over in his chair, staring directly into Mrs. Bogner's hysterical face. "Mrs. Bogner, Cindy isn't just *any* girl to me. Cindy and Kimberly mean more to me than you can possibly know. I would give anything if I could trade places with them."

Julie raised her head, a look of disbelief showing through her swollen eyelids. "What can we do?" She asked, now more controlled.

"First off, we can hope and pray that Bullock knows what will happen to him if he hurts those girls. Then we can trust that we're making the right decision by not notifying the police. Some time tonight, I believe Bullock will get a message to me with his demands. I will call you as soon as I hear from him. We can plan it from there."

Reed rose from his chair clutching his hat brim in both hands. He started to say something else when Julie walked toward him and wrapped her arms around his waist. Reed touched her shoulder while she laid her face on his chest and cried. "Everything will be okay," he said.

TWENTY-FOUR

Reed let out a tired sigh as he braked to turn off the highway onto the dirt road. Suddenly, a shadowy object, some distance from the cattle guard, caught his attention. His eyes never left the dark blotch as he made the turn and the headlights swept the sagebrush landscape. "Kirk's pickup, what is he doing here?" he said aloud.

Reed downshifted and approached the red Dodge at a crawl. When he was within a hundred feet of the vehicle, a man stepped out from the driver's side, carrying a white sheet of paper in one hand. The stranger stepped to the middle of the road, holding the sheet of paper above his head, with little waving motions. Reed recognized John Pratt, one of Kirk's hired hands.

Reed was slowly closing the distance to the other vehicle, when Pratt dropped the white sheet of paper and made a run for it. Reed slammed on the emergency brake, bailed out the door, and was on top of the frightened man before he could reach the perceived safety of his truck. Reed grabbed Pratt by the collar and dragged him across the ground until he could reach the note. Holding the struggling man on the ground, he read the short, printed note in front of the headlights.

All-the-while Reed could hear Pratt begging for his life. "Reed, believe me, I had nothing to do with it—on my mother's grave! Bullock made me deliver this. Said he would kill me if I didn't."

Reed slammed Pratt's body hard against the truck. "Stop babbling, you filthy scumbag, and start telling me where I can find Bullock and the two girls."

"I can't tell you anything. Bullock will kill me."

"If you don't talk you're gonna *wish* you were dead. Make your choice!" Reed said, while banging the man's head against the door.

Pratt was gasping for air, making choking sounds. "You can't tell Bullock, or honest, he'll shoot me!"

"I won't tell Bullock a thing. You tell me what I want to know, I'll let you go, and you can leave for all I care. Listen, Bullock is going to jail." Reed pushed him harder against the truck. "They're all going to jail. If you don't want to be keeping company with them for the rest of your life, you'd better start talking."

"Okay, okay, just lighten up so I can breathe. Bullock, Dubois and Rusling—they're all in on it. I *was,* but I ain't no more. Bullock said he'd make us all rich. We believed him."

"Where's he keeping the girls?"

"Locked up in Kirk's house—Kirk's bedroom. Bullock made us board the windows with plywood."

"Has anybody bothered them? And you know what I mean by that, you slimeball."

"Oh, no, Bullock said he'd skin us if we came close to the woman—keeping her for himself. We just push the food in the door and leave. Don't even speak to her."

"What's Kirk's part in it? Is he living in the house with the girls?"

"Kirk…? Kirk ain't been around for days, maybe a week or more—I can't remember. Nobody knows where he is. Left me a cell phone and said he was going to Denver to work on a case. That's the honest truth."

Reed loosened his grip and allowed the man to stand on his feet. "Okay, Pratt, relax. You can go back and tell Bullock that you delivered the message, or you can start driving and never look back. If you go back and keep your mouth shut, Bullock won't suspect that you talked and I'll never tell him. If you run, he's going to know you ratted, get scared, then who knows what he'll do, probably start looking for you."

"I'll do anything you want me to do!" Pratt said, trying to back out of Reed's grip. "I don't want no more prison, and I sure don't want to be killed by you or Bullock. Why did I let Bullock talk me into this?"

"You read the note. Bullock is demanding a hundred thousand dollars, or he says he'll kill the girls. I don't know how much Bullock promised you, but I can tell you how much he'll give you—not a cent. And you're stupid enough to risk the chair or spending the rest of your life in prison on that sleaze- bag's promises. Why don't you get smart, just one time, do the right thing, save yourself and the lives of those two girls?"

"I'll do anything you ask, and I won't scab, on my mother's grave, I won't scab. I'll die before I'll go back to prison. You don't know what it's like!"

"Okay, Pratt." Reed softened his tone and loosened his clutch on the man's neck. "Just go back, tell Bullock you delivered the message. Tell him I'll get him the money by tomorrow. Tell him to call me on my cell phone tonight. Between you and me, if I come for Bullock, I'll be coming alone. When the ruckus starts, you run fast; get out of there. I won't come looking for you and the cops won't hear from me that you had any part of it. But just you remember, if I see you anywhere near the girls when I come, you will be the first one to get it. And if you don't do exactly as you've promised, I'll come looking for you, with a whole train-load of cops following me. I'm offering you a life, Pratt. Take it—don't be a stupid fool."

Reed drove away, leaving him standing by the roadside. Reed's head was throbbing. Had he made the right decision by letting the man go free? What else could he do? He was trapped, just like Pratt was trapped. If Pratt ran, Bullock would know he'd talked and his hideout was exposed. He would take the girls, or kill them, and run for cover. If Pratt went back and kept his mouth shut the girls would be safe until he could get to them. Pratt's only hope to stay alive would be to play it straight, but was he smart enough to know that?

———

Shortly after six that evening, Cindy heard the lock rattle. She grabbed Kimberly, rushed her to the bathroom, cautioned her to be quiet, then positioned herself to watch the door. She cringed at the sight of Justin Bullock.

Bullock pushed his way through the door, closed it behind him and stopped to size Cindy up. A sinister grin spread across his face. He was holding a paper sack in one hand. "Brought you two pretty things some grub. Sweeten you up a little bit. Where's the brat?"

"What do you care?" Her face flushed with anger. Bullock was a coward—that, she was sure of. If her father or Reed were only here, he would be on his knees, begging for mercy. She had to be brave; not let this monster see how scared she was—stand up to him. She squared her shoulders, straightened her back, partly to hide some of the trembling and fear she was feeling.

"Oh, don't you have a temper! But don't you sass me. You and *me* are going to be real close from now on..."

"You're as close as you're ever going to get to me, you slimeball. You touch either of us, and Reed or my daddy will have what's left of you."

"You're funny too, aren't you? We'd have a little excitement right now—you and me—but I got other things to do, like worry about when your half-breed friend is gonna come up with my hundred thousand dollars, and plan a little reception for him."

"Reed isn't going to give you anything but a broken neck, and if you were smart you'd let us go before he catches you."

Bullock's smiled curdled. "You keep thinking that. You can think it all the way to Mexico in my pickup truck. You see, when I get that money, you and me, we got vacations plans, and that don't include the brat."

Cindy lowered her eyelids, clinched her fists. "I'd die before leaving here with you, and I'll kill you if you hurt my daughter."

Bullock let the bag of food drop to his feet, his face contorted into animal-like viciousness. "Listen, you're mine. The sooner you get that through your head the better off you'll be. You don't want anything to happen to that precious little brat now, do you?" He turned, walked to the door, slammed it, and clicked the lock. Seconds later, Cindy heard the sound of a vehicle pulling into the driveway, a car door shut, then muffled voices.

Cindy put her ear to the door and strained to hear dampened voices of men talking. Kimberly left the bathroom and padded to Cindy's side. "I heard him. Mommy he's going to hurt us, isn't he?"

Cindy picked Kimberly up and held her tightly. "No, honey, he's not going to hurt us—I won't let him. Reed and your grandpa are going to come soon. I just know they will. The man brought some food, darling. We have to eat to keep our strength up. Okay, sweetie?"

Cindy opened the sack of food on the bed. "See, honey, there's hamburgers, french fries, Pepsi, and two pieces of apple pie. Doesn't that look good? Let's eat, then we can watch TV for awhile."

Cindy choked down a few bites of her hamburger. She watched Kimberly eat, while Bullock's words about Mexico echoed in the back of her mind. There had to be a way out of here, she told herself. If only she could find a tool to loosen the boards on the window and break the glass without being heard, they could make it to a neighbor's house before anyone would know. She had peeked through a small knothole in the plywood several times, and hadn't seen anyone guarding the window.

———

Bullock strode out to Pratt moments after he skidded to a stop in the driveway. Pratt was out of the truck, brushing himself off. "You don't look so good, you little dink. What's the matter, you let that half-breed roll you in the dirt? You didn't fink or you wouldn't be here, but he sure didn't let you go for free."

"No, boss, I didn't fink." Pratt took a long breath. "He was gonna kill me, but I told him you'd waste the girls if he did. He believed me, so he let me go, but not until he roughed me up a little bit."

Bullock finished rolling a joint and pushed it toward Pratt.

"Well, what did he say?"

"He wants you to call him and tell him where to meet—says he won't give you the money without seeing the girls." Pratt was still knocking dirt off his clothes, out of breath.

Bullock laughed. "Tell me something new. I had that figured out. Maybe I'll take along a picture."

TWENTY-FIVE

Kirk returned to his condo after a quiet dinner at the Hilton in downtown Denver. He poked an unlit cigar in his mouth and used both hands to find the right key to his little hideout, as he enjoyed thinking of it. His cell phone buzzed as he was smoothing down his blue jacket and starting to loosen his red necktie. He laid the unlit cigar in a dirty ashtray and yanked the phone off his belt. "This is Kirk Carson," he said in a professional tone of voice.

"Is this the same Kirk Carson that sent me on a darn wild goose chase?"

It was a few seconds before Kirk could answer. Something had gone terribly wrong with his plan. "Is this Mr. Henson?"

"You're right this is Mr. Henson. This is the same Mr. Henson who might lose his job because a lying man forged a Power of Attorney, and the same Mr. Henson who paid several hundred dollars out of his own pocket to hire an appraiser to look at a ranch that you don't own. And this is the same Mr. Henson who's going to have you arrested if you don't cough up some money to pay expenses for an appraiser and all my costs. I'd call the cops right now if it weren't for my boss. He wants the money, and you better have it!"

"Mr. Henson, that Power of Attorney is good. Just give me a chance to show you."

"Sick mother! If anyone is *sick,* it's *you*! I *met* your mother, *and* your brother, who incidentally is going to have you arrested the first chance he gets."

"Okay, Mr. Henson, I'm sorry things didn't turn out for us. The Power of Attorney is good, but I realize I can't convince you of that. Tell you what, figure out your expenses to date and send me a bill. You have my home address. Fair enough?"

"Yeah, Carson, I have your address, but I'm not sure you didn't crawl out of a sewer pipe. You meet me at the Brown Palace at eleven o'clock tomorrow—and have some cash handy or you're going to jail."

"I'll be there, sir." Kirk laid the phone on the table, picked it up again, fumbled through the Yellow Pages, and dialed United Airlines. "Screw you, Henson, and screw you, Reed, and screw you, Lucy Carson!" he shouted to the wall, while waiting for his flight confirmation. By tomorrow at eleven o'clock he would be watching whitecaps over the Gulf of Mexico, looking forward to a traditional tourist welcome in Mexico City. The sixty thousand in cash he withdrew from his mother's account at the Garfield bank wouldn't last him forever. But he'd figure out something. Maybe he'd learn the language, take the Mexican bar exam—if they had one—and hang out his shingle under his new name.

Kirk was still on hold, nervously rubbing the cold ashes out of an old cigar butt, rethinking his carefully laid plans. Lucky for him, he'd taken the time to establish a new identity, social security card, birth certificate, driver's license, and passport all under his new name, Sam Kravitz. He breathed a sigh of relief that he'd had the foresight to deposit his newly acquired wealth under his new name in a Denver bank without having to take the chance of sneaking it past customs.

Mexico was a quick decision, and not his first choice as a hiding place. He'd been to Jamaica, brought back travel brochures, and studied their culture from books. But Mexico was close, quick, easy, and inexpensive. From there he could keep track of his mother through his friend in Gillette, Wyoming. He could easily find out what charges, if any, had been brought against him, maybe sneak back, when the time was right, and help himself to some more of the Carson Ranches' bank account. Anything was possible. Reed would always be after his hide, but Bullock would be in prison—no worry there.

"We're sorry, Mr. Kravitz," the operator interrupted his thoughts. "All flights to Mexico City are booked tomorrow. However, flight 2930, departing tonight at twelve-o-five is open, and if you'd care to go on standby, there is usually a cancellation or two on that flight. You would need to be here two hours early to check bags and go through customs."

Kirk checked his watch. It was eight-forty-five, plenty of time to pack and get a taxi to the airport. "I'll take it," he said.

———

At four o'clock the next morning, Sam Kravitz was winging it over a great expanse of water, occasionally checking out the porthole for the blinking lights of stray ships, allowing his thoughts to wander, and feeling safe for the first time since he could remember. This could be the first big break he'd had in his entire life. No one would know about his condition, and no one would *ever* know again. Money-grubbing Lucy Carson, he had stopped acknowledging her as his mother, was the reason his life was a living hell around that little hick community.

Sam Kravitz was high on Scotch, coffee, unsettled nerves, and still trying to justify his actions. His thoughts went back to that Sunday afternoon when he was eleven-years old. His mother had given him permission to take little Reed on a snowmobile ride. After crossing the smooth meadow, he decided to have a little fun in the deep snow in the sagebrush pasture across the canal. At full throttle, they screamed over the rough terrain. Little Reed, seated behind Kirk, was crying his head off. He remembered hitting the broken post, flying through the air, and the excruciating pain that followed—pain up and down his legs—and the blood.

He didn't remember old Doc Wisner putting him back together and sewing up his body parts, but he still felt the excruciating pain he endured the next week when the infection set in after his stay at the hospital where they removed vital parts of his body. He recalled seeing Doc Wisner shake his head as he was being examined before the operation, and he would remember the doctor's words to his mom the rest of his life: 'Lucy, why did you wait so long to bring this boy in? The infection has gone too far.' And Reed, you lucky son of a gun,

what did he get out of it; a broken nose, a few cuts and bruises? Shoot!

"Stingy old witch," he muttered to the porthole. "I'm not a man *or* a woman—what *am* I? She knows what I've gone through, and she doesn't care. She isn't through paying, yet."

———

Before reaching the cabin, Reed dialed the Bogner number on his cell phone. "Hello," a weary female voice answered.

"Mrs. Bogner, this is Reed Carson…."

"Reed! Have you found them?"

"Yes, I know where she is. She's safe, but I can't get to her, yet."

"Thank God. Where is she? When can you see her?"

Reed searched for the right words. "Maybe tomorrow, Mrs. Bogner, but please trust me, Cindy and Kimberly are not hurt, and please don't call the police … not yet. I'll call you again soon. Right now, I need time."

Hearing the loud sobs coming from the receiver, his shoulders dropped. He struggled to keep his voice steady. "Mrs. Bogner, I have to go now. Get some rest and I'll call you later."

———

"Come on in young man," Morgan greeted Reed, without turning from the stove. "I was just starting to hunt up some grub. A mite late for supper but we just got in ourselves."

Jesse nodded a welcome, then said, "If these winds don't die down soon your pasture is gonna look like the devil took a blowtorch to it."

Reed hung his hat on a wall peg, and moved to stand near the table.

Well, son, how'd it go with the Cadwallers? Jesse asked. "Are you a proud landowner, now? And, how's your mom?"

"Yeah, Dad, we struck a deal. The place is mine. I'll tell you about Mom later." Reed had to think about his father's questions a split second before answering. He hadn't thought about his mom *or* his new landowner status for what seemed like forever in his mind. Foremost on his mind right now was how to break the news to Butch Morgan that his daughter was in the hands of a maniac. Morgan would be going for blood, instantly. How could he control this bear of a man long enough to put together a plan of action?

Butch poured Reed a tin of coffee. "Better gulp down some of this mud, Reed. You look like you've been shot at and hit." Reed slumped in the wooden chair opposite Jesse, wrapped his hand around the cup, and stared into his coffee.

"We may have found where Bullock's been hiding," Jesse said. "About three miles from here a vacation cabin was ransacked, and someone's been living there. There are knobby tire tracks leading in and out that look like the ones we saw at the gate the other day. My guess is he stayed there until his supplies ran out and then lit out looking for another hideout." Reed never looked up or acknowledged his father's words.

The two older men locked eyes for a split second before Jesse said, "Know something we don't, son?"

Reed left his coffee on the table and got to his feet. He slowly walked over and stood behind Butch at the stove. Butch turned to face Reed, his eyebrows raised, questioning. "There's no easy way to put this, Butch," Reed said. "Sunday night, Cindy and Kimberly were kidnapped by Bullock."

"What?" Morgan inhaled several quick breaths, his facial color changed to a bright red. "I'll kill Bullock!"

"She's not hurt, and I know where she is," Reed quickly added.

Jesse stretched his frame from the table and moved to stand near Reed. "Where is she, son?" he asked, keeping his voice cool and calm. The last thing he wanted to do was give Butch any more reason to run off blindly after Bullock.

"Bullock is keeping her at Kirk's house. But Kirk isn't in on it." Reed said.

Morgan flew out the door, rifle in hand, pacing back and forth a few feet from the cabin, cursing.

"Never seen him like this." Jesse said. "Let him blow it out, then you can tell us what you know. How I'd like to get my hands on him!"

A minute later, Morgan clumped back through the door, eyes bulging. "What happened, Reed? What can we do?"

Reed dropped into a wooden chair and the two older men settled on the bench across the table from him. Reed told them everything that had happened, beginning from his first recorded message at Lucy's house. When Reed finished, the room became quiet.

From across the table, Morgan just looked at him, and he could feel the rage and frustration building in the big man. It was hard for Reed to gauge any emotions from his dad, who sat straight as a post and still as a rock, his black eyes staring past Reed.

"We all need to keep a cool head and agree on a plan," Reed broke the tense silence. "We can't just go busting in on him. But we have to get her out of there tonight. The Bogners wanted to call the sheriff, but I asked them to wait until they heard from me again. I think Butch should make that decision."

Jesse placed his forearm on the table and turned to face Morgan. "Whaddaya think Butch? We can call the sheriff for some backup, or we can go in there and do it ourselves. If they get involved it's out of our hands, and who knows what they'll do. We got more firepower than we need, and we know their habits. And, we know the layout of the house and every inch of the terrain."

Morgan took a breath, put both forearms on the table, and looked straight ahead at nothing. "This is no job for the sheriff, unless they've taken her out of the house and left with her. Let's see what we can put together." His voice was calm and determined now.

Reed found a pencil and tablet, and he settled into a chair at the table. Jesse removed the burnt deer steaks from the hot stove and tossed them out the door. The three men sat down at the little table. Morgan and Jesse watched closely while Reed sketched the house, yard fence, outbuilding, and pastures.

Reed sat straight in his chair and spoke slowly. "Pratt said the girls are being kept in Kirk's bedroom, and the windows are boarded up with plywood. If he wasn't lying, it was probably the first time in his life, but we have to go on something. I had him where the hairs were short, in a lot of pain, and his story sounded reasonable."

"It has to be a surprise attack," Reed went on. "Get the girls out fast, then go after the rats. I'm gonna lay out my plan. You can tell me it ain't worth anything, or you can add to it. They're all a bunch of crackheads and drunks, and unless Pratt talked, they don't feel threatened. My guess is by two in the morning they'll all be stoned and out to the world—that's when we bust them."

"What makes you think Pratt won't spill his guts?" Jesse asked.

"There's no way Pratt's gonna get himself killed out of loyalty. He hates Bullock, and he's scared to death of him. He would be dead in less than a minute if Bullock even suspected he told me anything," Reed said.

"Okay, what's your plan? The sooner we get moving the better," Morgan said.

Reed drew a sketch on a blank sheet of paper. "A mile from the house is a little road that leads to the river. We park the pickup in the cottonwoods on the river bank and go on foot from there. When we reach the house, you two will position yourself outside the door of the bunkhouse and catch them as they come out. The ranch house door will be locked. I'll bust in the outside door, call to Cindy, then knock down the door to her bedroom. By then, they should be rolling out of the bunkhouse, and they're all yours. I'll get the girls outside, then help you two finish off what's left from the bunkhouse."

The two fathers studied Reed's drawing for a long moment, without speaking. "What's to say one or all of them ain't sleeping in Kirk's house?" Morgan put in.

Reed didn't want that question to come up. He was pretty sure in his mind that Bullock would be sleeping somewhere in the main house, and he wanted him for himself. He had an old key to Kirk's house which, if it still worked, he'd use to slip in quietly, bust down the door to the girl's room, get them running free, then take care of Bullock. "Good question, Butch," Reed said. "Guess I just figured all those rats would be in the bunkhouse where their dope is stashed, smoking pot, and drinking. If there's anyone in the house, it will be Bullock, and you guys will have your hands full at the bunkhouse...."

"Wait a minute!" Morgan said. "Bullock belongs to me! If there's any chance he'll be in the house, that's where I'm gonna be."

Reed knew he was whipped. Anyway, he was feeling a little guilty about not allowing Butch the right to be the first one to see that his daughter and granddaughter were safe. "How about this," Reed offered. "Butch and I will take the house, and Dad, you can stake the bunkhouse and catch them one at a time. When the girls are out of the house, Butch can stick with them, and I'll help you with the others."

Jesse moved to the stove and shook the coffee pot. "It's ten-thirty, gentlemen. We have three hours before we move out. I know none of us have eaten since breakfast. What say we throw on some more deer steaks and recharge that coffee pot. It's gonna be a long night."

They were seated around the wooden table, cutting deer steak, each deep in his own thoughts, when Reed's cell phone rang. Reed made a motion with his hand for silence. He glanced toward Morgan's beet-red forehead and picked up the phone.

"You get one day, Carson...tomorrow. Have it all in twenties and fifties. Put it in a nice traveling bag. Saw Mill Road at ten o'clock tomorrow night—there's a turnout at a curve five miles west of Middlecamp. Be there, or I think you know what will happen. If you're not alone, I'll know it. Won't I?" The phone went silent.

Reed let go a big sigh. "Pratt didn't talk. Our plan is safe." He placed the phone back on the table, then related Bullock's words to Butch and Jesse.

Cindy washed Kimberly, walked with her to the big bed, and watched her crawl under the thick covers. She hummed a nursery rhyme and lightly rubbed Kimberly's back until she fell asleep. It was eleven o'clock. She tiptoed to the big leather chair, slouched, and watched Kimberly's slow, rhythmic breathing for several minutes. She hadn't stopped to take stock of the price her own mind and body had paid the last twenty-seven hours.

Since her encounter with Bullock earlier that evening, she had searched every inch of the room, without success, for a tool to pry loose the plywood from the window. She slouched lower in the chair and fell asleep, without intending to.

The sound of a door closing startled her out of a light sleep. She ran to the bed and stood beside Kimberly, afraid to breathe, while listening to a pair of boot soles scuff past her doorway. Her head was ready to explode with pain. She wanted to throw up as she eased herself down on the bedside next to Kimberly.

Unable to sleep, she stared at the dark ceiling and worried about how all of this was affecting the mind of her small daughter. How much did she really understand? Did she fear death, or was death something beyond her realm of understanding? Would Kimberly suffer from nightmares after this was all over? "My poor baby," she breathed.

TWENTY-SIX

The cabin door stood open. The wind had died to a cool breeze. Reed choked down a bite or two of his deer steak, scraped his chair back, and checked his watch. Eleven-thirty. Inside the little cabin, the air was tense, Morgan's face red, and Jesse was checking and rechecking his rifle load. Reed slipped into a chair across the table from Jesse, lit a cigarette, and watched his dad open a new package of Days Work.

A coyote called from the creek bottom, breaking the night stillness. The dog answered with a low, guttural sound from the doorway. The room became quiet again. Mister padded over to sit in front of Reed, where he cocked his head and stared up at his master. "Been thinking on our time schedule," Reed said, breaking the long heavy silence.

Morgan leaned his rifle against the wall and turned toward Reed. "Glad somebody's thinking. But who knows what my girls are going through while we just sit and think about it."

Reed raised his chin and looked squarely at Morgan, searching for the right words to calm the giant's raging frustrations. "Our plan to leave at one-thirty isn't written in stone. It might be better if we high-tailed it out of here right now, park under the cottonwoods, take our time slipping through the trees, get our positions and wait. We'll be well hidden, anyone comes or goes from the ranch we'll know it."

The three big men all moved at once. Reed checked the load in his 357 Magnum he'd purchased to replace the Colt 45 that Bullock had stolen. He shoved the long barrel of the Magnum deep into the new leather holster fastened on his belt and filled two pockets with extra shells. He'd take his Remington 30-06 and leave it in the pickup for Mister to guard, just in case things got really hot. Butch carried his 30-30 Winchester. Jesse hoisted a modified Mauser Action 30-06 to his shoulder and holstered a .38 Smith and Wesson revolver.

Reed was the last man out of the cabin, followed by Mister. Jesse looked at the dog and said, "Think it's wise to take the puppy? He could cause a ruckus and give us away."

Reed waved a hand and the dog leaped into the truck bed. "Don't worry about Mister. One of those guys is still nursing a sore tail from our last rodeo with that bunch of cowards. He'll stay and guard the pickup."

Three miles after Reed turned off the highway onto a dirt road, he stopped and switched off the lights. The night was as dark as a mushroom cave, but Reed was going to allow his eyes to adapt to the total darkness and drive the remaining five miles without headlights. A few minutes later, Reed fired the diesel engine again, shifted to low range, and eased forward at a snail's pace, crisscrossing the narrow road in the total darkness as they slowly moved closer to the little path that would lead them to the river bottom. Ten minutes, and two or three miles later, Jesse said, "We're getting close. We can't see well enough from the cab to spot the turn-off to the river bottom. I'll walk ahead. You wait here five minutes before moving."

They parked under a giant cottonwood tree, not thirty feet from the raging spring runoff in the Platte River. It was one-fifteen. The men synchronized their watches and took five minutes to go over their plans. As a tactical measure, they would each leave in three-minute intervals.

Jesse would go first, then Morgan, then Reed. When Reed joined Morgan at the front door of the ranch house, Reed would point his flashlight toward the bunkhouse and give three quick signals to Jesse. Reed would use his old key to open the front door, then while Morgan went for Bullock, Reed would break down the door where Cindy and Kimberly were held. Jesse would have his hands full at the bunkhouse when Pratt, Rusling, and Dubois heard the commotion and ran for cover.

Jesse and Morgan had left. Reed checked his watch, again. Fifteen seconds until he would trail Morgan to the house. Reed opened the truck door and rolled the windows down. Mister jumped on the seat and sat up straight with his ears drawn back. The dog cocked his head and gave out one pitiful whine before Reed spoke. "You stay here, old buddy, and keep an eye out." Reed checked his watch again and walked away from the truck, wishing his hairy companion could understand enough to be a part of everything.

"Cindy, I'm coming in!" Reed shouted, a split second before the door crashed to the floor. A flashlight beam raced across the room as Reed rushed to the bed. He grabbed Cindy in one arm and Kimberly in the other. Reed's flashlight slipped out of his hand and dropped to the floor. He stumbled toward the door in total darkness.

A gunshot sounded from another room. Reed felt a cold chill pierce his spine. Morgan had entered the house with him, searching for Bullock. Had Morgan been shot? Reed put Cindy on her feet at the outside door and handed Kimberly off to her. "Run! Take Kimberly outside and wait for me! I've gotta find Butch."

Reed rushed in the direction of the gunshot. Cindy held Kimberly to her breast, too stunned to move.

Reed moved off into the pitch-blackness of the house, cursing himself for dropping his flashlight. A figure moved in the darkness not ten feet from him. Reed saw the flash and heard the deafening sound of the gunshot. Reed lunged toward the flash, grabbing the arm of the shooter at the same time Cindy flipped the light switch. Cindy saw the pistol fly through the air as Reed wrestled Bullock to the floor. She squeezed Kimberly tighter and choked back a scream.

The pain came suddenly to Reed. He saw the blood spattered over Bullock's white T-shirt and suddenly realized that Bullock's shot had made its mark. He had felt a sudden jolt to his side when the bullet tore through his ribs, but there had been no pain until now.

Reed had Bullock flat on his back, pinning him to the floor, his fingers wrapped around the struggling man's throat. Reed landed a solid right straight down to Bullock's mouth and took a winding left on his own jaw in return.

Reed hit hard on his back. He was struggling to his feet when Bullock struck out to his injured side with a hard kick, doubling him up with pain. Reed rolled to escape another foot aimed at his head. He struggled to his feet with all the strength he had left in him. Both men were standing. Reed could feel his warm blood puddling at his waistline.

Bullock lunged, fists wind-milling. Reed caught Bullock with a left straight to the nose, sending him flying backwards, landing on his back within grasp of Reed's own stolen Colt 45. Bullock grasped the pistol in his right hand, smiled, and leveled the weapon at Reed's midsection. There was a loud burst of gunfire. Bullock rolled on his side, coughing blood and death.

Jesse lowered his rifle. "Where's Butch?" he said, stepping to Reed's side.

"I don't know!" Reed said, crawling toward an opened doorway. "He may be hurt!"

They found Morgan on the floor in a second bedroom, lying in a pool of blood, breathing hard. "Butch, it's Jesse. Don't try to move. You're gonna be alright." Jesse turned to Reed, started to say something, then noticed Reed's blood-soaked shirt. Shock registered on his face. "Sit down, son, I'll find a phone." He grabbed Reed's arm and helped him to a sitting position on the bed.

"Don't worry about me. Butch needs your help. How bad is he, Dad?"

"I've seen worse. Don't worry, he'll be okay."

"Dad, what about the others…Pratt, Rusling, and Dubois? Where are they?"

Jesse was holding the phone with one hand and punching numbers with the other. "Don't worry about them either," Jesse said, placing the phone to his ear. "Operator, we need three ambulances and a police car. Two men are shot and bleeding badly, and three more are hurt from other causes. The Kirk Carson residence, south of Medicine Park. No, I don't know the address. No, I can't stay on the line.—men are needing first-aid."

Reed sat on the bed and pressed his hand to his side. He watched Jesse tear sheets and make bandages. "Dad, where are the others…and Pratt?"

"I don't know, son, I guess Pratt is out there with the rest of 'em. Forget them, you gotta stop that bleeding." He was applying a folded sheet to Reed's wound. Jesse tore off another large piece of sheet and bent over Morgan. "You're sure enough hurt, you old rascal, but you ain't gonna die," he said to the bleeding man, while he wadded a bundle of sheet to his chest.

Morgan turned his head and smiled, weakly. "You sure about that, partner?"

"Dad," Reed said, "the cops will be here any minute. I promised Pratt he wouldn't go to jail if he kept his word. I told him he could run … get the heck out of here when the cops came."

"Might be kind of hard for that fella to do right now," Jesse said, still bending over Butch.

"I know he's a coward who'd shoot you in the back for pocket change, but he kept his word and I aim to keep mine. If he isn't gone when the cops get here, we're gonna lie for him."

"Suit yourself, son."

It all happened in less than five seconds, but it seemed much longer. Reed heard a familiar bark coming from outside the house. The next sound he heard was a beating of small feet across carpet—a scrabbling noise. Reed craned his neck to afford him a better view across the living room, where Bullock still lay in a pool of blood. Reed whistled, and his next perception was that of a black and white streak of hair cannonballing directly toward the body of Justin Bullock.

In a flash, Reed judged the dog hadn't seen Bullock before entering the room. The animal continued on a dead run, until coming to a sheering halt over Bullock's still body. The startled dog's body stiffened, as if frozen in space, hair bristling across his back. A split second later, he bounded over the dead man and onto the bed where he licked Reed across the face, as if that would set him in good graces for disobeying orders to stay in the truck. Reed hugged the dog and said, "That's all right this time, old friend. I could have used your help a little earlier, though."

Within a half-hour, the driveway was blocked with two police cars, three ambulances, and a fire and rescue unit. While medics stabilized Butch and Reed, readying them for the long trip to the Garfield hospital, Jesse talked to sheriff Jim Logan and his two deputies. "I figured Reed was going to try some fool thing on his own before this was all over," Logan said.

Jesse glanced toward the firemen administering first-aid to the three ex-convicts. "Reckon he had a score to settle, sheriff. Anyway, things happened so fast, it wasn't easy to get everyone involved."

The sheriff was holding a notebook in one hand, a pencil in the other, writing furiously. "Those three that look like they got hit by a dump truck …whadda'ya know about them?"

"Their names are Pratt, Dubois, and Rusling. I don't know their first names. Reed can fill you in when he's feeling up to it. Dubois and Rusling were in cahoots with Bullock. Pratt's a slime, ex-con, but he had nothing to do with the kidnapping. He just got in the way trying to help me with the other two."

Logan dropped the clipboard to his side and looked up at Jesse. "Pratt's a convicted murderer and an ex-convict, and you're trying to tell me that he was here all the time but wasn't involved in the kidnapping?"

"All I know is, he quit working for the South River Ranch about a week before anything happened. I saw him bumming around town, looking for a job. The guy came back to the ranch tonight to pick up some of his stuff, about the time everything went to hell. Guess he was trying to help out, I don't know. It was dark, and I just figured he was one of them."

"You're sure about this, Carson?"

"Yes, I'm sure. You think I'd want him to get off if he had anything to do with kidnapping that girl and her baby?"

"That's all I need from you now, Carson. I'm gonna finish my notes, then go have a word with Pratt. Something smells fishy here. And, I'll want some information from that hard-headed son of yours, as soon as he feels like it."

Jesse left the sheriff, walked over to Pratt, and shined a flashlight in his face. Pratt was sitting on the ground with a fresh bandage on his head.

A fireman was across the yard patching up Rusling and Dubois. Pratt squinted at Jesse. "Pratt," Jesse said, "Reed gave you a break. The sheriff has no cause to charge you. When you leave here, don't ever look back. If I catch you in this country again, I'll break you in half like a dried twig and feed you to the coyotes. Understand?" Pratt nodded, lowering his head between his knees.

———

Jesse had left Pratt to help a medic ease Morgan onto a gurney when he heard a boom that he easily identified as a shotgun blast. The ambulance, with Morgan on board, was pulling out of the driveway when Jesse glanced toward the bunkhouse to see sheriff Logan, with his shotgun pointed into the darkness.

"Pratt grabbed my pistol from the holster and made a run for it," Logan said. "Lucky I had my shotgun laid across the car seat."

Jesse stood at Logan's side and beamed his flashlight into the weeds past the bunkhouse. Logan was holding the shotgun, aimed at a body. Jesse placed a hand on the barrel and gently lowered it to the ground. Neither man spoke. Jesse walked over and shined his light on the lifeless form, lying face-down in a pool of blood. He slowly rolled it over with the tip of his boot. "Pratt," Jesse whispered under his breath.

The sheriff waddled over and looked down at the dead man. "Thought you told me he had nothing to do with this, Carson."

"I did," Jesse said. "I guess the poor miserable guy didn't believe it himself. He sure bought the farm this time."

_____

While holding Kimberly tightly to her breast, keeping the child's eyes averted from the injured men, Cindy divided her time between her dad and Reed. Silent tears rolled down her cheeks as she prayed and watched the four medics attach tubes to her father's arms and legs and place a mask over his face.

Morgan was the first to leave. Cindy watched until the flashing red lights disappeared before turning back to Reed, stretched on a gurney with more tubes and a face mask.

Reed removed his mask and turned his head toward Cindy.

"Cindy, are you and Kimberly okay. He didn't hurt you or anything, did he?"

"We're fine, Reed. Believe me, no one touched us." She bent over the gurney and lightly touched his arm. Reed tried to take a deep breath and emitted a painful cough. "Cindy, Butch is going to be fine too, believe me," he said hoarsely. "As for me, it hurts, but it isn't serious. These hoses attached to me are just for show."

One of the two medics working on Reed started the hydraulic lift to load him into the ambulance. Reed raised his hand and said, "Hold on there a second." He turned to Cindy again.

"Cindy, you and Kimberly ride with sheriff Logan. Mister will be happy to keep you company in the back seat. Logan won't like it, but tell him he'll have to deal with me if he leaves my dog here. My truck is parked about a mile from here, off a little side road that leads to the river. Tell the sheriff to get my rifle off the front seat and lock my truck." He smiled. "See you in town."

TWENTY-SEVEN

Reed sat on the wooden bench with his elbows resting on the table. He had a cup of coffee in one hand and a cigarette in the other. He was dressed only in his shorts and T-shirt. His gray Stetson rested loosely on his head. It was just two days after he'd been released from the hospital. He'd refused to fill the prescription for pain killers, and he hadn't slept well. The sound of a car engine brought him fully awake. Mister whined at the door. Reed jumped to his feet and grabbed his pants off a wall peg. "Yeah, I know, it's Cindy," he said to the dog. "You'd be barking your fool head off if it was anyone else."

Cindy held the cooler in both arms and tapped the door twice with the toe of her boot, then pushed it slightly open with her foot. Mister smelled her ankle, then he turned and dashed toward the barn. She gave the door another little push with her toe. "Anybody home?"

Reed turned away from the door as he finished buttoning the front of his pants. "Sure. Come on in. I'm half naked, but you've seen the other half of me in my hospital gown."

Cindy laughed and sat the cooler on the table. She reached up and gave him a friendly peck on the cheek, then she turned toward the table. "I brought you some breakfast. Are you hungry?"

"You know me better than to even ask. But, you didn't have to do this. I probably couldn't ride Lurch to town and back today, but I can open a can of pork and beans."

"I know that, but I wanted to see my favorite patient. How are you feeling?"

"Better. Just a little sore if I walk too far." He glanced toward the door. "Where's my little pal today?"

"She's with Mom. She wanted to come, but I left so early. Anyway, a day of quiet time with her grandma might be good for her."

Reed moved back to the table and sat down again on the bench. Between sips of coffee, he said, "Do you think she'll be alright, I mean, with everything that's happened?"

"Kimberly is a strong little girl. I've never lied or tried to hedge anything from her. She knows that we were kidnapped by a bad man. I think she was scared half to death, but she didn't see anyone get shot or the fighting. And, bless her heart, she believed every moment we were in danger that you and Dad would rescue us. She's amazing. We'll both have our share of nightmares, but she'll probably forget before I do."

"How's Butch doing?" Reed asked.

"He's fine—ornery as ever. Jesse was with him when I left last night." She took a deep breath. "But his doctor told me for the first time, yesterday, that it was touch and go during the operation to remove the bullet. He had lost a lot of blood and the bullet barely missed his heart."

"Dad didn't come home last night," Reed said. "Did he stay at your place?"

"No." She shook her head. "Now I see where you get your stubborn streak. I begged him to stay with me and Kimberly, but he would have no part of that. He said they'd put a cot in Butch's room and make do. He wanted to spend some time with Butch this morning, then get on out and check the cows. He said to tell you he'd be here before noon today."

"Guess he isn't used to sharing space with two pretty gals. Now, if you'd offered me...."

"Sure you would, you big liar. You don't remember me begging you to stay with us the last time you got out of the hospital. This time I didn't even bother to ask."

"That was different."

"By the way, the three of us had a long talk last night," Cindy said.

"That should've been interesting. They tell you some bear hunting stories?"

"Better than that, and they said I could tell you everything."

Reed sat up straight and gave her a suspicious look.

"Remember the first day your dad showed up at the cabin. We were all inside and Dad started to say something about what Jesse was doing in Cheyenne. Jesse asked him for a chew and ushered him out the door?"

"Yeah, I remember that. They were both acting kind of strange."

"Well anyway, Jesse had taken some gold samples to Cheyenne to have them analyzed by Arcade Mining Company. And, guess what, they want to buy Jesse's claim. Maybe for a lot of money."

"That's great, but what would those two grizzlies do with a lot of money?" Reed grinned.

Cindy laughed. "Well you'll just have to ask them, but they did mention something about buying a ranch in Montana. Dad would still have his claim, but Jesse said Arcade is interested in looking at it, too."

Reed turned his eyes toward the open door. "I'd hate to see them move so far away. I was just getting used to them being around."

Cindy turned away from the stove and met Reed's serious expression. "Would you miss *me*?"

"Yeah—especially you."

"Well then, I'll tell you some more about what Dad said. If they buy a ranch in Montana, he wants me and Kimberly to move there with him."

Reed lowered his head and spoke into his coffee cup. "Are you going?"

"Reed, I don't know what to do. They said it'll be some time before it's a done deal with Arcade, but they seemed pretty certain. I'm not married to that school job, and Kimberly would love it, with her own horse and everything. But if you want to know the whole truth, I'd kind of miss this little cabin."

"Fact is, this little cabin would sort of miss you, too. Whadda'ya think of that?"

Cindy smiled as she dished up scrambled eggs from a frying pan. She refilled his coffee cup, poured one for herself, and sat across the table with her chin on her hands. She smiled and talked above her hands. "Reed Carson, you don't really think for one minute that we're just all going to pack up and leave you here, do you?"

Reed finished his eggs. He drained his coffee cup with a long swallow and lit a cigarette. "This little house is gonna get mighty small with all of us bunking here."

Cindy reached across the table and pulled his hat down over his eyes. "Still a chip off the old block I see."

"Oh, before I forget," Cindy said, "I called your mother the day you got out of the hospital. She was going to call you on your cell phone. Did she call you?"

"No, but she drove up yesterday afternoon, after you'd left. She said she wanted to make up for not visiting me in the hospital."

"That was really nice of her. It's a long drive up here from her place. Did you two have a good visit?"

Reed laughed. "I don't know if I would go that far. But, I'm glad she came. It was good to see her, and we had a long talk."

"How did that go?"

"It was okay. Mom wasn't in a very good mood, though. She said Kirk cleaned out her Garfield bank account, and he hasn't been seen since. She claims she doesn't have a penny to her name."

"Reed, that's terrible! The poor woman! What will she do?"

Reed gave out a little chuckle. "Mom won't starve. I've seen a couple of her statements from the Cheyenne and Laramie banks. Those, and with her investments in stocks and bonds, you couldn't haul all of her money to town in a horse trailer in hundred-dollar bills."

"Does she want you to come home, back to the Homestead Ranch?"

"Oh, yeah—even after I told her I had bought her summer pasture out from under her. She wants me back, big time, with Kirk gone and most of her hired hands dead or in jail...."

"That's great, Reed!"

"Hey, not so fast. I didn't say I would do it, but I *did* offer her a deal she couldn't refuse." Reed smiled, and took a sip of coffee.

"Okay, smarty-pants, what was the deal?"

"I offered to buy the Homestead Ranch, cash money down, five-percent interest, with a fifteen-year note. Told her I would find some good men to run the other ranches, and oversee the whole shebang as long as she needed me."

"That's wonderful, Reed. I'm so glad for you."

Reed couldn't help himself, he gave out with a hearty laugh. "Actually, it wasn't that funny. She said, 'No,' without even blinking. I reminded her that she'd promised to sell me the ranch for eight years, ever since the day I graduated high school. She went on like I hadn't spoken."

"I'm sorry, Reed. Not just for you, but for her, too."

"No. Don't be sorry for either of us. Mom and I are okay, really. Our relationship won't change. She'll always be my mom, and I believe she will come around to thinking of me as her son again. And....I'll always be around to help her out if it's a real emergency."

"After Mom left, I got to really thinking about everything. Getting kicked off the ranch was probably the best thing that ever happened to me—and for Mom, too."

"Reed, do you mean that?"

"I've never been more confident of anything in my whole life. If Mom hadn't thrown me out, I would still be just another hired hand. Now, I have my dad, Butch, and two really pretty girls fawning over me."

"You had better take that fawning part back, Reed Carson."

"Okay, but Kimberly loves me. Seriously, though, Cindy, this is my big chance, the challenge of a lifetime. Even after being kicked in the head, shot, and robbed, I've had more good thoughts about myself these past few weeks than I've had the last eleven years. Sure, it'll be hard, managing my cow herd and working off the place part-time, but I'm free for the first time in my life, and it feels great. Someday, if Mom changes her mind and wants to sell me the ranch…well, I'll cross that bridge when I come to it."

"Now, you're talking like the Reed Carson I've always thought you were."

"Another thing," Reed went on, "after all these years, I'm just now getting a glimpse into Mom's head. You see, she needs all the ranches to be who she is. I understand that now, and I don't begrudge her a thing. Who knows, maybe if I was wearing her head I would feel the same way. Before moving up here, before Butch, you, and my dad, all I could think about was going home, back to the Homestead. You see, I think the problem was, for as long as I can remember, I always wanted what I thought I was supposed to want. I never once thought about what she wanted or needed. And that part I'm not very proud of."

"Do you think Lucy understands why you won't go back as her foreman?"

"I tried to explain everything to her, but she wouldn't listen. So, needless to say, our visit didn't go well. At the end, we both got a little hot under the collar." He seemed almost to be grinning now. "My very words were: Cindy and I will make it just fine in a one-room cabin with six sections of grazing land. I thought she would pass out right there in front of me."

"You told her *what*? Is that your idea of a proposal? If it is, the answer is, no. If I loved a man enough, I could live in this little cabin with him forever, but I would need my head examined if I agreed to marry a crazy cowboy with his head half screwed on."

Reed slapped his knee and laughed. He got up from the table and stood by the door with his hand on the doorjamb. "Is that a fact?" He put on a wry grin. "Well, just so you don't get a swelled head, that's *not* a marriage proposal. I didn't tell her that we were getting married, just that you would *be* here. She can think whatever she wants."

"Anyway, I just said it to get her dander up, and it worked just fine. And another thing, my head isn't *half* screwed on any more. I'd say it's like three-quarters. Maybe if I hang around you a little longer, who knows—it just might get screwed on a little tighter."

"You really think so?"

"Yeah. I've thought so from the first time you said, 'and what can Cindy Anne Morgan do for you.' You know, when I first met you at the school."

Cindy walked over to stand in front of him. She put her hands on his hips, stood back, stiff-armed, and turned her head up to look him square in the eyes. She grinned mischievously. "In that case, cowboy, why don't we just hang out and see what Cindy Anne Morgan can *really* do for you."

He reached out and pulled her to him.

ABOUT THE AUTHOR

DENNIS BOYKIN is a lifelong agriculturalist and conservationist who, after graduating from the University of Wyoming, enjoyed a successful career with the USDA Soil Conservation Service before becoming an independent rancher, businessman, and freelance writer.